The Westcott (

THE MUSIC MAKER'S DAUGHTER

A gritty historical saga of love, friendship and

loyalty

Madeline's story - part one

Gayle Wyatt

COPYRIGHT

This is a work of fiction. Key locations, primary characters and names are fictitious and the work of the author's imagination. The events in this story are set in an authentic historical context.

Second paperback edition: December 2021
ISBN: 979-8-7794-9749-7

DEDICATION

This is dedicated to my lovely husband who has patiently helped and advised me, supplied endless cups of tea and coffee, and given me enormous encouragement over the years.

I could not have done this without you.

To Beryl

With love from

Gayle

REVIEWS

The Music Maker's Daughter is a riveting story about bravery, ambition and the enduring power of hope. Tenderly told and expertly crafted, it's at times heartwarming, at others devastating. An immersive, epic tale of family and fortitude you won't want to miss.

-**Holly Miller**, bestselling author of *The Sight of You*

The Music Maker's Daughter is a beautifully written story that captures the essence of the 1930s, especially in the dialogue. I have not read a book that has touched me like this in a while. I ached for Maddy and everything she went through. I cannot wait to read the sequel.

-**The Online Bookclub**

A beautiful, heartwarming and captivating book with well-developed characters that you fall in love with. I couldn't put it down. It was heartbreaking and heartwarming in equal measure. A truly riveting read.

-**Aria Harlow**, *NetGalley*

CHAPTER 1

"JOSIE! WHAT IF I fail…?"

"You won't Maddy, you're brilliant…"

Maddy pulled the ribbons from her long golden plaits and ran her fingers through her hair as though the constriction was stifling her thoughts and feelings. She knew what she was capable of, but she also knew how hard the challenge would be. "I'd be very ordinary at music college." She glanced round at her friend and her face tensed with self-doubt. "Part of me desperately wants to try, and part wants to draw back and to have a normal, safe life."

"Look," Josie took her hands fondly, "you'll know what to do when you need to choose. Just imagine how proud your father would be."

Maddy smiled and nodded, and a little thrill of hope warmed her heart.

Her father was a great pianist. Few of those who knew

him really understood the extent of his ability nor how close he had come to success. He never spoke of it, almost as though he had turned his back on his past. He had been poised on the verge of playing to audiences across the world, then the appointments had been withdrawn and he retired from public life to come here, to be a church organist and to teach music.

He was good at that too.

If she succeeded then he would be intensely proud of her, and she knew he would be with her every step of the way. But if she failed she had a terrible feeling it would break his heart, make him relive the agony of his own failure. Life was hard enough for him without such hurt.

But thinking of her father reminded her of the tension that had been in the house this morning, and the reason for it. She had not dared to say anything to Josie or the other girls yet. She sighed. "I must hurry home today Josie. I've got a rehearsal in the church, and I need to show him this music first."

"Alright. See you tomorrow then," Josie nodded.

The girls went their separate ways. Josie continued on to the rambling old vicarage where she and her five brothers lived, and Maddy ran along the busy high street and up the narrow flight of stairs between the hardware shop and the green grocer's.

Their flat was a small place. A threadbare carpet covered bare floorboards, and the walls had been whitewashed so long ago that the surface was flaking and discoloured.

Her father, Angus Brooks, was working at the dining table but he looked round at the sound of her running footsteps.

She took one look at his face, at the weary despair in his

vivid blue eyes, and did not dare to ask the question that had been burning on her mind all day. She struggled to summon her enthusiasm, anything to distract him from this pain. "I've got some tremendous news Daddy!"

He turned fully round to scrutinise her, and made a visible effort to respond positively. "Oh yes, and what might that be?"

"They announced the programme for the end of term concert today and they want me to play the piano solo. *And* I'm only in the first year."

"Good. It's about time your talent was recognised."

"I've brought the music home. It's the Beethoven Pathetique. Mr Wrighton wants me to concentrate on the last movement, but I could do it all couldn't I?"

He took the music and flicked through the pages. Then he stopped turning and his strong fingers followed the accumulation of notes that soared densely across the page. His face had lost the echoes of despair. It was as though he was touching a past memory and playing once again to a big audience. Slowly he smiled. "It's a powerful work Maddy, you'll love it's passion and pathos. You're right, you could learn the whole of this in under a month."

"Then why did he suggest...?"

"Because he doesn't understand yet." He touched her cheek gently and his intense blue eyes were vivid with a mixture of hope and concern for her. "The gift you have is far beyond any of them, and you're still so young. They're obviously testing you by sending this home. I'm glad something has gone well today for one member of the family."

The sadness of his voice drew tears from her eyes, and she found it hard to talk around the lump in her throat.

"Didn't you get the job, Daddy?"

"No. So we'll be here for your concert." He turned quickly away from her, and she felt utterly helpless, faced with this silent uncommunicative hurt. Then he continued very quietly. "And you won't have to leave your friends."

Despite herself, an intense flood of relief went through Maddy. This was her home and she had some very special friends here. But then she felt passionately ashamed that she could be so selfish. If Daddy had got the job then the whole family would have lived once again in comfort and security. In a small voice, she murmured, "I'm so sorry. But other jobs will come along, won't they? Perhaps even here in Westcott."

"Perhaps," he murmured. But she could hear from his voice that he really meant the opposite.

"It's going to be hard isn't it?" she asked tentatively, almost afraid to enquire further. "I wish I could help."

He turned back to her. "You shouldn't worry about things like this at your age. Let's have a look at your new music, and then later, your mother and I have got something serious to discuss with you both."

The peace was broken suddenly as Matthew's vigorous footsteps stumped up the stairs and the front door went flying. The handle crashed back against the wall with a resounding thump and he stood there, covered in mud from a school football match.

They both looked around, and the lively eight-year-old dumped his coat and bag without thinking. "What a match! We lost three nil. They stomped all over us in the last ten minutes. Anything to eat Maddy? I'm absolutely starving."

"Come with me, you mucky pup," she laughed. "I'll see what I can find in the larder."

"Matthew, you can't leave your coat and bag in the

middle of the doorway. Kindly pick them up," her father said sternly. Then he looked from one laughing young face to another. A reluctant smile spread across his face as though their joy was warming him, and suddenly he nodded. He rose to his full height. "Go and wash Matt. I want you presentable. Maddy, brush your hair. We're going out. I shall need you both for some advice."

Maddy looked questioningly at him.

"Hurry along and get ready Maddy. I've made a decision. We have a lot to do before your mother gets home. You must have that rehearsal, and we have some serious celebrating to plan."

♪♫

Maisy Brooks arrived home from work that night to find the table set for a special occasion. The china and silverware had been brought out, reminding her of the gracious entertaining they had once done. There had been a time when their London flat had hummed with the discussions and ideas of hosts of talented and creative people. But that time was long past, the country was deep in depression, and she was simply grateful for a happy and loving family. The smell of cooking filled the little flat with a delicious aroma that instantly made her feel better. She hung her coat behind the door and gave both children a quick hug, turning her face away discreetly so that she would not breathe on them. "What's all this my darlings?"

Maddy's eyes sparkled. "Daddy and I have made dinner today. It's a little celebration. I've had some good news. I'll tell you all about it in a minute."

"It's a feast, and I've set the table," Matthew interrupted excitedly. "Come and sit down Mummy, it's all ready."

"Alright Matt," she smiled, but remained watching her daughter's face. "And did they really help you Maddy?"

"A little bit. They tried very hard, honestly," the girl smiled, and caught her mother's eyes and they exchanged a look of silent understanding. She knew exactly how ham-fisted boys and men could be, particularly if they thought the task belonged to a woman. It was a sort of agreement between them to make allowances for that.

"Well, it smells utterly delicious, dear." Then she turned as she heard her husband's footsteps coming from the kitchen.

He was a strong man, and even now she loved and admired him tremendously. But one look at his face told her that the celebrations were not for him. She moved quickly towards him and they held each other close.

She closed her eyes and swallowed hard, burying her face in his shoulder. They had become used to these disappointments, but this one was particularly cruel and difficult to bear.

Then finally he sighed and turned her face up so that she looked into his determined blue eyes. "Come and eat. Then I'm afraid we shall have to talk to the children. Are you ready for it now? Are you feeling strong enough?"

"Yes," she smiled and squeezed his hand. "It has to be done. Where did you get all this? I haven't seen so much food in months."

He drew the chair back for her with graceful gallantry. "I gave John Turnbull an extra lesson this week for his exam, and I thought what better use could I make of the money than treat you and the children? Maddy's a good cook, wait till you taste her stew."

Matthew threw himself into his seat with a vigorous

bump whilst Maddy brought the steaming casserole dish in and placed it in the centre of the table. Then she fetched the vegetables, and as she took her seat, her father looked around the gathered throng of his family and a strange expression of pain passed across his face.

He shook his napkin out and lay it over his knee. "Maddy, would you care to serve? We have an item of excellent news to celebrate today my dears, that's why we've created this feast. Tell your mother what happened at school."

♪♫

The meal left all of them replete and contented. Once the dishes had been cleared away and the silver polished and placed back in its velvet lined canteen, the two adults sat quietly near the fire and talked in hushed whispers for more than an hour, then at last Maisy Brooks turned to her children. She and Angus had decided on the best approach, and the time had come to break the news to the children.

She sat in silence for several minutes watching them at their homework, side by side at the dining table in the corner of the room, and gradually the grim future they had been discussing retreated from about her and the smile of affection returned, struggling for life against her weariness. The expression on her delicate pale face hardly changed, but her eyes warmed, resurrecting the cosy happiness that usually filled the little flat. She held her hand out to Maddy and forced herself to her feet. "Come on love. Let's try that new dress of yours one last time."

Maddy surfaced with difficulty from the intricacy of her mathematical homework and pushed her books away with a little sigh. "Mmmm. I'll just go and get it on," she hurried up the stairs, and by the time Maisy had caught up with her, the girl had slipped out of her school tunic and blouse, taken the elegant moss green silk dress from its hanger and was drawing it on a little anxiously. "I hope it'll do up, after all that dinner. I feel as fat as a pudding."

"Let's see, shall we? Stand perfectly still." Meticulously Maisy fastened the tiny buttons at the back of the dress, then turned Maddy round slowly and studied her from head to foot. Her daughter looked so grown up and beautiful that a lump of emotion filled her throat. It was not so long ago that she had been young like this and dressed with stunning elegance. The dresses of her early years had been very different, hem lines just beginning to creep up above the ankle. Then as a young woman she had instantly taken to the daringly short flapper dresses that had suited her slim figure and scandalised her mother: the chiffon scarves, beads, and long gloves and above all, the extravagance of the Charleston! But her life was almost over, just as the fashions and dances of her youth had faded into the past. She only prayed she had not passed the accursed disease on to any of the family. It was Madeline's turn to beguile and bewitch now. And she would do it splendidly. "It fits you perfectly. Let me show you how to do your hair. We'll have a dress rehearsal, shall we, and see what our gentlemen downstairs think?"

Maddy nodded and sat on the stool.

Maisy drew her daughter's hair out of its plaits and brushed it until it shone in the light and framed her finely carved face like a halo of shimmering curly gold. Then with a bold sweep of her hand the hair was gathered up into a perfect Chignon. A few clips were inserted to hold it in place, and suddenly the twelve-year-old possessed a graceful, elegant maturity. But the physical activity was more than the older woman could take, and she sighed and sank weakly onto the bed. "You look beautiful Maddy. How I wish I could be there to watch you."

Maddy was examining her reflection in the mirror and turned gracefully so that the silk swirled luxuriously around her. "You could come and listen from the vestry, couldn't you?"

Maisy watched her daughter hold her head up high and press her shoulders back, breathing in deeply as though she was about to sing. She had such poise and elegance that it was like a physical pain to realise she would not see her mature into an adult.

The wedding Maddy had been asked to sing at was going to be a society affair, and the guests were affluent and famous people from London. It was a great honour to be asked to perform at such an occasion. People all across Westcott had been talking about it for weeks, and there were rumours that guests were even coming from as far afield as India and Siam.

Maisy was finding it hard to breathe again, and her voice was muffled as she murmured, "You look so like your father, Maddy. I'm so..." her voice choked hoarsely with a mixture of emotion and weariness, "so proud of you."

The young girl turned quickly.

Maisy was struggling to suppress the cough that had destroyed her health these last few months. She had so much she wanted to say and so little time in which to say it. With a titanic effort she hauled herself to her feet.

"Sit down Mummy," Maddy rushed to make her sit, and the fear the young girl felt was naked on her face. "You should be resting. You've been hard at work all day. I wish you would go to the doctor!"

Maisy's determination was relentless. She struggled up, took her daughter's hands so that she would not come too close, and looked deeply into the girl's anxious blue eyes. "I have been Maddy, and we have to talk. Dr Morrison is sending me away..."

"Oh Mummy, *no*!" the young girl's mature young face paled and tears flooded into her eyes, and quite suddenly she was a child again.

Maisy reassuringly touched her daughter's golden curls although her heart was breaking. "Dr Morrison is sending me away immediately to stay in the sanatorium. When I've gone, Daddy will need all your strength and love. He'll be very alone. You'll have to care for him and Matthew as though you were me. You can, can't you?"

"I... I'll do my best." Tears flooded down the young girl's cheeks. "But I don't want you to go. Will you be gone for very long?"

"My dearest Maddy! They won't allow me home for a long while. I shall be too ill," her mother's voice was warm with affection, and gently she forced the girl's chin up. "You will be the lady of the house then, and I know you'll do well. I want you to remember one thing more. I've never regretted marrying your father, though my family tried to stop me. He is a marvellous man, and we've been very happy. That's what counts. One day, you must find someone you really and sincerely love, and don't let anyone take that happiness from you. There's nothing more precious in all this world. Remember that... always."

Maddy shook her head fiercely. "Mummy, I don't want to be someone's wife, I want to be a pianist. I want that more than anything on earth."

"You're still so young for all this," her mother murmured

and smoothed a wisp of hair away from the young girl's forehead and nodded in grave understanding. Then she patted her shoulder. "Strive for it Maddy, but ... that's not quite what I meant. When you're older..." but the cough was coming again, taking her breath away, tearing at her cruelly, and she could say no more.

♩♫

CHAPTER 2

BERNARD BELAUGH WAS a wealthy man, the head of an empire of his own building. He had no time for snobbery, but something in art of this quality touched him to his soul. He cupped the slender white statue in his plump fingers, stroking the smooth alabaster appreciatively, his eyes focused exclusively on the artefact that had just become his.

The voice at his shoulder came as a surprise and he looked up quickly.

"Trowbridge!" he cried, gratification spreading through him. "I'm disappointed. I'd expected a far tougher battle out of you."

"I had no choice. The funds weren't available. How much further were you prepared to bid Belaugh?"

"For this?" His eyes returned to examining the perfection of the statue in his hands, and he murmured softly, "It's beautiful don't you think?"

Indignation tinged the man's pale cheeks with pink, and he replied stiffly. "That statue belongs in a museum, not locked away in your private collection where you can paw over it."

Belaugh glanced at the other man. "It's a fact of life that art goes where the money is. Who knows, I may leave it to you in my will."

"Ye Gods, the final insult. I warn you, next time you'll not get another gem like this."

Belaugh's eyes hardened with an expression that was surprising on such a plump round face. Softly, he whispered, "Then I shall look forward to our next encounter very much." He nodded his head and turned away.

His agent was hurrying towards him with a thick file of papers in his hand. "We can begin loading now, sir."

"Good. Get to it then," Belaugh briskly handed the statue over. "I'll inspect the other acquisitions later today. I've got an appointment to keep now." He nodded briefly to the simmering Trowbridge, then left the great hall.

His car was awaiting him and he climbed in, pondering on the nature and arrogance of some of these arty museum types. They felt they had the monopoly on art, because of the fame and reputation of the institutions for which they worked. Yet he had a feeling that Trowbridge did not appreciate the sheer elegance and beauty of that statue. It gripped him with a powerful intensity that caught his breath in his throat. To Trowbridge it was simply a museum item, a cold possession of historic *artistic* value. Which of them really had a right to consider ownership?

An hour and a half later, the vehicle cruised softly up the long gravel drive and came to a halt at the front of a vast mansion in Bedfordshire, an elegant historic building set within a mature landscaped estate that pleased and relaxed the tired eye. The chauffeur came smartly around the car and opened the rear door. Belaugh was asleep, his chin had dropped open and he was breathing heavily. The chauffeur touched his shoulder and Belaugh's eyes gradually opened. He recognised the location, straightened his bulky slumped body, and glanced fiercely at his watch. It only took a moment to gather his wits, then he climbed out of the car and stumped past the ranks of removals vans and into the house.

The place was in turmoil, but the disruption was well ordered. Cotton covers were draped over stacks of furniture, and Phyllis Belaugh was quietly checking the inventory and directing its distribution into the huge echoing rooms.

A strong fine woman still in her middle twenties, she looked up at the characteristic sound of his footsteps and smiled. "Welcome home Bernard. Ignore the chaos, I've nearly finished. You'll be surprised at the change by this evening."

He kissed her cheek and nodded. "I'll take your word for it, Phyllis. Is everything here that should be?"

She nodded. "And in good order too, which surprises me a little. I expected items to be missing."

"Good. I shall soon be joined by Nigel Davenport and William Trepithic, and we'll need a room to use."

"Come to the library then, my dear. I'll have the covers removed," she slipped her arm through his. "In fact, I'll do it myself. I've got some replies to show you."

The library had not been changed in any way, and once she had swept the covers back, the literature of centuries looked down on them. Belaugh was hardly aware of it, his thoughts were on the forthcoming business meeting. He sifted through the pile of letters she handed to him, and intense professional satisfaction filled him. His fingers itched to get down to work. He looked around at the unfamiliar furniture. "There must be paper and ink here somewhere."

Patiently, Phyllis opened a drawer in the desk and lifted out a fresh ream of paper. "I've had new ink and pens installed, and you'll find I've compiled a guest list from the replies we've received. But I must return to oversee the arrivals. I'll send the men to you when they arrive."

He surfaced swiftly from his preoccupation and caught her hands in his. "How do you feel about the place after the first week, Phyllis?"

She nodded slowly, and there was obvious warmth in her eyes as she reached out and touched the laden shelves. "We made the right decision when we bought it."

"And the neighbours?" he watched her intensely.

Her firm, good looking face hardened. "I've had a visit from the Vicar, that's all."

"I thought as much. Bloody aristocrats. I don't want you buried here and unhappy."

She patted his arm firmly. "Don't worry about me. I plan to pay a few calls of my own once everything is set straight. And I'll have company when the children arrive. We should be able to send for them in another week."

He smiled and touched her cheek softly. "I've missed you. Never thought I'd feel like that."

She nodded but said nothing.

Presently, another car crunched up the long tree lined drive and two gentlemen climbed out. One was a soberly dressed mature young man, the other tall and elegant, his hair cut longer than was fashionable. This second gentleman possessed an aura of artistry and distinction that complemented his reputation for inspired design. Nigel Davenport did not follow fashion, he created it.

The two men were conducted through the house to the library, and Belaugh looked up from the stimulation of his mounting pile of paperwork and nodded.

"Good. Come and sit down."

The elegant designer shook the hand that was offered to him. "A pleasure to meet you again, Mr Belaugh."

Formalities over, Belaugh pushed forward the lists he was working on. "We're going to have a full house. All the major stores are sending their buyers, their best names, not their juniors. We've got that as a result of careful cultivation. What stage are your designs at Davenport?"

"Finishing touches are all that remain sir. I've commissioned the mannequins for the day and evening, and I'd suggest we also provide a wide range of fabrics for the buyers to study and choose from."

"Good idea, we will. And what's our production capacity, William?"

"The new machines are causing some difficulty at the moment sir, but that will ease once the men become more proficient. It's quite a change from the old machines, but starting on the first commission will speed them up."

"I agree. Get together, the two of you, and run a full line of designs. I shall need solid facts and figures by next week, Will. I want to know exactly what our maximum capacity will be."

The young production manager nodded briskly. "You'll have it sir."

"Good. The future thrust of Belaughs will be decided by this show, and I'm investing a great deal of money in it." He lay his hands on the papers in front of him, then rose to his feet. "Come with me and look around the house. I want suggestions and ideas. I want this show to rival the great fashion houses. We'll have buyers from Harrods, Liberties, Selfridges, John Lewis, Bentall's and many more."

He led them through the huge, shrouded house to the impressive entrance hall. Servants were busy removing covers and adjusting the small items of furniture. "We'll greet them here with a glass of sherry, then bring them straight through to the ballroom." His footsteps led them into a vast airy room. Deep windows stretched from floor to ceiling and gave access to the bright spring sunlight. He rubbed his hands together in satisfaction as his eyes scanned the decorative perfection. "It's Adam of course."

Phyllis came quickly towards them and held her hand out to each man in turn. "Welcome. We're just finishing the arrangements now. What do you think of it, William? We were fortunate. We could have had to wait years for such a property."

The two men were looking around, sizing up the potential of the room that was presented to them. "It's splendid, ma'am, a worthy home."

"Excellent proportions," Nigel Davenport moved forward carefully, and his eyes moved in a slow circle. "We'll need to hire suitable furniture for the show, complement it with flowers and drapes for the windows and stage. Everything must match my colour scheme of course."

Belaugh nodded. "Give me a full inventory of what you need, and some fabric swatches for the colour match. Only the best mind!"

"Leave that to me sir. Just give me a few days to wander round and get the feel of the place and I'll have the designs on your desk."

Belaugh nodded and glanced at his wife. "And the practicalities to you my dear?"

"Certainly." She glanced at Nigel Davenport and smiled. "Between us, we'll soon have the plans prepared."

The designer looked at her sharply, fierce parochial jealousy glaring from his eyes.

Phyllis smiled calmly. "It's practical, Mr Davenport. The catering and organisation will be in my hands. The artistic design in yours. Just tell me what you'd like me to arrange."

He nodded slowly. "As long as it remains that way."

She nodded, well accustomed to handling artistic temperaments such as his.

"Excellent," Belaugh smiled. "I'll leave you three to thrash out the details then," and he withdrew to the library and the stimulus of his work.

♪♫

CHAPTER 3

ST BARNABAS CHURCH in Westcott was open in a gesture of welcome. Its lawns were immaculately cut, the edges precise and straight, the ages old tomb stones softened with lichen and moss.

Cultured voices laughed and commented loudly as the guests and newly married couple milled around for a while on the lawn. The town rarely saw a motor vehicle on its roads. Deliveries were made by bike or horse and cart, and so the polished black vehicles drawing up one after another to carry the celebrants off to the reception at Ashforth House were attracting a vast crowd of observers.

Maddy, Emma and Josie were watching them socialise. They were colourful, the gentlemen immaculate in their morning suits, the ladies as ornamental as butterflies. They could see them through the church door and were fascinated.

Emma, whose father moved in those circles, leaned towards Maddy and pointed discreetly to one particular guest. Maddy coloured slightly and nodded. That *was* him: the well-dressed young man who had been watching her throughout the service.

To be the subject of admiring scrutiny from such an attractive young man, had taken her breath away. She could see him now, walking amongst the guests, and suddenly she realised that he was looking for her. A flare of heat burned her cheeks.

"You should go and say hello to him," Emma whispered softly.

Maddy glanced over her shoulder. Her father, dignified and handsome in his college robes, had just locked the organ and was talking quietly to the Vicar. She knew he would not mind her watching with her friends as she waited for him, but she did not think he would like her going out to mingle with them.

Behind her, the Vicar was asking, "Did you have any success with your interview Angus?"

"No. They'd decided on a replacement already. The interviews were merely a formality. I suppose I should have realised that." Her father's quiet face was suddenly weary and dispirited, and he looked far older than his thirty-eight years. "It would have been an ideal job. The post came with a house and education for the children. It's going to be extremely difficult now my poor Maisy has gone."

"I'm sorry Angus. If there's anything I can do, don't hesitate to let me know. The children are always welcome if you need help." The Vicar gripped his shoulder, and there was unaccustomed gruffness in his voice. "In my opinion, the Malthouse has made a terrible mistake. They've turned down an excellent teacher." He forced a smile onto his face. "But it means we still have you here."

Her father smiled. "Thanks Peter. You're a good friend."

The Vicar nodded. "And that reminds me, I gave your name to the Ashforths from the manor. Josie's playing has impressed them, and they're looking for a teacher for their granddaughter Avril." He hunted in the pockets of his cassock and handed a few pieces of paper to her father. "That's their address."

Angus studied the papers, and then frowned. He held a plain brown envelope in his hand and looked sharply at the Vicar. "And what's this?"

"I've just done the accounts and your fees are due. There was also the recital you gave last month, and..."

"You shouldn't do this," Angus Brook's face hardened, and he thrust the envelope back into the Vicar's hand. "I can't accept such a gift a second time, you know that. There are many families in a situation worse than mine. For heavens' sake give the parish charity fairly Peter..."

"I had a feeling you might say that," the Vicar nodded slowly, "so I prepared a small account. Every penny is specified, including Maddy's fees for singing today. They paid a handsome sum to hold the wedding here, I assure you."

Angus studied the Vicar's face for a moment, then the anger faded from his vivid blue eyes. "What a fool I am. You must forgive me." He looked down thoughtfully at the envelope and gradually his shoulders straightened. "Thanks. I shall be able to pay the rent now."

The Vicar clapped him on the shoulder and walked towards the open door. "I think it's time we congratulated your lovely young daughter on her singing today. It was beautiful. She's got quite a talent there, and the confidence to carry it off."

But encouraged by her friends, Maddy had slipped quietly out into the churchyard leaving the men to talk, and she stood by one of the gravestones, watching the young man as he searched.

He seemed quite determined, and when his eyes finally lit on her, she smiled shyly at him. His face brightened as though the sun had come out, and he hurried to her and then stood for a moment at a loss for words.

She held her hand out to him, breaking the awkward silence. "Hello. I hope you enjoyed the service."

"Yes indeed," he took her hand, and instead of shaking it as she expected, he leaned over and kissed it reverently. "Hearing your voice was the pinnacle of the ceremony. You sing like an angel."

She felt a shock flood up her arm, and her knees weakened curiously. Even her normally firm voice sounded slightly breathless as she replied, "Thank you."

"I hope to make your acquaintance properly at the reception…" he glanced over his shoulder in irritation as a name was called splendidly from the gate. "I must go now. My car is here. Whatever you do, don't disappear without seeing me."

"I won't be at the reception. I'm not on the guest list," she murmured quietly.

He had been about to hurry off, but he turned back to her urgently and took both her hands in his. "Who are you then, and where do you live?"

But her father's resonant voice carried sternly across the lawn. "Maddy. Come here immediately."

"I can't. I must go now," she said hastily, then turned and almost ran back to the vestry door. Behind her, the young man called after her, but the voice from the gate was becoming insistent. Reluctantly, he turned away from the church, and left.

♪♫

CHAPTER 4

THE FLAT THE Brooks family lived in reflected the tenderness and care of the mistress of the home. There were curtains and cushion covers lovingly made, that attracted the eye away from threadbare patches on the chairs. An appliquéd curtain hung across the door, weighted down by small pellets of lead sewn into the lining, and it kept at bay the draughts that whistled up the stairs, giving the room a snug welcoming atmosphere.

The Vicar's wife always felt at home when she visited them, and tonight she had brought her daughter Josie to keep the two children company until their father returned from teaching.

The clock was ticking placidly on the mantelpiece and beside it was the steady imperturbable glow of the oil lamp. On the floor, Maddy, Matthew and Josie leaned eagerly towards each other across the games board in front of a roaring log fire. The flickering firelight illuminated their faces, animating the Brooks children as they moved with restless enthusiasm, such a contrast to Josie's quiet, gentle discretion.

"Here you are my dears." Mrs Rogers bustled in with a big pot of steaming tea and three cups. "Supper time."

"Thank you, Mrs Rogers." Maddy shook the dice and threw it. "A five! Phew! That takes me past the snake. I'm safe. Let's have our supper now."

"Hang on a minute!" Matthew cried. "I just want to see if I can get that next ladder." He took the dice and concentrated every effort on his own throw.

The two girls ignored him. Josie opened a promising brown envelope while Maddy industriously brought the lamp over, and they huddled together eagerly around a batch of photographs. "Look! You've come out beautifully. It isn't a wonder that young man sat watching you all through the service."

Maddy clasped her hands to her cheeks and gazed at the picture of herself singing at the wedding. It had taken them hours to straighten her rebelliously curly golden hair and style it in the height of fashion, but the result had been well worth the effort, for her hair gleamed in discreet waves, and she looked more like seventeen than twelve.

Josie laughed, "And here's one of your mystery admirer. Everyone's been talking about him. Emma said he moped all through the reception because you weren't there."

Maddy felt little tingles of unaccustomed excitement run up and down her spine as she remembered the smile on his face and how he had kissed her hand. The picture told her that he must have been in his early twenties. His short hair was immaculately slicked back with cream, giving his face an air of distinction and character, and he wore a beautifully tailored suit and handmade shoes. "I'd have sung as flat as a pancake if I'd known. Are you sure he was asking for me? You're not just teasing me."

"No I'm not. But we can find out who he is from Emma if you like. He looks as though he could provide you with everything you could possibly need. You should have seen the car he came in! And by the way he was looking at you, he..."

"Don't you dare, Josie. I don't want to be looked after by anyone, I want to be a pianist."

"Then you'll need a very kind and affluent husband. Oh alright, I won't say any more," Josie laughed. "Here's one of the bride. Doesn't she look beautiful? And there's me," she glanced around quickly to make sure her mother was not within hearing range. "I hated that awful bridesmaid's dress, it was so old fashioned. I don't know why Becca chose it."

Maddy smiled. "She couldn't afford to have a beautiful young woman standing beside her, taking the shine out of her."

Suddenly a terrific thump came at the window, rattling the glass alarmingly, and they all looked round in surprise. Whatever had hit the window had done no damage and flew on down the street.

Maddy glanced at the clock. "I wonder where Daddy is."

"It's the first lesson he's given to Avril, so I expect he's chatting to her grandparents."

"Stop mucking around you two. It's your turn Josie."

Josie pulled a face. "We're going to finish the game later Matt!" She had five brothers of her own and was used to their irritating persistence.

But Maddy was restless now. She got up and went to

peep out of the window hoping to see her father's figure, or the glow of his carbide bicycle lamp somewhere in the distance.

The severity of the weather surprised her a little and she shivered. It was more like November than April. The wind was gusting intermittently, lashing the rain into cruel horizontal blades of water, making the deep puddles dance in the deserted street. The residents of Westcott were wisely within doors. There was only one sign of life to be seen in the road, and that representative of life looked miserable. A horse and cart laden with a few remaining sacks of coal were waiting just a few yards away. The horse was blinkered, its head bowed and turned away from the driving rain. The sack of oats hanging limply around its neck was sodden, and obviously held nothing of interest now for the poor beast. She saw the coal man reach up for the ears of the sack and turn his back dexterously, heaving the heavy load onto his muscular shoulders. Then he disappeared at a bent over trot down the narrow passageway to the back of the terrace of houses opposite. It was cold dark and inhospitable out there.

Josie crossed the room to join Maddy and touched her friend's shoulder in an attempt to reassure her. "There's nothing to worry about you know."

"I know." Maddy's throat tightened with sudden emotion. "I just wish he didn't have to go out on evenings like this."

Josie looked out at the gusting debris that was being impelled down the street, and she shuddered.

"Come on Maddy, it's your turn," her brother was sitting cross legged now, shaking the dice eagerly in his hand.

"Alright, let's get this game finished," she said briskly and hurried back to the friendly warmth of the fire, but the curtains blew agitatedly in the draught that forced its way around the window frame and she frowned.

Josie smiled and touched her hand. "We'll sort out some clean dry clothes for him and have a hot drink ready."

"That's a good idea," Maddy murmured with difficulty. It was the sort of thing her mother would have done, and she was missing her terribly. She knelt down by the snakes and ladders board and bent her fair head to study it, hiding the pain on her face. "Whose turn is it? Mine? Oh Matt, you've just slipped right back down to number five! What a disaster."

They played on and time passed quickly. Finally, the game ended and Mrs Rogers sent Josie home, then bustled Matthew off to bed.

Alone, Maddy gazed into the flickering flames of the fire, and curiously reached her fingers out to the heat, mesmerised and soothed by the constantly changing patterns of warmth and danger, and her thoughts wandered to her future. She had so many secret hopes and dreams. She knew deep within herself that she *was* capable of it. She could study at the Royal Academy of Music as her father had and go on to play with the best orchestras. But the path to that success was long and arduous, and the thought was daunting.

The flames licked up ruthlessly, devouring the coals in the fireplace, soothing her misgivings and replacing them with a burning hunger to play. She could vaguely remember being taken at a very early age to hear her father rehearsing with the London Symphony Orchestra, seeing him high up on stage with the orchestra in a semicircle around him, and a huge concert grand at his fingertips. That is when the fire in her had been kindled.

A hand touched her shoulder and she spun round but it was Mrs Rogers, not her father.

"You mustn't fret dear. You'll soon work out a routine for running the house. I was just thinking that I'd visit your mother tomorrow. Would you like to come with me?"

"Oh, could I? I'd love to!" Maddy rose to her feet eagerly. "I have so much to tell her."

"Come with me," the kindly lady took her by the hand. "We'll make a pot of tea and have a chat, and we'll see if we can find some biscuits for your father. If we have everything ready for him, and dry clothes warming by the fire, he'll soon forget the rain."

"I'll put one more log on, that should last us the rest of the night..." she halted suddenly as a firm knock sounded on their front door. Her father would be deeply disappointed if it was an enquiry from a new pupil and he was not here to take it.

"I'll answer it, Maddy," Mrs Rogers touched the girl's cheek and disappeared into the hall, and Maddy heard the door open. There was a sudden exclamation then a quick whispered conversation and footsteps headed for the sitting room.

Maddy stoked the fire then rose to meet the visitor. Her eyes widened as the village policeman entered followed closely by the Vicar. Both of them were soaked to the skin and dripping pools of rainwater onto the rug.

PC Wickens was a big gentle man with a loud voice, who had instilled considerable respect into the children of the town. Parents often took naughty children to him for correction, and he could always be relied upon to reinforce discipline. But he took his helmet off slowly and stood fingering it.

"What is it Mr Wickens?" Something about his behaviour suddenly made her very frightened, and she turned quickly to the familiar figure she knew. "Reverend Rogers?" But he too was bedraggled by the rain, and his face looked curiously old and haggard. He did not speak.

"I'm sorry Miss Brooks," the policeman sighed, and spoke slowly. "Sorry to come in here like this, but there's been an accident."

Maddy froze.

"It's difficult to say exactly how it happened. We'll know more in the morning, but with all this rain and the river running so high and fast, he was swept down just past the bridge. It was your schoolteacher, Mr Jenkins, who spotted the body and fished it out..."

"No," she whispered.

There was slow murmuring in the hall outside, then Mrs Rogers hurried into the room. Completely ignoring the policeman and her husband, she turned Maddy gently round and wrapped her up in a warm blanket, as though she was dealing with some minor childhood ailment. Her face was creased with distress, and she gave the young girl a fierce hug. "Poor child, such a terrible shock. But you mustn't worry, we'll look after..."

"Leave me alone," Maddy cried and swept the murmuring aside desperately, and she reached out to PC Wickens. "Where is he? There must be something I can do. Please take me to see him."

The policeman's firm reassuring face faltered, and when he spoke this time his country accent surged to the surface. "Miss, there's nothing you can do. The doctor has already certified 'im dead. The Vicar'll identify the body, so there's no need for you to have to see him."

"No, no! Oh *no*!" she covered her trembling lips with her hands and looked wildly around her. "It can't be. Reverend Rogers, tell me truly."

The Vicar's face was grim with his own pain as he nodded slowly and firmly. "It's true, Maddy. I'm so sorry."

"I have to see him! You can't just take him away!"

"Maddy, you can't," Mrs Rogers calmly took her by the shoulders and looked down into the young girl's wild eyes. "Don't you understand? Poor child." Then she looked pleadingly at the silent figure of her husband.

The Vicar came slowly forward and took Maddy's hands in his. "Listen to me Maddy. PC Wickens is right, there's nothing you can do for your father now. You must take care of yourself. You and Matthew can come and stay with us at the vicarage. Josie's getting your beds ready. You'll be comfortable and safe, and in the morning we can begin to think about things."

She shook her head numbly. "I want to see him, Reverend. He's my father! I *have* to see him. *Now*!"

"No Maddy…" Mrs Rogers began in perplexity.

But her husband touched his wife's arm with gentle authority to silence her.

"But she's so young!" Her face pinkened with indignation. "I don't think it's right."

He was still watching Maddy's whitened shocked face. "If we force her to desert her father, we could do terrible harm."

"Oh please. You must let me go. Look, I… it was my job to look after him. I t… tried so hard. I have to go."

"I understand. I'll come along with you Maddy. But first, you must have a hot drink and wrap up warm. The weather's terrible, and you'll need all your courage."

The Vicar caught his wife's eye. She was still frowning, but finally nodded her obedience. He ushered them both into the kitchen, then returned to the policeman. "We'll delay her as long as we can. Go quickly and make the body look presentable. I don't care if you have to knock the undertaker up and drag him out, but she needs..."

"I understand Reverend," the policeman strapped his helmet on quickly, relieved to be doing something useful, and hurried down the stairs to find his bike.

In the kitchen Maddy still could not understand or believe what was being said. It seemed to have no reality. In a daze, she watched a big pot of tea being made and poured. Three huge spoons of sugar were stirred into her cup, and she felt the warmth and comfort of the older woman's caring presence as the cup was lifted to her lips. She was enclosed in a comfortable embrace and encouraged to drink. She took a biscuit and nibbled it slowly, and coughed suddenly on a crumb.

As though it had released the understanding and grief, the tears came, scorching her. Daddy was gone, she would never speak to him again, never hear his voice or his music, never be protected by his strength and love.

More than an hour later, the Vicar took Maddy to the police station, and PC Wickens led her into a bare unfriendly room. This was the moment she knew instinctively that she needed. It seemed to her as though nothing would ever be real again unless she came to say goodbye.

She swallowed hard. The room was large and bleak, and the emptiness of it jarred in the stark electric light. At its centre was a table covered by an off-white cotton sheet. She clenched her fingers tightly together as the policeman lifted the sheet and pulled it back.

It was all true.

It was her father, beyond a doubt. He looked very peaceful. His handsome face was pale and serene, as though the water had washed it of colour, just as it had drained him of life. He was still her father, quiet gentle and capable. But he had withdrawn from her and was impossibly far away, behind the barrier of death.

There was a terrible pain in her chest. She wanted him back so much. She had promised her mother that she would take care of him, and she had failed. She reached out and touched one of the powerful skilled hands that were crossed over his chest, aching to shake him, wake him from this false slumber. But then she recoiled in shock. He was like ice.

Tears of anger and futility filled her eyes. It was so unfair. He deserved life, success and happiness, not this sad end.

She sank slowly into her knees and gazed at his face.

He had been so gifted, both as pianist and teacher. He had been kind and wonderful and had striven with all his strength and determination to provide for his family, yet at each turn he had been pulled down.

But then a quiet proud dignity filled her. He had passed on to her a priceless gift, his ability to make music. She took a deep breath and made a solemn promise. She would do her best to develop that ability, and wherever his soul was, he would be watching over her, and it would be his glory and joy as much as hers.

She tried to concentrate her thoughts on the anger and determination, so that she did not feel so bereft and utterly alone. But it did not work. The piercing thrust of grief and despair tore through her.

Daddy was gone, Mummy was dying in hospital, and she and Matthew were completely alone. They had been such marvellous people, warm, loving and able. And soon nothing would be left of them.

She touched his hand one last time, trusting like the small girl she could never be again. "Bye, bye Daddy. Watch over me. Please."

♪♫

CHAPTER 5

WESTCOTT ROSE EARLY as usual the following morning. Most families in the rows of red bricked terraced houses at the lower end of the village had known their streets well enough to hide within doors during the storm, and block their front and back exits with sandbags, for the river was prone to flood in such weather. Those who had taken such precautions opened their doors to collect the early morning milk expecting the worst.

There was a curious silence and joy about the day.

The sky was bright blue and absolutely clear, the sun lighting up the red brick of their homes as though warming and healing, lifting the weight and oppression of last night's battering.

The street was empty of all except the milkman. His cart was splashing through thick mud and oose that glistened, writhed and trickled as the last of the floodwater slowly seeped away into the fields beyond. The man had a cheerful smile on his face. He thought of himself as a mainstay of the community, helping the village to recover. And it was not a difficult task in this weather. His cheerful, "Mornin' missus, what can I do *you* for today then?" rang out again and again as he progressed up the road.

Many of them responded with a cheeky reply, a defiance against nature's attempt to conquer them, and approval of its bright start this morning. Others simply scowled. All of them knew it was going to take a lot of work to brush the mud from the walls of their homes, and on hands and knees to scrub it from the path into the road, make the village respectable again. But at least it was something different, something they would all do together. Still, the milkman kept up his cheery banter, aware of the blossoming of conversation and life that followed his progress.

Then one by one, kettles heating on gas hobs began to scream for attention and the women returned to the kitchen to prepare breakfast for their families, to polish shoes, light the fires, and make sandwiches. Later in the day, they would all emerge again, to gossip and laugh as they worked in the glorious sunshine.

♪♫

Maddy felt shattered when she finally emerged from sleep.

Nothing of the bright day entered her life. Her mind was muddled and sluggish. She recognised the room. It was friendly and she had often stayed the night here with Josie. But why was she in the vicarage, and why was there such a heavy weight on her chest? Slowly it all came rolling back. Alone in her friend's comforting bedroom grief overwhelmed her, and it felt as though the weight of the world was settling upon her shoulders.

♪♫

Josie stood rooted to the spot on the threshold of her room. She had been peeping in every fifteen minutes waiting for her friend to wake. But she had not expected this deluge of anguish and despair. She had no way of sharing those feelings or making them better, and what she saw happening to her best friend terrified her. It was beyond even her understanding. During her short life, she had always managed to find answers to problems, but she could do nothing for Maddy, and she wanted her laughing determined friend back.

She turned and ran down the stairs and reached the kitchen out of breath. There was a riotous hum of exuberant boys' voices filling the room with an air or normality. Mother handed her eldest son a pack of sandwiches and enough chocolate bars for one each, and held her hand up imperatively for silence. "A quick equipment check. Have you all got rods?"

There was a chorus of yeses.

"Who's carrying the bait?"

A young voice replied.

A placid smile animated her face as she surveyed the sea of heads in front of her. There were five of her own sons and young Matthew Brooks. "And have you got a bucket for the *enormous* quantity of fish you are going to catch for dinner tonight?"

"Yes Mum," the oldest, a young man about to embark upon his first year at university, laughed. "We've got two. So be prepared for the catch of your life."

"Good. It'll be fish for dinner tomorrow too, then." She looked at his lively mature face fondly. "Ron, you'll be in charge of the younger ones. Be good all of you and keep an eye on the time. You must be home by four o'clock." Then she turned to Matthew and tenderly pushed back the thick bob of hair that had fallen across his forehead. He was desperately pale and wan, a shadow that had lost all substance, and her maternal instinct made her long to hug him better. He had clung to her with such passion last night. She smiled encouragingly. "Here's a little something extra for you Matt. You need all your energy just now, don't you? I hope you have a nice morning."

His eyes widened slightly as he was handed another bar of chocolate, and suddenly he threw himself into her arms and gave her a big hug.

She returned the embrace. "There, sweetheart."

"Come on Matt," the boys were calling enthusiastically.

The young boy nodded, and Mrs Rogers watched him turn listlessly and join them on their expedition.

"Mummy," Josie called, once the clamorous horde had gone. "You must come quickly. Please! It's Maddy... We've got to do something."

Mrs Rogers turned. "Has she woken sweetheart?"

The young girl nodded. "It's terrible. We've got to do something."

"Come and sit down with me for a moment Josie."

The young girl came anxiously. "But surely we ought to do something. She's in such despair..."

The older woman took her daughter's hands gently in her own and shook her head. "I know it's unbearable to see someone you love feeling so bad. You want to heal the hurt, don't you?"

Josie nodded fiercely, her large brown eyes fixed on her mother's face.

Mrs Rogers smiled. "But there are times when you can't, and this is one of those times. Maddy has to feel these things before she can recover and be herself again. All you can do is give her time when she wants to be alone and be with her when she needs company."

Josie nodded and got quickly to her feet. "I'll go and see her now."

"Why don't you give her a little time to herself just now so that she can think. She'll come down when she's ready."

♪♫

Maddy emerged a long while later, exhausted by the vigour of her emotions. She found Mrs Rogers in the kitchen supervising the preparation of Saturday's dinner for her large family, and the kindly lady looked up with a smile. "Hello dear, come and sit down and have something to eat."

"Thank you," Maddy sat at the huge worn wooden table. The world around her seemed completely bleak and empty. She could never have believed that in the company of people she loved she could feel so utterly alone and desolate. She bowed her head and ate the cereal she was given.

The food helped, made her feel a little more like herself, and bit by bit she became aware of what was going on around her. The Vicar's wife was surrounded by a vast quantity of vegetables fresh from the garden, all in baskets and bowls, and she and the maid were scraping and paring busily as though life was still normal and cosy.

"May I help you Mrs Rogers? You've got an enormous amount of work to do."

"Thank you dear. You could prepare the beans for me." A knife, an empty bowl and a large brown paper bag of fresh beans was put in front of her. "Josie'll be back in a minute.

She's just gone to pick some mint for the potatoes and sauce. She wouldn't go away to stay with the Watkins after she heard what had happened."

"Wouldn't she?" Maddy felt a little flush of colour surge in her cheeks and she looked eagerly towards the door, then suddenly she frowned. "But the house sounds so quiet, where are the boys?"

"They've gone fishing, hence the unaccustomed peace." Her eyes flickered to Maddy. "I sent Matt with them, I thought it would do him good to get out in the fresh air."

"Matthew? Oh, poor Matt, I haven't even seen him today."

Mrs Rogers put her knife down and touched Maddy's cheek. "You mustn't make yourself responsible for everything. You're here with us and we'll help you."

Maddy lowered her eyes to the beans again and concentrated hard, but her mind was a riot of unruly thoughts and worries, all jostling for a place in her head. Tears filled her eyes. "There must be lots of arrangements that are usually made, and I haven't any idea what to do, or what will become of us."

"Poor love," Mrs Rogers left her work, and turned Maddy's face up. "Don't worry yourself about the arrangements, we'll see to that. Come with me." She took Maddy by the hand and bore her off through the unusually quiet house.

She tapped softly on one of the closed doors, then opened it and took Maddy in.

The Vicar was sitting at his desk. A small metal framed pair of spectacles were perched on his nose, and he was peering up at them over the top of the lenses, his pen poised, caught in mid-sentence. He saw his wife and Maddy, lay his pen down and came stiffly to take her hands. He looked as though he had aged ten years during the last few hours. But gentleness shone from his eyes as he murmured, "How are you, my child? Did you sleep?"

Mrs Rogers nodded. "She's had breakfast and is worried about the arrangements, bless her."

"Come and sit down," the Vicar pressed her gently into a chair, while Mrs Rogers left them to talk. He glanced at the notes and documents on his desk, then at the young girl's face. "I've already made most of the arrangements. Your father was a very dear friend, has been for years, and I'd consider it an honour if you'd leave that to me. As for the future," he played nervously with his spectacles. "We'll talk about that when you're feeling stronger. At the moment, I want the two of you to stay here with us, until we've sorted everything out."

"Th... thank you," she touched her burning cheeks. Everything was being done so quickly it was frightening. "But... but we can't stay with you for ever sir, can we?"

He turned to her and peered over the top of his spectacles. "Do you have any relatives, aunts, cousins, who might give you a home?"

"My father was an only child sir. I don't know much about my mother's family. They wanted nothing to do with us after she married Daddy." Maddy glanced down at her hands. "Mummy said they had a great deal of money, but I don't think they'll care much about us."

"Perhaps it would be best if I wrote to them and informed them of the situation. They may decide to give you a home. If they pay your school fees, you could come and stay with us during your holidays."

Maddy felt her cheeks colouring, and she murmured,

"You've been very kind to us sir, kinder than my mother's family have ever been."

"We'll see. We mustn't judge them until we hear their reply."

She nodded and yet another worry filled her awareness. With difficulty, she murmured, "Daddy has always tried to pay our bills sir. I've got to do that for him. He'd hate it if he owed money..."

"We'll talk about that later. You've quite enough to cope with at the moment."

"No! I've got to do it. Daddy was very careful to keep his accounts in order," she glanced at the accounts the Vicar had been working on. They *were* her father's; his writing was unmistakable. She gathered all her courage. "Does it mean we'll have to sell all our things?"

He flicked through the pages of receipts reluctantly, then looked up to meet her anxious gaze, and once again he seemed much older than his years. "It looks very much like it. I'm sorry Maddy."

♪♫

Maddy and her brother returned to the flat two days later. The two young people were quiet and withdrawn as they walked through the empty rooms. The furniture was still the same, but the warmth and joy had gone.

Someone had been here already, and there were price tags on the furniture. Even the piano had been costed and no longer belonged to them. Maddy touched it softly, feeling the memories and happiness surge through her once again.

She chose a selection of things that would remind her vividly of her parents, some of her father's music, and her mother's few pieces of jewellery.

Matthew took things that surprised her considerably. He wanted his father's medals from the Great War, handling them as though they meant the world to him. Between them, they sorted through the books and family photographs, and then looked around at the day-to-day functional items of life. Most of them were faceless articles that could have belonged anywhere, and now that the family had gone, they just looked old and tatty. They left the flat, hand in hand, shut and locked the door, and handed over the key to Mr Packard in the hardware shop beneath.

♪♫

CHAPTER 6

THE WHITE ALABASTER statue looked magnificent. The pedestal could have been made specifically for it, Belaugh decided. He glanced at the troop of people following him around the house. "We'll have Moet et Chandon. Three cases, to be on the safe side. Is your inventory complete, Mrs Cox?"

"Yes sir. Everything's cleaned and polished. We're using the Royal Worcester sir, and the Stuart Crystal."

"Excellent. I think the decorations have developed well." He stood back and surveyed their work. The hired tables and chairs were all in place and workmen were busy positioning the enormous wrought iron flower holders. Three days to go, and it was in safe hands. He nodded suddenly and waved his dismissal. "Thank you everyone. You've worked wonders in the time available."

The staff melted away, but Belaugh beckoned a uniformed policeman to his side. "One thing still concerns me. The evening could be ruined by undisciplined arrivals and departures. And you, Teagle, are just the man I need." He put his arm around the policeman's shoulder and walked him slowly across the ballroom to look out over the gravel drive. "I want a well policed marshalling of the cars as they arrive to deposit and pick up the guests."

"Yes sir. I can manage that. There'll be a charge for the service of course."

"Done. I'll pay you and your men double time for your trouble."

"Leave it with me sir," the policeman nodded in satisfaction.

Mr and Mrs Belaugh watched the staff hurry away, and once they were alone, a frown of anxiety creased his forehead. "Have we forgotten anything my dear?"

She linked her arm through his and patted his hand. "Everything is well under control. Surely you don't have any doubts? We've done this sort of thing time and time again."

His eyebrows twitched nervously and he took a deep breath. "I've invested heavily in this venture. Our future will depend upon this show, make or break. If it's break, then we'll have to sell the estate to recoup the money."

Her face paled. "God, Bernard, that was a risk."

"We're in an era of risks. We have to stride forward, or sink."

"Look, we could make some easy economies. For example," she paced away from him quickly, and began to tick items off on her fingers. "We could cancel the order of caviar. The Moet could be replaced by a sparkling white wine at a fraction of the cost. They would never know."

"No."

"But it's a shocking waste."

He smiled. "You're an unparalleled organiser and a

shrewd economist. But believe me, we can't skimp on anything. We must have the best and trust that it will tempt the buyers. They'll equate the quality of our product with the amount we're spending on the sales drive."

She watched his round determined face and nodded slowly. "You're right of course. You always are." She moved across the room to the pedestal near the door. "It's like this statue. I'd never have looked twice at it. You have an eye for the right fit."

He followed her and ran his fingers across the slender white alabaster figure. The majesty and purity of it sent a flame of awe through him. Then he touched his wife's shoulder affectionately, but that vital spark faded.

"Have you sent for the children yet?" he asked.

"No," she smiled. "Not with all these arrangements going on. It wouldn't be fair. When it's all over I can spend time settling them in."

He nodded slowly, but a great sense of loss filled him.

♪♫

CHAPTER 7

THE BRAITHWAITES LIVED in a rambling old Elizabethan house. The low oaken beams and huge fireplace, surrounded by panelled bookshelves and whitewashed walls, seemed appropriate to their advancing years. A small fire was burning even though the air had warmed. Now that the storms and foul weather of the last few days had passed, spring was continuing its course again towards summer.

Brigadier Charles Braithwaite was enjoying the last few hours of leave before taking up military duties in London. A fit energetic man of more than sixty, he sat erect in a hard high-backed chair whilst his wife Mathilda sipped elegantly from a bone china teacup before picking up her needle again. The maid curtseyed and placed a small silver tray on the table. "A letter has just arrived for you ma'am."

"Thank you, Emily. You may go." The tall elderly lady nodded graciously, picked up the letter and frowned as she examined the postmark.

Her husband looked up from his newspaper and watched her.

Mathilda slit the envelope open and spread the letter out, holding it up to the light. Her eyesight was poor and she squinted at it, turning the letter over. "From the church, some little parish of Westcott in Surrey. Why they should write to us is a mystery." She leaned closer to the paper struggling to read.

Suddenly she stiffened and straightened her back, and her pale cheeks lost the last of their colour. She dropped the paper on the tray. "Good God!"

"What is it m'dear?" he frowned.

She was breathing quickly.

Charles rose to his feet stiffly and glanced at the clock. He only had a few minutes to spare, so he came to grasp her shoulder. "Let me read it."

"No Charles. Allow me to read it to you." She snatched the letter up and turned slowly to give him the full benefit of her gaze. "Listen."

Dear Mr and Mrs Braithwaite,

I am writing to inform you of a series of events that should be brought to your attention.

Your daughter, Maisy Brooks, has lived for the last nine years in my parish. She and her husband have two children, Madeline aged twelve and Matthew aged eight.

You may already be aware that Maisy is gravely ill with tuberculosis and has been confined to a Sanatorium. Her husband, Angus Brooks, died three days ago in a tragic accident, leaving the children to all intents and purposes orphans.

I pray you can find it in your hearts to provide for your grandchildren. They are young and innocent of any harm.

They are staying with my family until their future is decided.

It is with regret that I inform you of these events, but I look forward to hearing from you.

Yours sincerely

Reverend P.K. Rogers

St Barnabas Church

Westcott

Mrs Braithwaite finished reading the letter and there followed a long, pained silence.

He was staring at her in pure disbelief.

She took a deep breath and whispered, "So there you have it." And she concentrated on folding the two pages and laying them on the tray.

"Good God!" he frowned. "I had no idea Maisy was ill nor did I know she had children. Did you?"

"No," the elderly woman was breathing with a little difficulty. "I've heard nothing from her in years."

"Surely you've made some effort to contact her. She *is* your daughter."

Her cheeks coloured. "She rejected us, Charles. She chose to marry a musician and cut herself off from us. I warned her what to expect, marrying into poverty. As for her children, we already have grandchildren."

"Mathilda!" he roared. "They're just children."

She stiffened with dignity. "We are not on a parade ground now Charles. The children would be completely out of place here. They've been living in rural Surrey and would be overawed by the life we lead," she shivered. "They probably won't even know how to use a knife and fork. I'll write to this Reverend Rogers," she opened the drawer of her writing table and took out paper and pens, then glanced at her husband. "I'll send him a cheque to help with their education."

"No. It's not enough."

She froze and looked at him. "I know what I'm doing Charles. They would hate it here." Then her eyes flickered quickly to the clock and her voice became persuasive. "Now my dear, you have important military duties to perform. You must leave the family to me as you always have done."

"I've had no option in the past, but they are my grandchildren, Mathilda. Extend to them such help as they require, and would you please find out where Maisy is being nursed."

Slowly she inclined her head. "As you wish Charles, I will write thus. Now it might be prudent to go and prepare yourself for your journey. You may leave it safely to me."

He continued to study her for a moment or two, then glanced once more at the clock and turned away. He had no other option.

There was something here that he was not comfortable with, and that disturbed him. He climbed the stairs to his bedroom. His bag had already been packed by the faithful Biddings and was waiting on the bed.

Methodically, he flicked through the clothes in his case, and checked that Biddings had packed everything he had requested. His wallet had been put out for him. He checked that he had enough cash, then placed the wallet in the inside pocket of his jacket and looked around.

Having served all over the world as a representative of a prestigious Empire with servants to provide his every wish, and spent the last ten years in the imperial splendour of India, his home country seemed more than a little small and squalid. And his wife had turned out to be a cold uncaring creature. He wanted his grandchildren cared for properly.

Ensuring that happened might prove a little difficult. The last few years before retirement were to be spent attached to the War Office in London and would entail a great deal of travelling. A slight smile warmed his eyes. This was going to be the most taxing job of his career and he felt a certain relish at the challenge.

In silence downstairs, Mathilda wrote the letter, enclosing a cheque. She mentioned nothing about further help for the children, nor did she make any enquiries about her sick daughter. Presently she sealed the envelope.

When he returned to bid her farewell, she smiled sweetly at him. "It is done. Now you must go and see Martin Grantham when you're home next, Charles. That new owner at Harborough Hall is putting on a vulgar fashion show for the trade next week."

He bent to kiss her cheek. "Well, that should keep you tabbies happy my dear, give you something to complain about. I'll write shortly and let you know when I shall be back. It may not be for some while. Please keep me informed when you receive news about Maisy."

♪♫

CHAPTER 8

THE RIVER WAS once again a quiet peaceful ribbon, winding like a gracefully discarded silver strand through the undulating countryside. It had subsided after the wildness of the storms and floods to its normal calm placidity and displayed no desire to hurry, neither glinting nor rushing under the warming sun of spring.

Out of breath from the invigorating two-mile walk, Maddy stopped by the roadside, and looked down at the grassy bank.

"Maddy." Josie caught up with her at last. The young girl was almost in tears as she beheld the sight of the accident. She averted her eyes and put an arm around her friend's shoulder. "It's not necessary you know. You mustn't ever doubt your father. No one will ever suggest such a thing again after the way Daddy spoke to them in church on Sunday."

"I've never doubted him, Josie." Maddy looked silently at

the deep gouges in the soft, muddy bank where her father had struggled to save himself from drowning after the car had knocked him off the road. Her father would never have committed suicide! It just was not in him to give up. Nor was it in her. There had been so many whispered comments made behind her back during the last week, spiteful suggestions that had been voiced just loud enough for her to hear, and she had fought back like a tigress.

She glanced at her friend's distressed face. Josie had loved her father like a favourite uncle and had reacted with surprising firmness to the unkind slurs that had been cast at him. It had surprised Maddy, who knew how timid and gentle Josie was, and this courage and determination warmed her more than anything else could have done.

Maddy smiled. "It's beautiful isn't it, in spite of what happened. I wanted to see it for myself, and there's something I've got to do. You don't have to stay if you'd rather not."

Josie smiled wanly. "Of course I will stay. Besides, it's our last chance to be together."

"I'll come back and see you in the holidays if they let me."

Josie's eyes filled with tears and she opened her mouth to say something, then shook her head suddenly. "I can't believe you've got to go away."

Maddy looked out over the rolling countryside, and despair touched her for a moment. Slowly she inhaled, breathed in deeply of the fragrant grass scented air, then knelt and began to pick the flowers.

Josie watched her for a moment, then knelt down onto the soft grass by her side. "What are you going to do Maddy?"

"Daddy loved flowers. I'm going to make the biggest

daisy chain you've ever seen, and leave it for him." Then impulsively she ran her fingers across the bobbing white flowers. "A daisy chain would put his memory to rest."

"Oh, let me help you," Josie reached out a little shakily and began picking the tiny blooms too.

The young girls remained on the grassy slopes for more than an hour, weaving busily. Maddy's fair golden hair shimmered in the bright summer sun, blown on a soft warm breeze so that it mixed with her friend's dark brown hair. Their heads were bent close together, intent on their work.

"There that's it." Finally, Maddy straightened and spread the long, lush chain out on the grass. She glanced at Josie and touched her arm. "Will you wait for me here. I've got to do this alone."

She gathered up the chain and crossed the road to the riverbank where she knelt by the deeply gouged marks. It must have been a terrible struggle in the pouring rain, numbed and half blinded by the deluge and badly hurt by the impact.

She arranged the chain carefully and tenderly over the marks, forming a beautiful and personal wreath. She looked at them for a long while, then touched them once as though communicating with him for the very last time. "I'll come back, Daddy, one day."

Maddy rose to her feet and a sudden surge of tears blinded her eyes. Her action had closed the door on her past. She was alone now, and she had to face her future.

She stood there for some while by herself, then finally Josie plucked up the courage to approach her. She put an arm around Maddy's shoulder, leaning close to whisper, "Come on Maddy. It's time we were going home."

Maddy nodded and tried to dry her eyes but the tears

kept defiantly coming, and she whispered, "What a fool I am!"

"You're not a fool! You're very brave, much braver than I could ever be. Oh, heavens, I'm going to miss you." Josie had to wipe tears from her own eyes, then she glanced at her watch and groaned. "Look at the time, come on, we must go."

♪♫

CHAPTER 9

SANDBOURNE WAS A large market town thirty-five miles from Westcott, and the two children, accompanied by the Reverend Rogers, made a long and lonely journey there in the back of a large black car that had been lent to them for the day by Mr Prior. Finally, they climbed down from the vehicle and stood side by side, each with a small bag of possessions at their feet. Two large terraces faced each other like combatants from opposite sides of the street, and they paused to look from one imposing Victorian facade to the other. A plaque on each door announced that they were council run orphanages. Fear bordering on panic filled Maddy, and she could feel Matthew shuddering against her, trying valiantly to be brave. She put her arm around him and squeezed reassuringly.

The Vicar placed a hand on each of their shoulders, his fingers gripping them gently, and he murmured, "Come on then my dears. Matthew, we'll come and see you settled in first."

They climbed the steps and pulled the bell cord, and presently the door opened onto a dark interior. As they entered, it seemed to Maddy that they were being swallowed into the stomach of an enormous whale and would never emerge to see the light of day again.

In less than half an hour Matthew had been taken away and it was Maddy's turn. They crossed the road and the great front door of the girls' orphanage opened before them. A figure stepped aside to let them in. "Madeline Brooks?"

"Yes." Maddy felt as though her voice had shrunk so that it seemed small and insignificant in the vast echoing hallway.

"Come on this way, dearie. Matron is waiting to see you."

Maddy picked up her case and followed in the woman's footsteps across a worn tiled floor that was illuminated in places by vivid pools of orange, red and green light from the stained-glass windows. They were taken into Matron's office, and Maddy found herself standing in front of a tall thin woman with a strict and uncompromising face.

"Thank you, Trent." Matron nodded to the lady who had shown them in. "I'll ring when I need you."

"Yes ma'am," and the door shut crisply.

Maddy could feel herself trembling now and a surge of despair swept through her. It was all happening so quickly, soon now she would be no one.

Matron was watching her solemnly. "There's nothing to be afraid of, Madeline. You will soon find that you'll fit in here. Sit down. I have some paperwork to finish with the Reverend Rogers." She turned to the Vicar and held her hand out to him. "I'm pleased to meet you Reverend, and glad that we've been able to take the girl in."

Maddy sat on the hard wooden seat as instructed and gazed blankly at her hands. She gripped them tightly together to control their trembling. This was like a bad nightmare. She and Matthew were being herded like cattle away from the people they knew, the life they understood, and dumped in this alien regimented establishment. He must be feeling even more frightened and alone than she was. She had to be strong, strong for them both, and help him through the next few months.

The Vicar's kind familiar voice was droning in the background, but the words did not sink into her bemused mind.

Matron rose to her feet and shook the Vicar's hand then turned to Maddy. "Say goodbye now child and come with me. We've got a lot to do."

Maddy rose slowly to her feet, her eyes wide with fright. She felt the Reverend Rogers kiss her cheek and speak to her, then Matron nodded and swept her away.

They climbed a wide flight of stairs that were exotically bathed in light from the coloured windows, and reached a long unlit corridor. Matron turned left abruptly and Maddy followed and found herself in a bright bedroom.

There were eight beds, four on each side of the room, and beside each bed stood a chest of drawers. The room was simple and orderly, the beds were all made, and she could see small cuddly toys and night dresses tucked under the pillows, slippers tidily under the beds, and the room was vibrant with life.

"Now Madeline, this is your bed. The girls on either side of you will take care of you for the first few days. You may unpack your things and put them in the drawers. You're allowed four items on the lockers. Now leave your case here for a moment and follow me."

In a daze, she was shown other large dormitories, she saw the white tiled scrupulously clean bathroom, lined with bowls and taps. And she was enchanted when she entered the nursery and saw a baby and two toddlers, too young yet for school. Their noise filled the room with life. Then she was taken downstairs to the dining room, to the sitting room and study, and finally to a large and empty assembly hall. Matron smiled. "Many of the girls prefer to spend their time here. They can play netball and games, and some of them enjoy dancing."

Last of all, Maddy was led into a large parlour at the back of the house, where several women were busy mending and polishing, and she breathed a sigh of relief. This warm room was most like home, with its air of industry and human cosiness.

"You girls are allocated jobs each day. Those jobs must be satisfactorily completed before you're allowed recreational time. The rota is put up here every Monday."

Matron's long bony finger pointed to a carefully drawn list consisting of names and tasks. Maddy looked closely at it and found her own name already listed. Her job was to help wash the dishes after each meal.

"You see," Matron continued softly, "we have to prepare you girls to run your own homes once you've left us. We pride ourselves on our girls. If you do your best, you will be well rewarded."

Maddy gathered all her courage and looked up into the thin strict face. "Shall I be able to see my brother? He's only eight and very frightened at being left alone. It's all happened so quickly..."

"Communication with the boys across the road is strictly forbidden."

"But Matron, he's only eight and..."

"That is the rule."

"But Matron, please…"

"However!" Matron's eyes sharpened, and she grasped her shoulder emphatically. "We provide the opportunity for families like yours to meet on Sundays after church."

Maddy smiled wanly and looked down at her feet. It was a small concession, but it was better than nothing. She would find a way to see her brother somehow.

"You'll soon get used to it, and so will your brother. He'll have more friends than he's ever had before." Matron turned away and threw open a large cupboard beside the boiler, then turned back briskly and straightened Maddy's shoulders. "Now! I have to measure you for your new clothes. Arms out straight please." The tape measure flicked around her with great dexterity. "You will have no further need of your old clothes, so I suggest you pack them away in the suitcase, under your bed."

With swift precise movements, Matron sorted through the piles of clothes in the cupboard, and counted out a set of crisp white blouses, navy blue serge skirts and cardigans. On top of that she placed voluminous navy-blue knickers, socks and two nightdresses. Matron looked at Maddy's pale face and smiled slightly. "We've arranged a place for you at St Michael's School down the road, so you'll be walking with the other girls in the morning. Up early, wash, breakfast, make your bed, and then off to school. By the end of next year, you will have to find a job and make your own way. Ah, Mrs Hardy, this is Madeline our new girl. Will you take her upstairs, give her a bath and check her hair please?"

"Yes, Matron." A plump motherly woman pushed aside her needlework and collected the pile of clothes Maddy had just been given, then took her by the hand. "Come on, my little maid, I'll give'ee a hand with your things if 'ee want."

Maddy could feel despair flooding through her as she was led along the corridor, and it suddenly overflowed in aching tears. The hand holding hers squeezed warmly. "I know, my little soul, have a good cry, it'll do 'ee good. Bath's the best place for that. You won't spoil your new clothes, and I'll stay clear of Matron's fire."

Maddy giggled in spite of her tears as she imagined Matron as a dragon breathing fire.

"That's better. This 'ere place come alive when the girls get home from school. On go all the lights, and my, what hullabaloo they make. Goes right through your 'ead, it do. But they all quiet down when Matron comes in."

Mrs Hardy gossiped as she ran the bath and coaxed her into the warm water. By the time Maddy had been scrubbed and dressed in the uniform clothes, she felt as though she had always known the friendly and warm-hearted woman. Even the indignity of having her long golden hair searched for lice did not trouble her very much.

"What beautiful hair you 'ave," Mrs Hardy breathed as she plaited it quickly. "But 'ee'll 'ave to keep it tied back I'm afraid, Matron's rules. Lots of rules 'ere, and you'll 'ave to learn em quick, my girl. But come and see me if you go wrong. Let's get unpack your things, shall we? You've lots of room in them drawers, so forget what Matron said. We'll put everything away safely, and you can see it whenever you've a mind to."

Later that afternoon, Maddy sat alone on her bed, looking down at the music on her knee. She felt a little better for touching it, and as she looked at the print, she could hear the music running through her head. She would survive. She was determined to.

She heard the huge house come alive suddenly with voices and activity, and then she looked up quickly. She was already beginning to recognise Matron's footsteps. She slipped the music away into her drawer just as Matron opened the door and beckoned her briskly. "Come with me Madeline. I want to introduce you to the girls."

♪♫

That night, the Reverend Rogers sat alone in his study, his head in his hands, the table lamp giving a gentle light. He needed darkness to hide and heal the anger and self-disgust that filled his soul. Neither of them were particularly Christian emotions.

Presently, the door opened and his wife crept in and placed a cup of tea on the leather framed blotter in front of him.

Her hand touched his shoulder tenderly and squeezed. "You couldn't do anything more to help them, Peter. You mustn't blame yourself." She drew a chair up and sat opposite him.

"Sometimes I wonder whether there's any Christianity left in the Church," he said painfully. "There is certainly none in the Town Council. When I think how much Angus has done for the parish... you should have seen those poor kids when I left them today, all alone and terrified. I don't know how I managed to do it, yet I smiled at them as I said goodbye! I felt like Judas."

"I wish we could have taken care of them. It would have been no hardship, and Josie would have loved it."

The Vicar's face tensed once again. "It all comes down to money in the end. Very few of those who have it are prepared to share it with those who haven't. The only man who has made any contribution towards their care is John Prior, God bless his soul."

"Perhaps there's still something we can do ourselves if we try really hard." Eagerly she drew towards her the red clothbound book in which they kept their accounts and opened it restlessly.

He smiled and gently encouraged her to shut it. "I've tried, Laura. Every night, I've sat here and worked through the accounts, trying to find something we can cut back on. But there's nothing, and it's only going to get harder. When Ron goes to Durham in the autumn, we're going to find the fees and expenses prohibitive. Then there will be William who's bound to want to go to university the following year, and in a few more years..."

"It makes me feel so selfish!" she murmured and looked down at her hardworking hands, at the calluses and dry skin. It took constant physical work to care for such a large family, cleaning and scrubbing the house, growing the vegetables, and making and mending clothes that had to be passed down from one to another.

He nodded sombrely. "Angus would have moved heaven and earth if it had been our children."

"You have tried Peter!"

"Yes. And damn it, I'm going to keep trying." He drew towards him a pen and paper. "I shan't let the Braithwaite woman forget this, nor the Church, nor the Council."

♪♫

CHAPTER 10

ALTHOUGH IT WAS early June and the weather glorious, Harborough Hall was illuminated like a Christmas tree. The long, elegant windows emitted an exuberant intensity of light and sound that had not been witnessed for a generation, not since the once proud Lord Harborough had hosted vast summer balls for his guests. Well trained waiters had been hired from London for the occasion, but local people had not been overlooked. Nearby farms supplied meat, fruit and vegetables, with only the exotic produce being shipped in from the capital. Young girls and women were paid to help in the kitchens and receptions rooms, and their menfolk were drafted in to tidy the gardens and lift and carry. Meanwhile it fell to the village constables to supervise the flow of traffic.

Belaugh was a man they could do business with. His tastes and direct style were reassuringly down to earth, and he paid handsomely for their services.

One by one, sleek black cars drew up at the house, and out climbed a lady and gentleman, each splendidly dressed to display their affluence and influence.

As the couples entered the house, they were greeted by the Belaughs, the gentlemen presented with a cigar and the ladies with a corsage of fragrant flowers. Discreet waiting staff served sherry and conducted them through to tables in the ballroom.

The entire process worked remarkably smoothly and the Belaughs had nothing to do but receive and impress their guests. There was little in their demeanour to hint at the vital importance of the occasion to their financial wellbeing, for they performed with impeccable style.

Belaugh, in a black suit hung with gold watch and chain, looked every inch the self-made businessman. He knew each of the buyers, having cultivated their acquaintance and dealt with them over many years. They in turn had learned to respect his round, mild featured face, knowing that a shrewd and competitive brain was concealed behind it.

Phyllis Belaugh was a fine woman, chosen by her husband from the many who had thrown their caps at him, for her strength, honesty and capability. He wanted nothing in the least bit weak or faulty to pass on to his future generations. He had no pretensions to gentility and no desire for it, indeed he judged many of the quirks and mannerisms of the upper classes to be an expression of weakness. The wife he had chosen was discreet and well able to hold her own amongst any group of people. He could trust her to handle shop-floor workers effectively, and to do him a credit at the Masonic ladies' evenings. He could ask for no more.

Phyllis Belaugh was dressed in the most beautiful of the evening gowns created by Nigel Davenport for tonight's event. It had taken some persuading to entice the designer to entrust her and not one of the gorgeous young mannequins with the task of modelling his prize creation. But now, seeing her display it so elegantly and with confidence and character, he understood the wisdom of Belaugh's demand. She had a strong, attractive personality which gave it greater value in the eyes of the middle-aged female guests. After all, it was women like these who would be buying the gowns, and he was gratified to see veiled glances of admiration and envy.

The Belaughs observed their guests discreetly during the show, gauging their response to the fashions they were seeing. Then once the easy part of the evening was over, the wines and champagne had been drunk, the lavish food consumed, and the buyers were in a mellow frame of mind, Bernard and Phyllis rose from their places to perform the much more difficult task of selling the product and clinching deals. They mingled amongst their guests, encouraging them to get up from their seats and view the collection a second time on the static models that had been placed around the house.

"Quite a show Bernard," a large ponderous figure, the most important of the buyers present, watched Belaugh approach his table.

"What did you think of what you saw, James?"

Sir James Monaghan rose slowly to his feet and leaned his head back to draw deeply on his cigar. He released the button on his stretched waistcoat, tucked his thumb into the pocket and allowed his stomach to expand. "Design is excellent. No quibbles. What I want to see is the quality of output from your factories. Have you got any lines up and running yet?"

"We've produced a couple of hundred of article six, the cotton summer dress. We'll be expanding the fabric selection soon. We've also produced a small batch of fifteen of the evening dress Phyllis is wearing tonight, just three of each size, a limited edition. That dress deserves special consideration wouldn't you agree?"

"Ah! The lovely Phyllis," cigar smoke curled from the man's mouth, and his bright brown eyes were instantly keen and alert. "Now that does interest me, very much."

"Then allow me to take you to see the batch. I have it on display. Perhaps Lady Monaghan would care to join us?"

"Love to Bernard," a thin lady, as impressive as her husband, but a complimentary opposite, rose to her feet and came to take his arm, and Belaugh led them through the hall to the dining room to view the gowns in question.

Meanwhile, in the room they had just left, Nigel Davenport was working his magic with artistic extravagance upon several other interested parties, and Phyllis was conducting a group of abandoned wives around the displays, providing them with another glass of wine and leaving their husbands to talk business. Many people underestimated the influencing factor of the wives but not Phyllis, and she worked hard but with discretion.

The last guest did not leave until two in the morning, and once the sleek black cars had finally scrunched away down the drive, Phyllis sighed and let the bright act slip. She sat down and eased her shoes off and just gazed around at the debris. The staff were still dutifully collecting up glasses from all possible horizontal surfaces. The tables had been cleared hours ago but had been repeatedly cluttered with glasses and spillage from the ash trays.

Belaugh smiled at her, and she could see the eager gleam sparkling in his eyes, and it made her laugh. "How could you, Bernard?"

"I'm good for another few hours yet. May I visit you tonight?" He rubbed his hands together with relish.

"Tonight?" she looked at him in dismay. "My feet ache, my back aches and I'm exhausted."

"It's my lucky night, my dear. I have a feeling about this. The show went well, and we have plenty of them nibbling at the bait. We could be lucky in other ways too."

She pulled a face. "You may as well return home every time a black cat crosses your path. That's pure superstition. I am genuinely very tired."

His face suddenly showed the grit and determination that lay at the root of his character. Firmly, he said, "You know what they said at the clinic."

Her shoulders slumped slightly, and a deep pang of pain reminded her of her failure as a wife and mate. "That's unfair. I've done my best Bernard."

"And I intend to do mine. I'll be waiting for you." He turned on his heel and made towards the stairs.

Phyllis sighed and eased her throbbing feet back into the shoes that were now pinching her and forced herself to get up. She beckoned the butler over and smiled. "The staff have performed really well tonight, Parstow, you've done us proud. I want you to send all the village staff home now, and our own people to bed. They must be exhausted. We'll begin work again at nine in the morning."

"Yes ma'am." He inclined his head graciously. "Thank you."

She made her way slowly up to her suite and opened the door cautiously.

Bernard was looking at himself seriously in the mirror, and she almost laughed. He did not have a very impressive figure, but he was admiring what he did have like a peacock preening itself.

She straightened her face. It was not fair. His figure in no way matched his intellect, and she had a great deal of admiration for that. She entered, and his eyes moved to study her.

"I really am tired, you know," she said quietly.

"I know." He turned and placed his hands on her shoulders, but he did not allow them to rest there. His hands moved slowly down her back, exploring and caressing her with searching possessiveness. "You know how success makes me. I'll never sleep now, until I've had you. Just look at you in this dress. Every woman tonight wanted to be in your shoes."

His fingers were wrestling to find the new-fangled zip under her arm. She let him reach it, with a sense of resignation.

She was exhausted and could make no real response to his desire for her, but that did not matter much to him. In this mood, he would not take long, and then he would take his clothes and retire to his own room for the night.

Once he had satisfied his restless desire and gone, Phyllis touched her flat stomach and tears filled her eyes. She prayed vehemently to God that he was right. They had been married for five years and there had been no sign that their marriage would be graced by a child. And it was not for lack of trying. The absence was like a bleeding wound in her heart, and to be acting as mother to three children who were not her own only made the hurt worse.

But she was too exhausted to think for long tonight. Sleep hit her and she did not wake until breakfast was brought to her at ten.

♪♫

CHAPTER 11

THE HUGE DINING room at the orphanage accommodated thirty-two girls, and on a hot July day like today the windows were thrown open and a cool breeze blew through, making it the most comfortable room in the house.

Maddy was hot and tired after a long arduous day at school. They had played netball this afternoon, and she was aching for a long soak in the bath. It was her turn tonight, but she would have to wait until she had finished her chores. This week she had been assigned the task of helping bathe the toddlers and baby each day and changing the sheets on their cots and beds. A gleam of laughter came into her vivid blue eyes, and she glanced sideways at the girl who had befriended her, and whispered behind her hand, "I hope that wretched little Paula doesn't wee on me again today. I could still smell it when I got up this morning."

Tina choked with laughter and Maddy giggled too, remembering the moment when the child had drenched the front of her dress. Tina had made a hilarious comment, and Maddy had laughed out loud. That was when the barrier between them had collapsed, and they recognised each other as like spirits. Bubbling with fun and daring, Tina secretly hungered to achieve things.

Matron looked up repressively from her position and fixed her eye on the two girls. Hastily Tina coughed and hid her laughter behind her handkerchief. Then as Matron looked away, she whispered, "You'll be the death of me Maddy Brooks, we're not supposed to speak at the table."

Maddy smiled mischievously and lowered her eyes to her food once again. They were released from their silence once all the plates had been removed. Matron dismissed them to their tasks, and Maddy glanced at the piano leaning against the wall. As they filed out, she touched Tina's arm and nodded towards it. "Is anyone allowed to play that?"

"Heavens no!" The girl's voice was shocked. "It's far too precious for our grubby little fingers. You'll be thrashed if you're caught touching it."

Maddy followed her friend up the wide echoing stairway to the nursery. Then as they opened the door, all the noise and exuberance of the little ones assailed them, and her disappointment and irritation were forgotten. The little girl who had wet her yesterday came toddling straight for her with precarious determination and lifted up her arms to be cuddled. Maddy broke into a laugh and leaned over to oblige, and she smiled as the child pulled at her long golden plaits. "Yes, you little monster. You have quite a thing about me and my hair, haven't you? I suppose that was some strange baptismal ceremony you performed on me yesterday."

"You'll just have to make sure she has a nappy on when you pick her up next time, Maddy." Tina came into the room behind her, and it was her turn to be assailed by an eager child.

By the time the two girls had completed their chores and the little ones were cleaned, polished and ready for bed, most of the other girls were already in the hall and sitting room. Maddy turned away from the throng nervously.

Tina touched Maddy's arm and held her back. "Don't go and sit all by yourself again in the bedroom. Why don't you come and join us?"

"Thanks Tina, but I was going to have my bath." Maddy hesitated for a moment. "Look, I don't think I'm quite ready to be with you all yet. I'm not used to being so close to people all the time."

Tina frowned and bit her lower lip between her teeth. "You won't get used to it either, unless you come in, at least for a little while." Then she linked her arm through Maddy's persuasively. "I have an idea. We've got some homework to do. We could do it quietly together in the study, couldn't we? That'll be a start."

Maddy looked at the bright chirpy face of her new friend and relaxed suddenly. "Yes, I'd like that. You're right, I'm just being silly."

"Good, come on then."

Tina turned and ran exuberantly down the stairs, then froze to a halt as a strict voice boomed, "Who is that behaving like a gazelle? You're a young lady, not an animal. Walk please."

They continued on their way with ladylike decorum and found a spot in the study where they could sit together and work on their mathematical problems. The work did not take Maddy long, and soon she was idly looking along the shelf of well used dictionaries and encyclopaedias. Hundreds of children must have passed through here, fingering the volumes so that the spines were shredded and bare.

It brought back a vivid memory of home. Their furniture had been worn bare too. Now it had been sold and even Daddy's piano belonged to someone else.

Her thoughts veered away from the darkness trapped within her, and she glanced quickly at her companion's face. Tina was frowning in concentration. "Stuck?" she whispered.

Tina nodded and pulled a face. "I hate arithmetic. I don't think I'll ever conquer it."

"Let's see." Maddy pulled up her chair and leaned over Tina's shoulder and peered at the neatly written figures for some while, then at last she sat back. "I see what it is. Look. You must always do the sums inside the brackets first. Everything else is perfectly correct."

"Ah, that's it! I'd forgotten about that. Thanks." Tina began to scribble away again furiously.

Later, when they were packing up their books, Maddy's thoughts kept returning to the old piano in the dining room. The sight of it had made her ache with the longing for the lost magic of her father. She touched Tina's arm. "Look, would you come with me Tina? I couldn't do this on my own, I haven't the courage. It's that piano." She shrugged. "It reminds me so much of the one at home, it hurts. I just need to touch it."

The other girl stiffened a little. "It's forbidden you know. There would be terrible trouble if we were spotted." But then as she studied Maddy's tense face, her expression softened, and she smiled. "I understand. There were things like that for me too when I first came here. I'll come with you."

Maddy breathed a sigh of relief. "I won't get you into trouble. You can stay outside if you like. It's just that I'm frightened of what I'll feel."

"Come on then. We'll go together." Tina lifted her satchel onto her shoulder and hurried her along. "You'll feel better when you've done it."

A few minutes later, the two of them cautiously pushed open the dining room door and peeped in. The vast room was empty, the rows of tables already laid for breakfast the following morning. Maddy exhaled slowly. Her heart was pounding so heavily she had to force herself to breathe naturally. She crept across the creaking wooden floorboards with Tina close behind her.

It was not just an illusion. It was very like the piano at home. The wood veneer was beginning to flake in just the same places. She reached out to touch it and experienced a strange sensation almost like shock. The suppressed emotion came bubbling dangerously close to the surface, and she shrank away quickly, not daring to allow it any more reality.

"What are you girls doing in here?" a sharp voice demanded from behind them, and they spun round quickly.

Tina was struck dumb with fright, and Maddy glanced at her friend with a desperate feeling of guilt, then stammered, "I'm sorry Miss Trent. It was my idea to come in. I... I don't know why, but... I needed to..." she could feel her throat tightening up.

"You girls are not allowed in here between meals, and touching the piano is forbidden."

"Yes Miss Trent. I'm sorry. It just seems such a shame..."

"Silence!" The woman's face was drawn and tired, and her irritation struck fear into both girls. "This incident will be reported to Matron. Now get out of here, and don't do it again."

The two girls fled and waited in dread to be summoned to Matron's office.

They waited more than half an hour in growing terror, and then stiffened as Miss Trent appeared in the doorway and beckoned them. Nothing was said, and they followed her severe outline to Matron's office. The door was opened, and they were ushered in.

Matron rose to her feet and came slowly around the desk towards them. "Girls. I'm surprised at your behaviour. What have you got to say for yourselves?"

"We're sorry, Matron," Tina whispered in a small voice.

"Very well. However, the rules of the house must be obeyed. Now present your hands," and she turned to fetch a fine cane from the corner of the room.

Tina extended her hand obediently, but it was more than Maddy could bear. "Matron, all I did was touch..."

Matron turned quickly, and the authority in her eyes silenced the girl. "You broke the rules child. You clearly need to learn obedience."

Her hands were trembling now in fright, but she gathered all her courage. "Yes Matron. I'm sorry. But Tina didn't do anything wrong, it was me."

"It was her responsibility to inform you of the rules, and she has either failed in her duty or abetted you in breaking them. Now present your hands both of you, your left hands please."

There was no choice. Maddy did as she was told and closed her eyes, screwing them up tightly as Matron came towards her first. She could almost feel the strict presence crossing the room to stand threateningly in front of her, and her legs began to tremble ominously. Then the small thin stick thrashed wickedly across the palm of her hand and she gasped, pulling her hand away involuntarily and clutching it to her chest.

"Hand!" Matron said sternly.

Maddy took a deep breath and extended her hand once again, watching in fascinated horror. The stick thrashed again, and two angry red weals appeared on her skin.

Matron looked into the young girl's eyes as they rose from the scored palm to look in shock at her, and more than a little gentleness softened her expression. She closed the rigid thin little hand and patted it. "You must remember Madeline. The rules are there for a purpose, and I cannot permit you or any of the girls to break them. I've been lenient with you today. If you intentionally digress again, then the punishment will be six thrashes. Remember that."

♪♫

CHAPTER 12

LATER THAT NIGHT, Maddy lay in bed and looked across the darkened room at Tina's outline. "Are you asleep yet?"

"No," Tina murmured instantly. "My hand hurts too much to sleep."

Maddy leaned up on her elbow. "Mine too. Look, I'm sorry, Tina. I should never have asked you to come, it was all my fault. But it's not very fair, we'd done nothing really wrong."

"It's the rules. Matron was right, I should have been a better friend and warned you properly," the girl's voice was stifled by a deep sigh. "Going with you reminded me of when I first came here. It was that big red chair by the fire that got me. We had one just like it. Even now it's my favourite, and I've been here three years. I don't think you ever forget how it was."

"Did it get any easier?" Maddy asked around the constriction in her throat.

"Oh yes, eventually. Life seems quite real and normal here, now."

There was a long pause, and just as Maddy began to think her friend must have fallen asleep at last, the voice whispered, "Must have taken about a year."

Maddy looked at the regimented outlines of beds just visible in the darkened room. "I keep thinking I'm going to wake up in a moment and I'll be in my own bed, and all this will have been a dream."

"So did I. Nothing here was like home, except that chair. You're fairly local, aren't you? You're used to the farms and fields and hedges. I bet you even came to the market sometimes."

"Yes," Maddy had a sudden vivid recollection of coming here with her mother before she was ill. The memory was precious, and with difficulty she murmured, "I can't talk about it."

Tina was silent for a while then, "You ought to try Maddy. It helps."

"Does it really? It just seems to hurt."

"Tell me about it in the morning, and I'll tell you about my home." The young voice suddenly filled with surprise. "Do you know, I think I'll be able to sleep now."

"Goodnight," Maddy whispered and turned over, but her mind wandered through all the memories that she treasured. They seemed to belong to another existence, as though they had happened to a different girl and had nothing to do with the Maddy Brooks who lived here. She tried hard to concentrate on her home and her parents, and slowly some of the blackness inside her began to retreat.

At breakfast the next morning Maddy kept her eyes firmly away from the closed instrument in the corner. She did not want to go through that painful experience again. It was better to put the past firmly behind her.

She succeeded very well for a long while, until one evening some three weeks later when the girls were getting up to leave the dining room, she brushed up close to the piano. It was too much, and she did the unmentionable. She touched the flaking wood, and her thin strong fingers pulled eagerly at the lid.

Her hands fell away. It was locked. Oh, how she longed to touch it, to run her fingers over the ivory keys. Maybe then, she would find herself again, and wake up from this strange existence.

She glanced over her shoulder. No one was watching her. She only prayed her transgression had not been observed.

♪♫

It was nearly midnight, and all the girls were in bed and asleep. Matron looked around the gathered staff as they sat before her in her wood panelled office. Her hawklike gaze was often quite sufficient to silence an unseemly word. Now it was used to impose her wishes upon the staff. "You are to ensure that the girls receive a far more generous helping of vegetables. What I saw last night was disgraceful. They cannot live on bread alone for their substance. Mrs Alcock, when the market opens tomorrow, I want you and your girl to go straight there. Come to me before you leave, and I'll give you a purse."

"Yes, Matron."

Matron glanced down at the agenda and her face became gentler. "Now. The new girl. She's in your room, Mrs Hardy. How is she settling in?"

"Settling in quite well, Matron. She be a tidy maid. But

she's holding herself in."

Matron nodded. "I've been watching her and I think the same. She and Tina seem to be getting on well, but she hasn't opened up to anyone else has she?"

They all shook their heads, so Matron looked down at her notes. "Well Tina will certainly benefit. Madeline was apparently given a Grammar School scholarship at her last school. I've been reading through her papers. There must be something here that will bring her out. I have the feeling we're missing something, but of course it's early days yet."

"I'll have a chat with her tomorrow night, Matron." Mrs Hardy crossed her hands placidly in her lap.

"Yes, do that." Matron fixed her sharp gaze on the kindly woman. "You can usually get through to the most stubborn of them in the end."

Mrs Hardy frowned over her thoughts. "She ain't mentioned nothing about herself. I have a feeling she's still full of the past and brooding over it."

"Go gently then, she's still very newly orphaned."

Mrs Hardy nodded. "I know what to do Matron."

Matron glanced back at her agenda. "Good. The next item is not so pleasant. The problem of Daniella has arisen again."

"She can't stay in my room no longer Matron," one of the other staff shook her head firmly and looked around at the other faces in the room. "What that maid needs is a spell on her own to teach her how to behave. T'others can't abide her, and she pays no notice to us."

"Hmmm." Matron folded her hands thoughtfully on the desk. "We'll try that, but I don't believe it will make any difference. Her problem is deeper. If solitary fails to calm her down, we'll have to get her transferred to a hostel where they can cope with her. She's having a detrimental effect on the other girls, and we can't have that."

There was a general consensus of approval, and a short while later, the meeting was dismissed.

♪♫

Matron watched the new girl carefully for the next few days. It was a normal pattern of grief, and there would eventually be a trigger that would bring her through it, and then they would begin to see a happier smile and a more open reaction to other girls.

♪♫

CHAPTER 13

PHYLLIS BELAUGH WAS elegantly dressed for church. She had adapted very quickly to her new environment and was now a relaxed and natural part of it. As a thoughtful mistress of Harborough Hall, she had earned the trust and respect of her servants, but her husband was not at home often enough to have developed a similar relationship. He still disliked the quiet of the countryside and appeared out of place in the impressive splendour of his classical surroundings. Phyllis glanced at his plump outline in the drawing room window and pulled her gloves on. "You're full of bright ideas this year Bernard."

"This particular project was the Vicar's." He turned back to the highly decorated drawing room. "Apparently the fete has always been held here in the grounds. There will be nothing for you to trouble over. Parstow can make the arrangements, just as he did for old Lord Harborough."

She nodded. "Then it's agreed. We'll inform the Vicar that

we'll continue the tradition next summer. Although I intend to play a good part in arranging it all. Parstow will have to become accustomed to that." She smiled as she detected a note of caution on his face. "There's nothing for you to worry about, we worked well together for the fashion show. He's an excellent man, adaptable."

Belaugh nodded and turned quickly. The door opened and three children were ushered in for inspection. His eyes warmed at the sight. The oldest of the three was a girl of fifteen, a plump rounded child with a delicate little face that had filled out to a moon shape with puppy fat and pampering. The middle child was a slender athletic boy of twelve who moved with controlled grace and precision. His dark thick hair and black eyes were a stark contrast to the northern pallor of his skin which was not even relieved by a summer tan. The youngest child was a girl of ten, a shy retiring little flower with chestnut brown hair that flowed in well-groomed order down her back and was so thick and strong that it never tangled or became untidy.

Phyllis smiled at them and nodded quickly. "Come on now children, the car is waiting."

They attended the morning service in quiet obedience, but as they were leaving, the Belaughs fell into step behind two well-dressed distinguished ladies whose loud conversation was audible even over the thunder of the organ.

"...a large marquee. Of course, all the best families in the county will be invited. The other team's being organised by Lord Draycott."

"I've spoken to Charles and he will take time off to umpire for you, though his cricketing days are over. How on earth did you manage to persuade Jardine to play? That was a scoop."

"Need you ask? I knew his mother, dear."

"It always pays to send girls to a good school. Well, he'll be in good form after sharpening his teeth against India. We'll wipe the floor with the opposition."

"I'm not so sure, James Draycott has a shrewd head on his shoulders and quite a few contacts of his own at the MCC. I have a feeling he has a similar surprise or two up his sleeve. It'll make the game more entertaining."

The noise of the organ was receding a little now as they left the church, and the taller of the two women held her hand out graciously to the Vicar. "Good morning Reverend. An excellent sermon this morning."

"Thank you, Mrs Braithwaite. How is Charles? Recovered from the bronchitis I trust."

"Yes indeed. He's returned to his duties in London."

"I'm pleased to hear it." He turned to the shorter lady but there was a marked degree of iciness in his demeanour. He extended his hand in a polite salute, then turned away to greet the rest of his congregation. "Ah, Mr and Mrs Belaugh. Welcome among us indeed, and I'm glad to see you've brought your young family."

Bernard Belaugh shook the Reverend's hand firmly and nodded. "Been giving thought to your request Reverend. We'd be pleased to oblige. Make whatever use of the grounds you can."

"Ah excellent." The Vicar shook his hand again vigorously. "Thank you very much."

"Not at all. I'm just sorry we weren't able to oblige this summer."

Mathilda Braithwaite turned discreetly to study the Belaugh family, and she murmured under her breath, "Very much as I expected. Every inch a self-made man. Can you imagine that beautiful house in his hands? He'll destroy it."

"Very likely. And the Vicar's dignified him by arranging to have the fete there next year. And would you believe it?" the woman stifled a laugh behind her hand. "He's chosen the very same date as my cricket match. Now isn't that a coincidence? Most people will come to my function in preference to the fete. It will be the social occasion of the summer."

"My dear how very clever of you," Mathilda Braithwaite gave a small smile of malicious pleasure. "Allow me to help you with your arrangements."

The Belaughs were leaving the Vicar now, and the two women turned back along the path and remained just a few paces ahead of them, speaking in deliberately loud tones. "No, I haven't paid them a visit. I don't know whether it's just rumour, but can you imagine anything more grotesque than using Harborough Hall to sell clothes?"

The smaller woman shuddered visibly. "It will be sadly altered. All those tasteless statues and modern paintings I hear he's been introducing."

"Old Lord Harborough must be turning in his grave. If it's any consolation, none of our friends will set foot in the place."

"Then there will be no need to invite Belaugh or his wife to my event next July."

Mathilda Braithwaite smiled at her friend pointedly. "You won't need to. I understand they will be holding the village fete there on the same day. I expect the Belaughs will feel far more at home with the villagers."

"Oh heavens." Patty looked anxiously at Mathilda Braithwaite and murmured, "You don't think he hunts do you?"

"Shouldn't think he knows a stirrup from a strop, dear."

"True, his sort never do. Ah, there's my car. Would you care to call in for a glass of sherry on the way home?"

"Thank you, I'd love to."

"Good. Hop in then."

The two elderly ladies left the church grounds together, and as their car drew away they were gratified to see Belaugh's face had turned scarlet with fury. They were still chuckling gently to themselves when they arrived at their destination.

In the churchyard, Phyllis linked her arm urgently through her husband's and her firm strong grip covered his hand. Under her breath she whispered, "Leave it Bernard. Take no notice. They're just a pair of spiteful old biddies."

"That's not the point. Just who do they think they are, making judgements like that?"

She laughed gently. "Judging by the sound of them, they believe the world revolves around them. They're wrong, but I don't suppose they will ever know any better."

"They are excluding us from the local social life, and on what grounds? Because I busy myself with work, and don't sit on my arse all day making judgements on other people and shooting at helpless animals. That makes me inferior? Christ all-bloody-mighty..."

"You're in a church, Bernard," she murmured sternly. "Please contain yourself."

"I'm sorry Phyllis, but it makes me mad."

"I know." She patted his hand again and her stern expression softened coaxingly. "But you'd hate every minute of their life. You'd find yourself conversing with people who spend their time in leisure, and nothing drives you to distraction more quickly than squandering time and money in that fashion. We're well out of it."

"You're right." He took a deep breath and straightened his shoulders, and she was able to release the restraining pressure on his arm. "But that doesn't excuse such malice. Those two women need to be taught a lesson."

Phyllis glanced at his face a little anxiously, but she did not reply. She knew from experience that it would be better to work on him when his anger had cooled, and he was more open to reason. He was a formidable man when his temper was aroused.

He looked sideways at her. "Besides, I don't want my wife excluded."

She smiled and folded her gloved hands in front of her. "I have no desire for such contact Bernard. I have more than enough to do with the schemes I've started already. And of course, the children are here now."

He nodded slowly and gravely. "You'd hate it as much as I would."

"Yes," she agreed, trying hard to suppress the fond amusement in her voice.

♪♫

CHAPTER 14

MATHILDA BRAITHWAITE WAS concerned at her husband's silence. He had come home on leave, snatching just a few days in the country before returning to London to prepare for an overseas tour of duty. Having flicked through the letters that had been awaiting him, he had hardly spoken a word.

She sat down to her needlework placidly and asked in a casual voice, "How were the family, Charles?"

"Fine." He looked up absently from the tray of letters on his lap and gazed at her face. "Jeremy's down from school for the week, Jessica's going to bring him to stay tomorrow."

"And you didn't think to tell me!" Indignation brought a pink tinge to her pale cheeks. "Charles Braithwaite! What are you thinking about?"

"I have other things on my mind." He rose to his feet sternly. "I asked you to make enquiries about Maisy and her children, yet there is nothing among the correspondence.

Have you had any reply from this Reverend Rogers?"

She plied her needle with great care and lowered her gaze to her work. "Nothing my dear, so we must assume that they are alright."

"We can assume nothing of the sort." He placed the tray of letters on the table and turned to face her. "I want to know where they are, and in what manner they are living."

She paused for a moment, her needle poised, then she stabbed down at the material and drew the thread meticulously through to the back of the work. "Whatever for? They're perfectly settled. It would distress them beyond measure to be presented with a grandfather they don't know. We're from a vastly different world to theirs..."

"*This* should be their world Mathilda, not some deprived charity existence!"

"But my dear, you have no time for such diversions. Every moment you have is occupied with your work, why you've not been home since you were ill, and you're shortly going abroad again."

He looked down at her and murmured with deceptively quiet authority, "I intend to see Maisy and the children, and provide them with what they need. So, I would like you to write again and furnish me with the details as soon as they arrive."

She put her sewing to one side and folded her hands precisely in her lap and smiled sweetly. "Very well, if that is your wish. I will write again to the Reverend Rogers."

He nodded, and a little smile curled his lips, leaving his eyes curiously cold and uncompromising. "Be sure that you show me the letter before it goes. I'll post it for you."

Her eyes flashed with sudden anger, but the expression was speedily veiled.

♪♫

Maddy felt a discreet tug on her plait. She turned quickly without breaking her stride and raised an enquiring eyebrow.

"After dinner?" one of the younger girls asked eagerly.

She nodded and turned back to glance at Tina. The two girls smiled conspiratorially, and Maddy tossed her long golden plaits joyfully. The day was glorious, sunny warm and successful, and her eyes shone with the energy and fun that was slowly returning to her. They had both been doing well with their work at school and had been chosen to take part in a concert at the end of term. In her satchel she carried three songs, trios to be practised this evening.

The girls hung their coats and satchels up, and bustled around for an hour until dinner, doing their chores. Then after they had eaten, Maddy rose from her seat, and once again she brushed against the old piano. A pang of unbearable longing went through her. Softly she touched the closed lid, but the memories did not hurt so much now.

A firm hand grasped her shoulder and she gasped nervously. Matron's bony fingers drew her to one side, out of the flow of girls. The tall thin woman did not speak for several minutes, and Maddy found herself stiffening and trying not to shiver. Her heart was pounding with dread. She was appalled at the idea of being thrashed again, and what she had done was so utterly trivial.

She saw Tina glance back at her anxiously, but Maddy shook her head, knowing her friend could do nothing to help her.

When all the girls had gone, Matron carefully shut the door then looked thoughtfully at Maddy. "Come here child."

Maddy approached the fearsome figure.

Surprise shot through her. Matron was not angry. The older woman took a bunch of keys from her pocket and carefully unlocked the lid of the piano. Her eyes turned to the keyboard as though hypnotised, it was in surprisingly good condition considering the state of the wood veneer on the exterior.

Matron drew the stool up and patted Maddy's shoulder. "It hasn't been tuned for a long while my dear, but I'd like to hear it played."

"May I really?" she spun round eagerly to look at Matron.

"Yes," Matron nodded, and watched Maddy keenly.

She hesitated for a moment, then ran her fingers softly over the notes, making no sound, simply enjoying the feel of the cool ivory keys. She took a deep shaky breath, and floods of memory and hope surged through her, filling her with deep yearning.

She had imagined what this moment might feel like, and now that it was here, she hardly dared to play lest the promise disappear.

She slid round the stool and made herself comfortable, relishing the familiar feeling that came into her fingers, into her mind. She stretched her hands out and played a sonata that she knew she would not fluff even after so long without practice.

The first notes jarred like a bolt of anguish through her senses and she grimaced. The piano desperately needed tuning, and the discordant sounds grated, desecrating her precious memories. Her fingers slid from the shiny, smooth keys, and her shoulders slumped. She was after all only an orphan, just one among many on the council register. There was no more magic, no more music. She took a deep breath and rose from the stool. She turned to Matron and murmured with some difficulty, "Thank you. I won't touch it again now."

"Is it that bad Maddy? I have no ear for music."

She nodded. "A piano needs to be played not shut away. It's badly out of tune."

"Your father was a music teacher, wasn't he, child?"

She nodded.

"I'm really quite cross that you didn't tell me. I've had to wait for a letter from the Reverend Rogers to explain it all to me."

Maddy kept her eyes lowered to her feet. "I'm sorry, Matron. I couldn't. It hurts too much to talk about it. I just couldn't."

Matron lifted her chin up and smiled gently. "I'm not an ogre child. I do understand. Did your father enter you for any exams?"

She nodded, and the memories she treasured so dearly came flooding back and were visible in her eyes: a shimmering tender vivid warmth and pain. "We used to go to the Royal College of Music for the exams. He always came to London with me and sat outside waiting." She wrung her hands, unaware of the action. "I've done all my grades and Daddy was very proud."

"Did you do well?"

She nodded.

"I can see how much it means to you Maddy." Matron nodded slowly and then patted her shoulder with finality. "I must think deeply about this. Run along and join your friends now, I expect they're waiting anxiously for you."

Maddy glanced one last time at the open piano and the

swirling memories and feelings that had been resurrected here, then she turned away and left the room. Once in the privacy of the corridor, she leaned her back on the wall and closed her eyes.

Every part of her had been shaken by this encounter with her grief and loss. Behind her, she could hear small movements where Matron was closing and locking the piano and putting the stool away. She had to move. She did not want to face Matron again.

Then hurrying footstep whispered like blowing sand across the wooden floor. Tina took her hands and squeezed them anxiously. "What happened Maddy? Are you alright?"

"Yes. And I've so much to tell you. But come away or Matron will find us." She linked her arm through Tina's, and the two girls hurried away.

It was not until she was lying in bed again that night and Tina had fallen asleep at last, that she suddenly realised she felt better. Her friend had questioned her unmercifully until she had confided everything to her. She had told her again and again all the things Matron had said, and finally given in to the insistent questioning, and described her family and home.

Maddy lay in peace with the rustling sound of breathing all around her, and strength flowed through her wrought limbs. She was proud and immensely fond of her past. Now she could talk about it and it was part of her again.

Maddy was a new girl when she got up the following morning. She sang like a bird as she brushed her teeth and washed, and very soon many of the other girls joined in, infected by her enthusiasm.

But when the girls arrived home from school that afternoon, Matron was standing by the door, waiting.

They fell silent and filed through the open door in good order, then dispersed quietly in various directions to do their chores.

Matron only ever waited at the door if one of the girls had committed some terrible misdemeanour. The tall, thin, gaunt figure descended like a vulture, and it was Maddy Brooks who felt the hand on her shoulder and was drawn away from her friends.

Matron took Maddy to the dining room. The young girl was not frightened this time. She could see by the expression on Matron's face that this was not going to be a punishment. Indeed, the older woman seemed pleased about something.

"Try it again Maddy and tell me what you think." Matron shut the door and turned to watch her curiously mature young charge carefully.

The piano was open, the stool invitingly ready. Maddy glanced back at Matron's face but there was nothing in her expression to read. She nodded and sat down. Bracing herself for the excruciating discord, she played a few scales. The sounds that rang in her ears this time were perfectly in tune, and even the tone of the notes had improved and rang brightly.

She spun round, her blue eyes glowing with excitement. "Matron, it's been tuned."

"Yes, child." Matron grasped her shoulder gently. "It's years since we've had anyone here who could play, and as you say, a piano should be played. Play me something."

Maddy turned back to the keys, closed her eyes and the music just came flooding out. There were a lot of wrong notes but correcting them was not important. The floodgates had been opened on her memory. It did not hurt as she had expected it to, it was just a great relief. She had no idea how long she sat there, but she played all that came to her, all the music she had been taught, all the popular songs she had enjoyed playing, then finally she folded her hands in her lap. It had been so long since she had done this. It was good to have the magic back in her life.

Matron's stern, aloof expression had relaxed, and she was smiling. She came to kneel in front of Maddy, took the young girl's thin strong hands and turned them over and looked at them carefully, then sighed. "You have a very rare gift. Even I can hear that, young lady. When you've finished your chores each night, you may come and play as much as you like. I'll leave the piano unlocked for you. And if any of your friends want to join you, then they have my permission. Would you like more lessons?"

"Oh, I would love it Matron. But how can we manage to pay for it?"

"Don't you worry about that." Matron swept a small wisp of hair away from Maddy's forehead. "I'll find a way. Trust me. I always do when my girls need something. This could be the making of your life, do you realise that?"

Maddy was at a loss for several moments, then burst out enthusiastically, "If there's anything I can do to help pay for it Matron, I'll do it. I used to do a cleaning job to earn money, before I came here."

"Did you?" Matron's eyes were watchful. "That's something to fall back on if all else fails, child. But there are many avenues to try before we do that. Would you, for example, play for Mrs Kirkpatrick's dancing class, or help with the Choral Society?"

"I could try." Maddy nodded slowly. "I've never done anything like that before but, yes." She glanced up, her eyes shining in sudden determination. "I've turned the pages for

Daddy when he used to do it. I know what to do. I could also teach some of the girls if they want to learn, and in that way I can share the knowledge."

"There. That's an excellent start. Now just leave the rest to me." Matron rose to her feet and frowned slightly. "Don't pin your hopes too high just yet Maddy, but keep your fingers crossed."

Maddy smiled, and there was a great deal of confidence and hope in her now.

Gradually it was all becoming real again, the promise she had made to her father. Matron's permission to play was the first step on the way. The rest was up to her.

♪♫

CHAPTER 15

LIFE SEEMED TO take flight for Maddy from that day forward. Within the month she had begun accompanying Mrs Kirkpatrick's dancing classes. Girls came from all over the area to learn ballet and tap, and as the year went by, parents and grandparents heard her playing, and she was asked to play for the Choral Society when their accompanist was ill or away.

At the orphanage, she worked out a routine to wake up early and practice before anyone else got up, then the rest of the day was as normal. One night each week Mr Tomlinson the local piano teacher came to give her a lesson.

Her circle of friends grew, and she settled in very cosily. Christmas came and went with carols, mince pies and a visit for everyone to the pantomime. The following spring saw her working early each morning on music for a recital at the Church, and then busy most evenings with her friends and her tasks at the orphanage. By the end of the first year, she was completely at home.

♪♫

Meanwhile, Charles Braithwaite did not achieve his desire. Little more than a month after he had asked his wife to contact the Reverend Rogers, he and a small group of military colleagues were posted abroad. He went gladly, for it was a task he had be arguing for, and yet he took with him the knowledge that part of his family was in serious difficulties and he had failed to find and help them.

All through the winter and spring, the small group of elderly gentlemen drank, danced and betted their way across Europe, spending the government's money and enjoying themselves as though they were carefree civilians. Wherever they went, they renewed contact with old friends and were absorbed into social activities drinking, partying and entertaining with the elite of society.

They idly talked politics and warfare, in the manner of most elderly military men, reminiscing about past glories and disparaging the style of the younger soldier of today. But they watched and listened to replies from all quarters and absorbed far more than anyone knew. They committed nothing of this to paper, it was far too sensitive. Everywhere they went, they assessed the changing political situation, the ominously resurging military attitude, and the growing expertise and arrogance of the Nazi soldier.

All thought of family paled beside the threat that he could see coming.

♪♫

The following summer, just as Charles Braithwaite was sitting in London writing reports and meeting with numerous military and political figures, Matron summoned a small but important meeting at the orphanage. The Reverend Rogers arrived first and grasped Matron's outstretched hand. "Good afternoon ma'am. I read your invitation with some trepidation. Nothing is amiss I hope?"

"Reverend, I'm as much in the dark as you. Mr Tomlinson will be able to give us his reasons for calling the meeting when he arrives."

The Reverend nodded and frowned anxiously. "How is she?"

"Settled at last, thanks to her playing."

There was a knock on the door, and an elderly man in his late fifties entered the room diffidently. Matron rose quickly to extend her hand in greeting. "Please come in Mr Tomlinson. This is the Reverend Rogers, Madeline's nearest relative."

The Reverend rose to shake the teacher's hand. "I'm pleased to meet you."

Matron gestured to the chairs. "Please be seated." The two men made themselves comfortable and Matron looked enquiringly at the teacher. "You have something of importance to tell us about young Maddy, Mr Tomlinson?"

The music teacher steepled his fingers and spoke with slow deliberation. "Young Maddy has a great deal of talent. I'm sure you're both well aware of that. Unfortunately, we've reached the stage where I must resign my job teaching her."

"Whatever for?" the Vicar leaned forward anxiously. "She's a good girl and works hard. Is there some problem?"

"No problem as far as her progress and enthusiasm are concerned. The trouble is that she's far too advanced for her age, and for me. There's nothing more that I can teach her. She needs to be tutored by a music professor; she needs to attend an academy of music."

"That's out of the question Mr Tomlinson. We're an orphanage!" Matron said sharply. "Our task is to provide our girls with the basic skills of life, and I can't do more than that. She will have to begin working for her living very soon now. If you can give her support until then, she'll at least be able to use her talent to her best advantage."

"I could do that. I could coach her through a great deal of music, but I don't think you really understand the nature of her talent or her problem. She could easily go on to be a top concert pianist. She has precisely the right temperament. She has a prodigious memory for the music, discipline, sensitivity, and above all, she responds to the tension of playing to an audience. Have you noticed how her public performances always outshine her practices? We've got something here that must be nurtured and brought to fruition."

"That may well be true," the Reverend Rogers said, "but she's also a vulnerable child, one who has already been badly hurt." He took off his glasses and began polishing them vigorously. "What she needs is peace and stability, but you're suggesting that we push her into a bitterly competitive and public environment. It's a cruel and unforgiving world, as her father discovered to his cost."

"She needs a good sponsor, Reverend, one who can bring her directly into the musical world. She needs to hear concerts, play to audiences and learn from the best pianists."

"That's beyond our means and you must resign yourself to that," Matron snapped irritably. "Maddy has worked her fingers to the bone to pay for her lessons. We must be content to provide for her safe future."

The teacher did not speak but reached into the pocket of

his jacket and brought out a page of newsprint. He unfolded it and placed it carefully on the desk. "Read that."

Ringed in black pencil was an article in the distinctive Telegraph type. It contained a large picture of a mild looking plump man of about forty.

ARTS PATRON PRAISED

Patron of the Arts, Bernard Belaugh achieves one of his greatest ambitions. Young protégée, Michelle Davis, 16, gains scholarship to study at the Paris Conservatoire. Her talents were recognised at the age of eleven, by the music loving Belaugh family who have given the child a home, education and thorough musical training.

She has sung to audiences country-wide, and won the scholarship ahead of a class of thirty young hopefuls.

Mr and Mrs Belaugh are delighted and will continue to sponsor Michelle through her study.

Mr Belaugh said: "Michelle has a tremendous talent for creating music, and such a gift should be shared with mankind. These talented children deserve every encouragement."

The Belaugh family also sponsor the career of Patrick Anderson, who hopes to be accepted to the Royal Ballet School in another year, and clarinettist Janet Taylor, just eleven years old.

Conductor and composer Sir Edward Hamilton Harty said of Michelle's success: "It is a tradition that music has great benefactors. The list is illustrious, and their achievements monumental. This country needs such men. In the years to come, the Belaughs may well be recognised as the English equivalent of the Esterhazy family."

Matron looked up finally and removed the small pair of

reading glasses that were necessary for the appreciation of such print. "Are you seriously suggesting that we propose Maddy to this man?"

"If we don't, then we're failing the child," he stated flatly.

The Reverend Rogers' cheeks coloured slightly. "Taking her from here and placing her in such an establishment would be cruel. She's happy and settled. She's still only thirteen and has just come through a considerable trauma. It may be kinder and better for her career to give her stability until she is old enough to attend college. If it's in her, nothing will be lost by waiting a few years."

"And then who will pay her expenses? Even if she wins a scholarship she will need music, transport, food and accommodation. Who will be with her and care for her?" the music teacher demanded with suppressed vehemence. "I can't, you can't, and the training she needs won't come cheaply."

Matron bent her sharp eye on the Vicar. "Have you heard anymore from her grandparents?"

"Nothing. They wanted nothing more to do with her. I've written repeatedly, but to no avail."

Matron nodded slowly. "I think we should speak to Maddy and discover what her wishes are in this matter."

Reverend Rogers rose to his feet. "Would you allow me to do this Matron?"

She nodded briskly. "I expect you'll find her in the hall. You may take her into the study, or for a walk if you wish."

He nodded, and left Matron and Mr Tomlinson talking earnestly.

Maddy was in the hall, engrossed in a game of hopscotch with a cluster of other girls, and he paused to watch. She had grown up considerably in the year she had been here. Her lively face had lengthened, the features had become more feminine and expressive, and it was easy to see that in another year or two she would be a fascinating young woman.

She cried out with surprise when she saw him and came to give him an enthusiastic hug. "Reverend Rogers! I'm so glad to see you. How are Josie and the boys?"

"Very well my dear and they send you their love. You look very well. Matron's given me permission to take you out for a walk. Would you like that?"

"Oh, yes please. But just before we go, I'd like you to meet someone." She turned and smiled. Tina had been hovering uncertainly in the background but came forward eagerly when she was beckoned over. Then Maddy looked back at the Reverend. "This is my friend Tina, Mr Rogers."

The Reverend held his hand out to the young girl and smiled gently, very aware that life in an all-female establishment like this made young girls deeply uncertain about how to communicate with men. "Maddy's told us a great deal about you in her letters. My daughter Josie's looking forward to meeting you if you'd like to come and stay this summer. There's lots you three can do together."

Tina offered her hand, and a shy smile lit her mobile fast-moving face. "I'd like that very much, sir, thank you. I've never been away on holiday before."

"I've just been making the arrangements with Matron. I'll come and pick you up in three weeks' time, on Saturday."

Tina blushed slightly. "We haven't got anything special to wear sir, only these old things," and she pulled in disgust at her uniform.

He laughed. "You look lovely as you are. As long as you enjoy yourselves whilst you're with us."

Tina blushed more vividly this time and found it very difficult to make any reply.

♪♫

Fifteen minutes later, Maddy was walking across the park with Reverend Rogers and she looked out over the flat green lawn with the swings and roundabout in the far distance, and she frowned. "No, I don't mind doing it at all, it's worked out very well. It's good fun playing for the ballet classes, and I'm earning enough to pay my own way." She glanced at the Reverend's face. "Why do you ask?"

He took a deep breath. "It just seems a lot of hard work for someone of your age."

Her eyes sparkled with laughter. "It's fun. Playing the piano is a great relaxation. The hard bit is the schoolwork."

"Your playing will be a great asset to you," he smiled. "Have you considered what you want to do with your life?"

"I've always known that." She looked down at her hands, the long strong fingers that so closely resembled her father's. "I promised my father the night he died that I would make my music the success that he should have had."

"He wouldn't want you to do anything that caused you hurt, you know," he interrupted hastily.

"Music won't hurt me." She looked up into his eyes. "I want more than anything to be a pianist. I'm not sure how to set about it yet, but I will! It's something I have to do. I think I shall have to find a job in London, and somewhere to stay. If I save *very* hard, I could probably manage a few terms at college. I want to play as my father should have." Tears of vehemence filled her vivid blue eyes. "I want it so much that it hurts!"

His expression grew bleak as he watched her intense

face. "You've set yourself a great mountain to climb, Maddy. I only hope you can do it safely."

♪♫

The library at Harborough Hall was inundated with letters. Each morning when the post arrived, Phyllis Belaugh opened the batch and read through the begging letters. It was difficult, and many of the letters hurt because all the children deserved help.

She selected from the batch only those that described children with exceptional talent who were still young enough to benefit. Several times she shook her head, angry with herself for feeling such a desire to help them all.

From the batch, there were usually only one or two each day that were suitable for serious consideration.

By the end of two weeks, she had prepared a selection of twenty letters for Bernard to read and assess, and he sat down with her on Saturday morning, going over the letters time after time, until they had narrowed the list down to five gifted children.

Then finally he sat back. "I'll visit each of these children over the next month and observe them."

"Can you afford to take the time off my dear?" she frowned anxiously. Their financial affairs had not flowed well since the fashion show. There had been a number of promises but very few completions.

He smiled, and the fire that lit in his eyes told her more than words could have done. Eagerly she gripped his hands. "What is it, Bernard?"

"The contract was signed yesterday. Monaghan has ordered the complete limited edition of evening gowns, and a large run of winter clothes."

He rose to his feet with dynamic energy. "I'm taking you out tonight to celebrate. We'll treat London to a splash it'll never forget. We've done it!"

♪♫

CHAPTER 16

MADDY AND TINA arrived back from their holiday with the Rogers family, refreshed and still bubbling with excitement. They gossiped for ages as they unpacked their belongings and folded them tidily into their drawers. They had had a marvellous time, and the three girls had got on very well. Poor Josie had been in tears as they had left, and they had made promises to write each week and meet again at Christmas.

As they were talking, a splendid Bentley cruised up to the front door and a plump middle-aged gentleman climbed out. The driver rang the doorbell for him, then returned to the vehicle to wait.

Presently the door opened and the gentleman was conducted to Matron's office.

The two of them eyed each other for several seconds before speaking, then Matron held her hand out. "Mr Belaugh."

He grasped her hand firmly. "I read your letter about Miss Brooks with interest. I'd like to see the girl and hear her play. Is she well behaved?"

"Yes." There was a steely edge to Matron's voice. "We insist on that from all our girls."

"No insult intended, but I've always found children who have suffered trauma to be more difficult." He nodded briskly. "Miss Brooks is one of five children on my shortlist. The recommendations from her music teacher are excellent. Would you fill me in on her background?"

Matron told him all that she knew about Maddy, and Belaugh listened carefully. When she mentioned her grandparents, he took little notice, until she mentioned their name and location, then his attention was caught.

The Braithwaite family!

He felt as though illumination had come at last to a dark and uncomfortable recess of his life. He had always believed her to be proud and cold-hearted, and this proved it. Moreover, to be in possession of her impoverished and abandoned granddaughter would be an exquisite weapon against her snobbery.

He rubbed his hands together and almost laughed to himself. To wound that Braithwaite woman would be deeply gratifying.

More than an hour later, Belaugh was conducted along the corridor to a well-lit dining room. He glanced at his surroundings as he went.

The entire establishment was humming with the noise of children. There was laughter and chatting, the chirping of voices raised in excitement, and it surprised him to think that any child brought up with this noise and social pressure could develop individual musical talent. But before he reached his destination he could hear her playing, and it was enchanting.

They entered without disturbing her and stood just inside the door. She was a slender graceful young girl, already halfway to adult. And she had complete command over the powerful instrument before her. She had thick golden hair, tied in two plaits. But little wisps had worked loose and framed her pretty face with a shimmering halo that glinted in the sunlight.

He could feel his breath catching curiously in his throat.

He knew instinctively that it was all here. His intuition had always been reliable, and it made the final decision for him now. This was the child.

He watched for a long while, fascinated by what he saw and heard, then he glanced at Matron. The woman was watching him. He nodded in a business-like fashion. "I've seen enough."

Back at the office he said abruptly, "I've made my decision, Matron. I will sponsor Madeline."

Matron's lips tightened to a hard line. "You have made a very quick decision Mr Belaugh. Before we reach agreement, I shall need to know exactly what you plan to do for her, and we will have to put the proposition to her directly."

"I see. I wasn't expecting that." He raised his eyebrows in surprise. "She will live at Harborough Hall with my two other children, from there she will attend school. I'll provide her with expert piano tuition and coaching in all aspects of music. I and her tutors will encourage her to enter competitions, we'll secure concert opportunities for her, and when she's old enough, send her to college or conservatoire. In short, we will provide the best preparation to further her talents."

Matron nodded slowly, but there was still a frown on her face. "We'll be sorry to lose her. She's a dear girl."

"If you're having second thoughts Matron," he rose to his feet, "then you've been wasting my time."

Matron fixed him with an icy gaze, and even Belaugh was intimidated. "I only do what is best for my girls. They have no one else to fight for them, and each girl receives what I believe is the best for her. Madeline Brooks will not leave here unless I'm convinced that what you propose will make her happy."

The excitement of the hunt flashed through Belaugh. It was little different to bidding for a priceless statue or painting. He wanted that girl. "My protégées are provided with everything: a home, excellent schooling, and unparalleled opportunities in their arts. If Madeline joins us there will be three of them again, living as a family. I can't guarantee happiness, that rests in the nature of the child. What I can guarantee is the opportunity to excel. Her references indicate that she would respond well to such a chance."

Matron sighed and nodded reluctantly. "Wait here Mr Belaugh. I will fetch her."

♪♫

"He wishes to sponsor *me*?" Maddy asked incredulously and ran her fingers up and down the keyboard. Her thoughts turned instantly to college, to all the opportunities Matron had spoken about, and a powerful surge of purpose filled her.

She would be following in her father's footsteps, and this would give her the opportunity to achieve the success that he should have had. She would strive for it, and do it for him, as she had promised all those months ago.

Matron was still talking, and gradually Maddy began to listen to what she was saying. "...in a large house, Harborough Hall. There will be two other children living there, both of them sponsored like you. He will become your official guardian, but we'll keep in contact with you, I promise."

A cold dash of dread drenched Maddy, and she looked around at the familiar scene. "I'd have to go away from here?"

Matron touched her white cheek, then stood up and placed her hands on the young girl's shoulders. "Take your time. I'll send him away now and tell him to wait three days. Don't make a rash decision. We'll talk it over together."

Maddy's hands were shaking now. The opportunity that was being offered to her would never come her way again, and yet she felt safe here with her friends. "Couldn't he sponsor me and yet let me continue to live here Matron?" she looked up earnestly. "Perhaps if you asked him..."

Her sharp eyes warmed. "That's not possible my dear. Think carefully about it. Will you promise me?"

Maddy nodded slowly, but not in answer to Matron's question.

If she did not take this opportunity and try, then she would be failing her parents a second time. She stood up, gathering all her courage and determination about her. "I know what I have to do Matron. May I come and meet my patron?"

"Already? Are you sure child?"

Maddy nodded, and her voice grew husky with memories. "I made a vow that I would do this over a year ago."

♪♫

111

CHAPTER 17

THE BENTLEY RETURNED for Maddy Brooks several months later. She walked round and round the home during the hour before the car arrived, rather like a caged lion prowling its terrain. She wanted to see everything for the last time and enjoy the things she knew.

Her departure had been kept from the girls until the last possible moment and keeping such news secret from Tina had been the hardest thing Maddy had ever had to do. But now that the announcement had been made, Maddy understood exactly why Matron had insisted on it. Two of the older girls came down the stairs, and pointedly crossed out of her way, lifting their noses in the air, one murmuring spitefully, "Little snob."

Maddy ignored them as best she could. But when she reached the dormitory and Tina deliberately turned her back on her she could have wept. "Oh Tina. Don't *you* treat me like this too! Please."

There was not even the slightest hint that Tina had heard the words.

Swallowing her hurt, she came and sat on the bed beside her friend and touched her hand coaxingly. "Will you come down with me Tina? Saying goodbye is going to be agony, and I don't know if I..."

"Just go away and do it quickly."

"Is that what you really want?" Maddy demanded, the hurt mutating slowly into anger. "You're just going to erase me from your life, are you? That's very unfair don't you think, after everything we've done together?"

"It's not unfair." Tina rounded furiously on her. "That's exactly what you're doing to me. Look, I thought you were my friend. I never imagined you'd leave me like this... go off to some posh house and become a spoilt little rich girl. And you didn't even have the courage to tell me! How could you Maddy?"

"Matron forbade me to tell you, Tina. And I'm *not* going to be a rich girl. This is a music scholarship. I shall have to work extremely hard. I won't be living a life of ease. Look, if I don't take this opportunity, I'll be stuck for the rest of my life. You know I could never afford..."

"Really? You'd be like the rest of us then. I bet you soon get so wrapped up in your airs and graces that you pretend you were never even here."

Two bright flaming spots of colour flared in Maddy's cheeks, and she rose to her feet with icy dignity. "If you think I'm like that, then I'm sorry you've ever been my friend. I made a promise to my father, Tina. I can't go back on that."

"But he's dead Maddy. He's not bothered any more about what you do. I'm here and I care. It's going to be horrible when you've gone."

Maddy sat down and much of her anger seeped away. She touched her friend's shoulder. "I won't forget you or desert you, you silly thing. Look... I shall write, and I'll need your letters and support even more. It's going to be very lonely in this new place. Everything they do will be different. The things they say and the way they behave, even the food they eat. I'm going to be *so* out of place and alone. At least you'll still be here with the others."

"But you don't have to go!" Tina sat up at last and grasped her shoulders. "Really you don't."

"I do." Maddy touched her fingers to her cheeks. "I've got to let the music out, do you understand that? I've got so much inside me, it's just bursting to be free. But when I think of what lies ahead of me I'm frightened half to death."

Tina looked resentfully at Maddy. "Oh alright. I'll come down with you. But I don't think you should go."

The Belaughs' chauffeur was a quiet aloof man who waited in silent patience as Tina gave Maddy a hug of farewell. He opened the door and helped Maddy into the car. She settled herself in the luxurious comfort of the back seat and the door closed on her with a soft thud. Suddenly she was utterly alone and fear began to overwhelm her.

She did not belong in this soft luxury!

The chauffeur climbed into the driving seat and asked over his shoulder, "Are you ready, miss?"

"Yes." Determinedly, Maddy clenched her hands together in her lap.

The car pulled away quietly, and she managed to keep her poise until the outskirts of Sandbourne had disappeared into the distance. Then, alone in the back of that enormous luxurious vehicle, having said goodbye to everyone she knew and loved, she burst into floods of tears.

The driver glanced quickly over his shoulder at her, then pulled into the side of the road and turned in his seat. The aloofness had evaporated and his face was very kind. He lifted her chin up insistently, and Maddy looked out miserably through the tears.

"Now miss, there's no need to cry like that. Have one of these. Here take them."

A bag of bull's eyes was put into her hand, followed by a neatly pressed handkerchief. "Dry your eyes. Mrs Belaugh's been getting your room ready for you all this week."

"I don't want to go," she whispered.

"Yes, you do. This is only a momentary pain. It'll all be worth it, you'll see."

Maddy nodded and wiped at the tears. She knew he was right, but it still hurt unbearably.

The journey across England took more than six hours, and those hours would have been formidable but for the friendly companionship of the driver.

By the time she arrived at her new home, she knew all about Briggs, his family and some of the people who worked at the house, and she had built up a vivid impression of the highly respected and capable Mrs Belaugh.

Harborough Hall turned out to be a vast stately mansion, much larger than anything she had imagined it to be. And it hit her suddenly that Tina was right about the airs and graces that she would have to assume. Belaugh had not seemed a sophisticated or well-bred man to her, yet if he owned this gracious estate, he would expect his wards to behave in a manner that befitted the place.

She took a deep breath and climbed from the car.

"This way miss," Briggs murmured gently. "Mrs Belaugh will be waiting for you, and once you've met her everything will fall into place."

"You really think so?" she asked with a doubtful smile.

"I know so," he laughed encouragingly. He led her up the grand steps, between gleaming classical pillars and through the impressive front door.

She stood quietly looking around at the ornately decorated, spotlessly clean marble-clad entrance hall, while Briggs exchanged words with another member of the staff. Then he guided her through the house, their footsteps echoing importantly on the marble floor. They were approaching a closed door now, and Maddy stiffened, drawing about herself all her courage. This was the moment that would change her life forever.

She followed Briggs into an enormous drawing room, where he stepped aside and gestured for her to come forward. "Ma'am, this is Madeline Brooks."

She had expected to see a grey-haired lady with an awe-inspiring but benevolent air of authority, and she froze for a moment in surprise. A much younger lady rose to her feet and came to meet her. The lady had kind eyes and a firm comfortable, face. She was holding her hands out in a warm greeting. "Welcome to your new home Madeline."

Maddy found herself tongue tied, and wordlessly held her own hands out in response.

Phyllis Belaugh smiled understandingly and placed an arm reassuringly around her shoulders, then turned to Briggs. "Thank you, that will be all for now." Then she turned back to her young charge and gave her a small hug. "Now come with me, and I'll show you what I've arranged for you. I hope you're going to like it."

Maddy could feel her awkwardness finally seeping away, and she managed to reply a little huskily, "I expect I shall, ma'am."

Warmth touched the lady's eyes as she led her up a grand staircase to the upper floor of the house. "You'll soon get used to living here. You children are very adaptable, it's we adults who take longer to adjust. I still find it utterly surprising when I wake in the mornings surrounded by all this history. It can be a little overwhelming."

"Oh!" Maddy looked at her in surprise. "I thought you'd always lived here."

"No," the lady laughed gently, then met her eyes with open honesty. "We have been here nearly a year and a half my dear. Before that, we had a house in London. It's been quite a challenge becoming accustomed to the quiet, and to the size and splendour of the rooms. I sometimes have to pinch myself. I often have the impression that history is alive here."

"I understand what you mean." Maddy nodded slowly and looked around at the enormous rooms, and her imagination suddenly took flight, fed by the books she had been studying at school. "This is like something from a Jane Austin novel," she breathed. "I can just imagine the ladies sweeping through here in their long gowns."

"Yes, indeed," Phyllis smiled, opened one of the doors and led Maddy into an enormous bedroom. "This is your room, Madeline."

The bed was made, the covers turned down invitingly, and her heart suddenly leapt. There was a beautifully appointed doll's house awaiting her attention on the table. It was no toy, but a sophisticated and beautiful thing that would delight a young woman of any age. But that was not all. Books she knew and loved were scattered by the bedside lamp and her battered old suitcase was waiting for her just inside the door.

A little dazed, she wandered into the room and looked around slowly. It was bright, sunny and comfortable. She touched the exquisite furniture in the doll's house and knew that she was extremely lucky. Phyllis had gone to great lengths to make her feel welcome and at home.

Then a great pang of grief went through her, and she almost cried out in pain. She was going to miss her friends. None of them would be able to share this with her.

"Let's unpack your things, then I'll show you round, and you can meet the others when Briggs brings them back from school."

♪♫

Several hours later, Maddy found her way back to the drawing room. Already she felt different. She had been dressed in new clothes by a strict seeming nanny. Her hair had been liberated from its plaits and brushed and pinned into a style that made her look far more mature than she actually felt. And all the while Nanny had been instructing her on the routines of the house, repeating again and again the habits that would be expected of her, so that she was confident that in time she would learn exactly how to behave.

Phyllis was waiting for her in the drawing room, and they chatted comfortably for a while, discussing plans to go shopping later in the week and buy everything Maddy would need for school and for her musical studies.

She had tutors to meet tomorrow, and exams and competitions to begin planning for. It was daunting. She was just beginning to panic that she might never be able to fulfil the Belaughs' high expectations, when Phyllis smiled, stood up abruptly and took her through to the music room.

"This is your practice space, Madeline, and you will probably spend much of your time here." Maddy's eyes swept around the bright space in growing awe. There were tall windows stretching almost from floor to ceiling, which allowed great shafts of sunlight to fall in bars across the marble floor. Above her, the ceiling was decorated with ornamental figures and those same designs had been woven into the central rug.

Then she saw the piano.

A full-sized concert grand was waiting for her in the middle of the room.

Her eyes widened. The panic evaporated and her fingers itched to play. She hesitated for a moment, not wanting to be too forward, then Phyllis touched her shoulder encouragingly. She needed no other sign but sat herself at the instrument and played. Joy surged through her. She had always dreamed of playing a piano such as this, and its tones filled the room with grandeur. She played through much of the music she loved and was hardly aware of Phyllis nodding to herself and retiring to leave her to become acquainted with her practice space.

A short while later, the tranquillity of the house was shattered by the sound of children running up the stairs. The footsteps stopped and the music room door opened.

Maddy turned as she heard a whispered conversation behind her, and she found Phyllis holding the hands of two other children. Nervously, Maddy rose to her feet and came towards them, looking from one to the other. "Hello."

"Madeline, I'd like you to meet Patrick and Janet. They'll show you around the house, and make you feel welcome I'm sure. You'll find out all about them very quickly. You'll almost be brother and sister."

Maddy was extremely nervous now. She found herself being sombrely studied by a boy of about her own age, with dark brown burning eyes framed by a pale, intense face. He was at that curiously sullen stage between childhood and adulthood, and walked towards her with insolent grace and ease, as though his body simply flowed through the air.

"Patrick," Phyllis said sharply.

He held his hand out to her disdainfully. "Welcome to Harborough Hall, Madeline Brooks."

"Thank you," she returned the gesture with equal formality. A quiet withdrawn young girl several years their junior eventually let go of the older woman's hand and came forward too. Although she must have been around Matthew's age, she did not have any of his exuberance and energy. In its place was a curious resolute calmness. Maddy held her hand out to the girl and was surprised by the sharp birdlike grip that touched her for a moment.

Then the girl withdrew and murmured, "Would you care to come with us now Madeline? We usually play for a while when we get home. We'll show you the gardens."

"Run along now all of you," Phyllis nodded. "We dine at six, Madeline, and Nanny will expect you in your room at five."

Maddy tried to smile but she was too nervous of these strangely withdrawn children to do it properly. She was used to vigorous fun-loving folk, and her smile went awry.

Janet's eyes warmed shyly, and her reserve melted a little. She took Maddy's hand confidingly. "Come on, quickly. I've been hoping you'd be another girl. I've got something to show you."

Once out of the house they seemed to relax even more

and ran across the grass with joyful liberation, just like any other boy and girl. Maddy gathered up her flounced skirts and dashed after them, drawn on by Janet's eagerness and excitement. She laughed as the low hanging branches of a huge and ancient tree reached down to pull her carefully brushed hair into a tangled mess.

"Where are you?" she called suddenly, spinning round to look all about her. They were gone, and she was completely alone. She peered quickly around a huge tree trunk. "This is a trick isn't it? Oh, come on. I've no idea where you are."

There was a stifled giggle that told her they were very close indeed. Then she heard Patrick crossly admonish the younger girl. She ran around the tree again and then she saw it, a narrow hollow low down in the enormous girth of the trunk from which Janet's laughing face was peering out and watching her.

"Oh, come on in and see!" Janet reached out to grab her wrist. "It's such fun."

Maddy went onto her hands and knees and squeezed in and found the centre of the tree completely hollow. It formed a big dark dry vault that extended in great cobwebby secrets above their heads. "Oh, this is marvellous. Does anyone else know it's here?"

"You idiot, Jan," Patrick hissed angrily. "You shouldn't have shown her. Not until we know we can trust her. She might be on his side."

"We can trust her Pat, I know we can," Janet whispered, and squeezed Maddy's hand. "Don't be so hateful. You know what it's going to be like. You can't let her..."

"We haven't got any choice now have we, big mouth? Oh alright. Look Madeline, you must never tell anyone about this place. We come here when we need to be alone. It's *our* secret, and if they ever discover it, then it would be spoilt."

"I won't tell a soul, I promise," she murmured. "You're very full of commands aren't you, Patrick? There's no need to be so unpleasant."

"Someone's got to be in charge and you'd better remember that. You'll have to be very careful coming here, no one must see you. We usually take it in turns to get fresh straw each month. You'll have to take a turn too."

She reached down into the sweet-smelling dry straw that lined the floor. "I thought I smelt straw. Where do we get it from?"

"The stables of course. That's if you have the courage to go there. I hope you're not as timid as Janet. She's terrified of the horses."

"Are there really horses?" she asked quickly. "I've always wanted to learn to ride."

"Oh really?" Patrick demanded, scepticism dripping from his voice. "You can't get round me like that."

"As though I'd want to!" her cheeks flushed with irritation. "Alright bossy boots, if you want to be like that, I'll show you. You'll eat those words."

"Well," he laughed, "you've got more fight than Janet, that's for sure. If you really want to ride, Green'll teach you just as he does me. Do you want to come and see or are you chicken?"

"No. I'll come," she raised her chin defiantly.

Patrick nodded and squeezed out of the secret den, but as she made to follow, Janet caught her arm anxiously. "You must keep this secret. No one knows about it except us... not even Briggs the chauffeur."

"I won't tell a soul, I promise. Look, I'll be back as soon as I've seen the horses. I'll be as quick as I can." She frowned, and on a sudden impulse she grasped the girl's hands. "What is it Janet? Is it just the horses, or is something wrong?"

"No," the girl looked away quickly. "It's nothing. You'll see."

♪♫

CHAPTER 18

THE FIRST WEEK passed very quickly as Maddy began to learn about her new home. She gathered up all her courage and threw herself into finding out as much as she could, hoping that it would help her feel at home more quickly. The horses were tremendous, and she began her first riding lessons.

It was now Saturday, and she looked out at the vast green curve of the gardens, at the open spaces, the enormous trees and glades, all cunningly designed and planted by some famous landscape artist generations ago. It had been great fun climbing the trees and Patrick was an expert, a vigorous capable boy who goaded her unmercifully with both her riding and climbing. He and Janet had nothing in common, for she was a quiet retiring, trusting creature who craved gentle company. They had had a great deal of fun, and she soon forgot all traces of awkwardness and discord.

But there was tension in the house this morning.

There was no school at the weekend and the routine was vastly different. The children spent the morning practicing but that did not explain the feeling that pervaded.

Maddy left the letter she had been writing and went to wash the ink off her fingers and frowned. Neither Patrick nor Janet had spoken at breakfast this morning. They had not even looked at each other or her.

She dried her hands and looked at her reflection in the mirror. There would be a strict admonition from Nanny if she appeared downstairs with her hair out of place.

♪♫

In the drawing room, Phyllis touched her husband's arm fondly. "Just go gently with her Bernard, you're rather an overwhelming presence to the children you know."

He smiled slightly, and his fingers ran across the smooth surface of the statue absently. He knew every detail, every texture and contour of this priceless object now, and its pure beauty still managed to thrill him. "I'll be gentle my dear. Do you realise who that young girl is?"

"No, is it important?"

"Could be." He glanced at his wife's handsome strong face. "She's the granddaughter of the Braithwaite woman."

Phyllis blinked quickly, then her cheeks coloured with indignation. "You shouldn't play with a child's life like that Bernard."

"I'm not!" he replied quickly. "I chose her on merit; you've heard her play. But I *am* curious to know why that evil woman ignored the girl and left her languishing in an orphanage. What sort of woman would do that to her own flesh and blood?"

"It is odd," Phyllis nodded slowly and sighed. "She's a

dear thing, and she's coped very well with the upheaval. In fact, she's brought the other two much closer, they both like her." Then she glanced up at her husband and her voice broke. "She's just the sort of daughter I'd love to have."

His face tensed. "I'll be with you tonight. Don't despair Phyllis. I'll be home more often now young Trepithic has the new production lines operating. We'll give ourselves a chance. I could be home most nights."

"Good," she nodded and turned away hastily, fighting to control her pain.

He leaned across and kissed her cheek then left her.

He was still thinking of Phyllis as he entered the music room, but his thoughts soon changed. Madeline was sitting at the piano, working intensively on her scales and arpeggios. She was dressed beautifully now, her hair shimmered around her face and her slender arms moved quickly and gracefully up and down the keyboard. He could sense the strength and intensity in her, and it thrilled him.

She paused and looked round at him, and he nodded briskly. "Morning Madeline. How are you settling in?"

She folded her hands shyly in her lap. "Very well thank you sir."

"Good. You can play to me later but come. I want to show you where the others are and what they're doing." He reached out his hand to her.

She rose to her feet eagerly, a graceful, sprightly young creature that reminded him vividly of the beautiful statues he adored. And dressed as she was, the last vestiges of the orphanage child had fallen from her.

"I'm very grateful for all you're doing for me sir," she said earnestly.

He took her hand and patted it reassuringly. "You young

people are special, don't you know that? All three of you are capable of great things. My role is merely to provide you with the tuition and support you need."

"If my father had been given an opportunity like this," she continued slowly, "then I know so much would have been different."

"It is not good to dwell too much on the wrongs of the past Madeline, you can't change that. What you can do is build your own future. Now come."

He took her upstairs and opened a door that gave access to what initially looked like an empty room. All the furniture had been removed. A barre had been screwed to the wall, and the long mirrors that were a decorative feature of the room now had a different function. They no longer enhanced the shape of the room and emphasised its contents, they gave Patrick an all-round view of his posture and appearance.

The boy was limbering up. An accompanist was playing in the background, and he was going through a series of gracefully controlled movements under the watchful eye of a delicately featured lady with silver-grey hair that had been swept up into a bun. Her eyes flickered to the newcomers for a moment. She nodded slightly and returned to studying her pupil.

Patrick turned slowly, effortlessly, with almost insulting ease. Then he saw them.

His eyes skimmed over Madeline and widened as he saw Belaugh. His movement faltered for a second, then his concentration snapped back, and the graceful movement resumed.

Belaugh watched the exercise a little longer, then he glanced at Madeline and beckoned her and they left the room quietly.

Janet had a music studio of her own and they could hear her clarinet from some distance. She was alone, practising a difficult passage again and again. She had no idea they were there, her back was to them, and all they could see of her was her long perfectly brushed hair which seemed to ripple slightly as she moved and expressed the music.

Again, they did not interrupt, but left quietly. As they walked through the house Belaugh murmured, "You're an extremely talented group, as you can see."

"Yes, sir. I've seen them both practicing this week."

"You're good friends then?"

Maddy nodded.

"Good." He held the door of Maddy's music room open for her and followed her in. "Then show me just what you can do with this piano. You'll find that I come to watch your progress at the weekends so you mustn't be nervous of me."

The young girl sat down, and he watched her flick quickly through her music. He could see she wanted to play well for him, her movements betrayed a slight nervousness. She placed the music on the stand, then closed her eyes for a moment as though she was gathering her inner musicality together. She took a deep breath and allowed the music to flow through her.

She was mesmeric to watch, and a curious breathless tingling swept through him. He was witnessing something very special indeed.

When the music came to an end, she turned enquiringly to him. "What did you think sir?"

His breath was still clamped within his chest. She would take the musical world by storm.

He saw a little constriction of concern cloud her eyes and he smiled reassuringly. "That was exquisite my dear. You play well. I shall look forward to following your progress."

Relief was visible on her delicate face, and she smiled in delight. "Thank you."

"Keep up the good work." He nodded and left her to her practice.

♪♫

On Sunday night, Madeline sat down to write another letter. She had already written in glowing terms to Josie and Tina, and now she was writing to her brother.

It's really very exciting. They have been very kind to me and there is so much being planned for my career. Already it looks as though I have a definite path to follow. It's such a change from the orphanage, although I really miss seeing you on Sundays.

Mrs Belaugh gives a big party each Christmas, and she would like you to come and join us. She will write to Matron, and she'll send the car to collect you. Please please come! I'm dying to show you all the things I've discovered, and then there are the horses!! You'll love it. I just wish you could be here all the time...

Her thoughts flew instantly to the horses, her eyes grew distant and the ink began to dry on the immobile pen nib. She had chosen a beautiful chestnut mare called Sunny Suzy. Her imagination was so powerful that she could almost smell the stables around her, feel the nuzzling snout taking bran from the palm of her hand. The groom, Jack Green, had taken her to view the horses earlier in the week. It was almost as though they had been made for each other, the beautiful, elegant beast had greeted her visit by nuzzling gently against her neck.

Janet had been terrified. But from that moment, Maddy

had known there was something special about that mare, and she had been right. Riding her had been a dream.

There was a discreet tap on the door, and she looked up. "Come in."

The door opened and Janet peeped in cautiously. "Am I disturbing you Maddy?"

"No! I was just writing to my brother. He's still living in the orphanage. Come on in."

The young girl came in timidly, reminding Maddy of a mouse crossing a large open space and wary of predators lurking close by. She had been quiet and withdrawn all weekend, hardly speaking a word to anyone. It was an immense relief to Maddy that she was coming out of her shell again because the silence had been quite uncomfortable.

Janet perched on the edge of Maddy's bed and clasped her hands together tightly. "I just wanted to tell you that I'm really glad you're here Maddy. It's been so lonely since Michelle left. You see, Patrick's always so loud."

"He's just a typical boy!" Maddy laughed. "A pain! Ignore him. He'll grow up one day."

"What's your brother like? He can't be as bad if you're actually writing to him."

"Matthew's very shy and quiet these days. He didn't use to be." She frowned and looked down at the letter she was writing. "He worries me, Jan. I think he's lost himself. I wish he were here, sharing this with me."

"I would imagine..." she murmured shyly, "I expect you feel a little bit lost too, don't you? It must be an enormous change, coming here from an orphanage. Life here is so polite and ordered. And solitary."

Maddy looked up quickly, and when she saw the anxious questioning look on the girl's face, she reached out to touch

Janet's hand. "You are very sweet Jan. But Mrs Belaugh has been so kind that I don't feel awkward. A little lonely perhaps. She's marvellous, isn't she? No one has ever done so many lovely things for me before."

The girl nodded, but there was a strange look in her eye. "So, you like it here?"

Maddy nodded, and her enthusiasm game bubbling through. "It's like being in heaven. It's such an opportunity too. All I had to look forward to was playing at small provincial concerts and accompanying the local choirs. Now, my future is what *I* make it." She looked down at her hands and turned them over, feeling the determination flow through her.

The younger girl looked at her admiringly. "I wish I could be as strong as you."

♩♫

The following week was filled with rich musical experiences, meeting and working with people that she had previously only dreamed existed somewhere in the world. But as the weekend approached, an unbearable tension returned to the house. Janet and Patrick fell silent once more, withdrawing into themselves as though they were afraid to communicate with each other and thus expose their inner selves.

Confused, she went quickly to her piano and played until she had completely relaxed and lost herself in the music. She did not hear the door open and shut, nor did she hear the slow heavy breathing of a visitor listening and watching her every move. It was not until footsteps broke the spell she had woven around herself, that she realised she was not alone. She spun round to find Belaugh's vast bulk crossing the floor towards her.

"No, don't stop playing my dear. Keep going."

She turned back to the piano and picked up the phrase she had been playing.

He came to stand behind her, so close that she could feel the texture of his coat against her back and the movement of his breathing.

Then when she had finished, there was a long awkward silence and Maddy turned anxiously, hoping she had not offended him. He was watching her. Their eyes met and he took a deep breath. "I hear reports that you have been working hard young lady. I'm very pleased. But you must make sure you keep up the effort."

"I will sir. This means a very great deal to me." And without knowing quite why, she turned quickly back to the music so that his presence was once more behind her. "Would you like me to play something else?"

"Yes." He straightened and placed his hand on her shoulder, and his finger stroked her neck softly. "You must get used to having an audience."

Later, when she was alone again, she tried to still her uneasiness. It was hard. Eventually she went to the stables where she knew the horses would take her mind off her anxiety. There, she found Sunny Suzy in the bright sunlit courtyard undergoing a thorough grooming. Jarvis, one of the game keepers, was as skilled with the horses as the head groom, and when he was not riding the estates and watching over the pheasants, he was caring for the horses. On this occasion, he looked up at the sound of her footsteps and smiled. "Mornin' miss."

Her heart grew lighter as the lovely animal whinnied and turned her head in eager greeting. She reached out to grasp the bridle. "She's a beautiful animal, isn't she?"

"Certainly taken a liking to you miss." He straightened up and patted the animal's flanks. "She'll be a loyal friend if you treat her right. There's good blood in this mare. Would you like me to saddle her? I could take you for a ride."

She nodded eagerly. "I'd love that, but will it be alright? I've only ridden her a few times."

"Don't worry. I'll keep an eye on you."

But that night, when she came to write to her friends again, she could not quite communicate the same enthusiasm that she had the previous week.

And yet the following week passed calmly and contentedly, and Madeline was so happy that she began to think she had just been very silly at the weekend and had let a trivial matter bother her.

♪♫

Phyllis was a very kind and placid guardian, providing a calm and encouraging environment for all three children. So when Madeline was summoned to the drawing room one morning, the young girl wondered what she could possibly have done wrong. But Phyllis smiled at her and indicated that she should make herself comfortable in the chair. "Maddy, I have been thinking about this for several days. When was the last time you visited your mother?"

Maddy felt her heart lurch and she paused to marshal her thoughts. "It was… I last saw Mummy just before Daddy died. That was several years ago."

"I thought that might have been the case. I've made some enquiries at the Sanitorium, and if you would like to do so, then we could go and visit her. There is no pressure on you if you would rather not, but if you…"

"Oh, I would love to!" she rose quickly from her seat,

unable to contain herself sitting.

Phyllis smiled, folded her hands in her lap and waited for the young girl to calm down slightly then continued. "Then I shall take you this weekend. But remember that she is very poorly, so you must have plenty to talk to her about. Perhaps we'll take her some fruit too."

The wait for the weekend seemed endless to Maddy and anticipation wiped away all other concerns and doubts from her mind.

♪♫

CHAPTER 19

AT THE SANATORIUM, when the news of the impending visit was broken to Maisy Brooks, the older woman wept. Her family had been her life. What would Maddy feel when she saw such a sick and helpless wreck instead of the mother she remembered? The poor girl had already been burdened with responsibilities and cares beyond her years, it would be terrible to burden her with this also.

Then the innate strength and courage of Maisy's character resurfaced. She ached to see her daughter, surely it could be done without hurting her.

Maisy sat up determinedly in her bed and sent one of the nurses for a mirror, an item she had not been allowed in more than a year. Within minutes, sister arrived at her bedside. "Now, Maisy dear, you know we don't allow such things on this ward. It's not good for a woman to dwell on her reflection."

"Rubbish!" Her voice may have been weak, but she

projected into it the full authority and strength of her upbringing. "Please have the goodness to find me a mirror. My daughter is visiting me tomorrow, and I will *not* have her seeing me in this condition. If the nurses could help me with a little makeup and some attention to my hair, I can give her a far more encouraging sight to remember me by."

What Maisy saw in the mirror came as a terrible shock. She was desperately thin, emaciated, her eyes hollow and dark rimmed, skin yellowed to the colour of ancient parchment. It would strike horror into the fourteen-year-old Maddy. No wonder they forbade mirrors in this establishment!

The following morning, with the help of several nurses she carefully styled her hair, dabbed colour onto her cheeks with a little borrowed makeup and succeeded in hiding some of the awful pallor and hollow lines of disease. Finally, she touched a few remaining drops of her favourite perfume to her wrists and behind her ears.

When the hour of the expected visit approached, she felt almost sick with nervousness. Whatever would she say to Maddy? It seemed a lifetime ago that they had been together as a happy family.

Maisy glanced once more at her reflection, patted her hair firmly into place and practiced her smile. Then suddenly she remembered how she had used to sing to the children each night at bedtime. Her heart ached. She wanted to see her daughter so much.

♪♫

Maddy had spent the intervening days mulling over the things she could talk to her mother about, and she had so much to tell her. Yet as the car crunched up the long drive to the hospital, fear and apprehension began knotting in her stomach. This place had terrified her when she had come here with Mrs Rogers, and that horrifying sensation was sweeping through her once more. It was the sight of the grimly functional, white painted building sitting starkly in large open grounds that did it. There were no flowers, no bushes or trees, no signs of colour to relieve the severity of it.

This was so silly, she told herself, it was Mummy she was coming to see!

Maddy glanced sideways at Phyllis. That kindly lady was sitting at her side in the car, but she seemed to be anxious and uncertain too, and that unsettled her even more. When the car finally drew to a halt at the front entrance, Phyllis took her hands gently in her own. "There's no need to be nervous Maddy. I know how much you've been longing to see your mother. Would you prefer it if I wait out here for you? I don't want to gate crash on your reunion. It will be a very personal occasion."

"No, no, Phyllis!" Maddy gripped her hands earnestly. "Please come in with me. I would rather not go alone. And I'd love Mummy to meet you."

"Very well." Phyllis nodded in relief, and patted her hands. "Are you ready then?"

Maddy nodded, picked up the bag of fruit and took a deep steadying breath.

So it was that when Maddy entered the vast airy ward with its huge open windows and cold spartan atmosphere, the kind and caring Phyllis was walking at her side.

The sight that met her eyes was even more daunting than she remembered. There were long rows of metal framed beds, each with standard white cotton sheets and a gaunt, sick patient. There was no hint of human comfort or individuality anywhere.

Each bed was occupied by a frail shell of a woman. She followed the nurse through the ward, looking from side to side, searching for the face she knew and loved. But a little spark of indignation was beginning to smoulder in her. How could anyone have consigned Mummy to this alien and unwelcoming environment? She was such a warm-hearted and loving person, one whose vibrant personality could turn even the barest of rooms into a homely haven.

Then she saw something familiar at the far end of the ward and her spirits soared.

One painfully thin figure was watching their approach, and unlike all the others on the ward there were traces of colour on her sunken cheeks. But what caught Maddy's attention was the tender smile that was emanating from her blue eyes. It brightened the room, filled it with colour, and created a warmth that not even this terrible place could quench. "Mummy!" she breathed.

Maisy held her hands out and Maddy went to her, sinking into her mother's arms, unable to speak for a moment. She felt her mother touching her golden curls, a gesture that she remembered from when she was very small and it evoked a flood of wonderful memories of comfort, safety and love.

"I've missed you so much," Maddy managed to say at last. She breathed in slowly, and as she inhaled the cold disinfectant laden air, she caught an unmistakable whiff of the perfume her mother had always worn. It had even permeated the starched white cotton of the hospital sheets, and brought back another host of precious memories.

"There, dearest. I've missed you too." Tears trickled down the older woman's cheeks as she hugged her daughter to her heart. Then she took Maddy gently by the shoulders and held her away so that she could see her clearly. "Oh my, you are a beautiful young lady, I always knew you would be. Come and sit down by me and tell me everything you've been doing."

Then Maisy looked over Maddy's shoulder towards Phyllis, who had been hanging back tactfully. Their eyes met, woman to woman, and after a few awkward moments Maisy suddenly smiled. "And do introduce me to your friend, dear. I believe I owe her a great debt for bringing you here today."

Maddy nodded and drew Phyllis forward to the bedside and made the introductions, then she settled herself in the chair to chat. "I have so much to tell you, Mummy. But before I do, look. We've brought you some fruit."

"Oh, why thank you dearest..."

Phyllis only stayed for a few minutes, long enough to be certain that Maddy was not going to be overwhelmed by the experience, then she slipped away discreetly to leave them alone.

Maddy found it very easy to talk to her mother, telling her the details about her new life, her friends, her hopes and ambitions. The sound of her mother's gentle voice questioning and replying was a great joy. The visit did the dying woman a great deal of good, but on the return journey to Harborough Hall Maddy sat silently in the back of the car.

She was reliving every moment of her visit, but her silence was due to more than that. She was acknowledging and facing up to an inevitable and shocking truth. Her mother's health was continuing to deteriorate, in spite of this prolonged period of treatment. It had not needed the Doctor's solemn pronouncements as they were leaving for her to understand that her mother would never recover. She was going to die.

"Oh Mummy," her breath caught suddenly in her throat, and in spite of her best efforts to hold the emotion at bay, tears filled her eyes, and she wept.

Phyllis draw her gently into her arms, cradled her close and kissed her forehead. "Shh sweetheart. It must be so terrible. I only hope I did the right thing by bringing you today."

"I'm so grateful that you did, Phyllis," Maddy said jerkily. "Just imagine if we had not come today and I'd never had the chance to see her again! I would like... would it be possible to return again soon? It's just..."

"I understand," Phyllis stroked her hair gently. "Would you like to come again in another month?"

"Oh I would love to." Maddy's eyes shone suddenly through the tears. "And I promise you that I will work even harder to make up for lost time."

♪♫

Belaugh came to Maddy's practice room late that evening to check on her progress. He did not approve of allowing her a day each month away from her work. They had never done it for the other children, but Phyllis had persuaded him to agree against his better judgement. He stopped in the doorway and watched her working.

The music she was playing had a deep and intense sadness, and he could sense suddenly that she was expressing what she must have felt at meeting her sick mother. Poor girl, her mother was going to die. Phyllis said the doctors had given up hope of a cure.

Yes, he nodded to himself. It was right that she should

visit each month. And then surprise filled him. It was amazing that she had the power to express so much through the medium of music, that she had been able to change his convictions.

When her hands finally came to rest, the magic that had held him enthralled evaporated. With a sigh, he stepped forward and took her chin in his hands and turned her face towards him.

Her blue eyes flashed to his in surprise. His fingers wandered across her cheek and under her jaw and he whispered softly, "You will achieve great things Madeline Brooks. The audiences will worship you. They could not fail to."

She rose quickly to her feet, her eyes widening warily, and she stepped back from him so that his hand dropped from her face. "I don't want to be worshipped, sir," she said, her voice slightly unsteady but determined. "I want to make music that people will enjoy."

He stiffened, suddenly aware of what he had been doing, and hastily stepped back. "You do that already young lady. Continue with the good work."

♩♫

Once Belaugh had left, Madeline found herself trembling, and she stood with her fingers pressed to her burning cheeks.

That night as she lay in bed, she hugged the blankets close under her chin. Anxiety was buzzing horribly in her stomach. She had never experienced this before in her life. She had grown up knowing she could give the Reverend Rogers an enthusiastic hug. Yet the touch of that man's plump soft fingers on her neck and the way he had come so close to her had left her feeling invaded.

She thought then of her father, of the orphanage, and she yearned for their honesty and kindness, not this unnamed darkness.

She remembered the look on Patrick's face when he had seen Belaugh watching him, the little things he and Janet had said and the silence that enveloped them both when the businessman was in the house. They were even more afraid than she was and that appalled her.

She would give anything to be away from here.

She covered her face with her hands and wept silently, trying to hold the sobs back. She was too frightened to let anyone hear her lest they came to investigate and ask questions.

Then finally she managed to calm her fears. She had to be brave. This was her one chance to do well, and she had promised her father.

Dear beloved, father!

She forced herself to focus on the future, on the training that was being mapped out for her. It would be foolish beyond belief to throw it all away because of a few ridiculous qualms. There would never be another opportunity like this.

♪♫

CHAPTER 20

CHARLES BRAITHWAITE PARKED his car in the lee of a bare horse chestnut tree and looked for a long while at the rambling old vicarage. It was a big place and must cost the devil of a whack to maintain. He took a deep breath. There was no point in putting the moment off. It had taken long enough to track the man down. This was going to be difficult.

He opened the car door and pulled his stiffening body out of the driver's seat into a biting December wind, but he felt better as he straightened his shoulders and strode up the path.

Presently the door opened before him, and he was met by a kindly-faced man wearing a dog collar. "Reverend Rogers? Pleased to meet you. I'm Charles Braithwaite."

The Reverend Rogers' eyebrows rose in surprise, and he slowly extended his hand. "This is unexpected, sir. You must come in, come this way."

The vicarage was alive with the sound of young voices,

and Charles looked around appreciatively. He chuckled and his voice echoed back from the walls as he said, "You have a large family of your own I see."

"Yes." The Reverend showed him into a well-used book lined study and ushered him to a chair. "I have six children, five boys and a girl. But that's not why you're here, is it? What can I do for you?"

"I'm trying to find my daughter Maisy and my two grandchildren. I've been stationed in Europe throughout the last year, so it's been impossible to enquire about them until now. I can only apologise for the length of time it's taken to come and see you. My wife's eyesight is poor, and she copied down your address incorrectly. I eventually had to visit the Bishop of Salisbury to obtain your location."

The Reverend Rogers pursed his lips and his eyebrows rose in disbelief. "Really? My first letter to you was over a year ago and I've written several times since then asking for help for the children. Every one of those letters has been ignored, Brigadier."

"As I said," he stated firmly, "I've been abroad until this month."

The Reverend blinked hastily. "I must have written six times in all." He removed his spectacles and spent a few moments polishing them. "I am no judge of family matters, Brigadier Braithwaite. That's for you to decide. But I would suggest that you look into it." Then he placed the spectacles back on his nose. "However, knowing something of Maisy's family background and the disagreement with her mother, I am not surprised by what you say. What is it that you want of me?"

Charles Braithwaite was aware that he was being observed by a pair of a shrewd and piercing eyes and he rubbed his forehead. "I want to find my daughter. There are several things I deeply regret in my life. One of the greatest being she did not come to India with me. The last time I saw her she was sixteen, passionate, spirited and full of life, and we became good friends." He sighed. "Her husband must have been an inspiring man, to gain the devotion that he did from her."

The Reverend's smile this time was far kinder. "He was indeed, and he was also a very gentle character. They were an admirable couple."

Charles nodded and smiled. "Would you kindly tell me where I might find her."

"Be prepared for something of a shock when you see Maisy. Her health has deteriorated, and she's extremely frail."

Charles looked searchingly at the Vicar's face. "Was life here particularly hard for her?"

The Vicar appeared to age suddenly, with a mixture of weariness and anger. "They lived in a small flat and struggled. It's terrible to watch friends struggle and be unable to help. Angus taught, but he should have travelled the world and earned fame and fortune. He was capable of it you know; just as young Madeline is."

"So, she takes after her father?"

"A little after them both." A fond smile filled the Vicar's eyes. He rose to his feet and went to pour a glass of brandy for himself and one for his visitor. "She has her father's gifts, and her mother's spirit and energy."

Charles took the glass that was offered and sighed. "Can anything be done to make Maisy more comfortable?"

"Small details for her daily comfort, yes. But I believe a visit from you would do her a great deal of good. She's always spoken very highly of you." He looked quickly at Braithwaite's face and smiled. "And I can see the resemblance between you. But don't on any account take your wife. I know they had a catastrophic breakdown in their relationship."

"I certainly shan't do that!" the old man's face tightened as he recalled Mathilda's uncaring and callous comments about Maisy and her family. "It sounds as though my daughter and her husband were well respected here."

"They were. Angus did a tremendous amount for the community. As for your grandchildren, I'm surprised you haven't seen young Maddy. She's living very close to you. She's at Harborough Hall. Her talents have earned her a scholarship from a very distinguished benefactor."

"Belaugh! Good God! Yes, I have seen her!" He frowned and looked out blankly into the middle distance. "I had no idea who their new protegee was!"

"As for young Matthew, he's still at the orphanage and deeply unhappy." The Vicar perched his spectacles on the end of his nose and hunted in a drawer. He peered at several papers, and then took out the most recent report. "This is from Matron. If you'd care to read it, you'll find he's regressed into himself since Maddy left. He was always quiet and shy. He used to love sport, but he's even shrinking from that. He needs to be part of a family to rebuild his confidence."

Charles frowned and took the letter. He had to squint to read the congested handwriting, and by the time he had finished he felt more than a little ashamed of his lack of urgency in searching for the children. "Poor little soul." He glanced up at the Reverend Rogers and found the man watching him steadily. He placed the letter back on the table. "If I forced my wife to take him in, it would lead to nothing but pain for the boy. I came here with the intention of providing him and the girl with good schooling, but clearly that won't be enough to replace the security of his lost family."

"So, that's what you wanted." The Reverend thought for a moment, then a shadow of a smile illuminated his face, and he nodded. "If you could place Matthew in a good school, he can stay with us during his vacations and exeats. He's a good lad and will be company for my boys."

"And when he needs uniforms clothes and books, write to me in London, not to my wife."

"I'll do that." The Reverend nodded and drew towards him a large sheet of paper. "Meanwhile, here are the addresses where you can find Maisy and Matthew. And I'll give you a letter of introduction to the orphanage." He looked up suddenly and frowned. "If you have the opportunity, will you also speak to Maddy? I have a feeling that all is not well with her."

"In what way?" Charles asked in surprise.

"It's hard to define, but I think she's frightened. She used to write long open letters to my daughter Josie and to the girls at the church, all about her friends and her thoughts and feelings, but she never mentions her friends now, and seems to have no feelings."

"It may just be that she's growing up. She must be fourteen years old now, and the life at Harborough Hall will be very different to the one you lead here."

The Reverend nodded. "You may be right, but I would feel happier if I was sure that's all it was."

"I'll speak to her."

♪♫

CHAPTER 21

CHRISTMAS CAME TO an end and Maddy reluctantly said goodbye to Matthew and Tina, waving them off as Briggs drove them back to the orphanage. She was going to miss them, but her thoughts turned to the coming year and the challenges ahead. She had been at Harborough Hall for four months and had settled into a strict routine of study and work. The concentration on music was utterly thrilling. Her tutors were greatly knowledgeable and gifted, and in a short space of time she had learned more than she had imagined possible. But she had also been at Harborough long enough to discover exactly what was going on.

She smoothed her gloves on primly and rose from the pew, carefully withdrawing into the background and averting her eyes from the plump presence that liked to press close to her. She turned and followed Mr and Mrs Belaugh out of the church. Gradually she became aware that an elderly gentleman who had been sitting several pews back, was watching her closely. He had done that several times now.

She handed her hymn book and prayer book to the verger and stiffened unbearably as Belaugh put his hand on her shoulder. It took all her courage not to shake him off, but she looked up enquiringly into his rounded, misleadingly gentle face.

He smiled. "Have you noticed the elderly couple who were watching you today? Why don't you go and speak to them? I believe they have something they wish to tell you."

Belaugh never said anything without a purpose, and she longed to demand why. But she had been strictly trained by Nanny, and it was more than her life was worth to be so rude to him in public.

She glanced enquiringly at Phyllis and the kind lady smiled reassuringly. "Go on dear. I think you'll be very glad if you do speak to them. We'll wait for you in the car. Take your time."

"Yes ma'am." Maddy took a deep breath and looked back at the couple.

The elderly gentleman was standing with his wife in the dimly lit aisle by the font, talking quietly to some acquaintances, and she hesitated for a moment. Then he saw her. An alert smile touched his grey eyes, and he beckoned her over.

He was a tall erect man who looked as though he would be very much at home in command of a cavalry brigade. He must have been handsome in his day. Curious now, she stepped forward to meet him.

The elderly woman at his side turned, expecting to find more friends approaching, but when she saw Maddy she froze. An ugly expression flashed across her face. She spun round and glared at her husband. "Speak to her if you will, Charles, but I certainly shan't have anything to do with her."

Startled, Maddy hesitated.

The gentleman nodded calmly. "As you wish." Then he left her and came towards Maddy. "Miss Brooks?"

"Yes sir." She held her hand out politely to him.

He smiled charmingly and gripped her hand with open warmth. "I've been wanting to speak to you for some days now. I have some news for you. Would you care to walk with me for a few minutes?"

Maddy glanced over her shoulder. "But your wife...?"

"Take no notice. Her anger is not directed at you. Shall we take a turn around the grounds?"

Maddy allowed herself to be guided out into the chilly winter air. The day was bright and cold, with just enough of a breeze to sting the cheeks and invigorate the blood. They trod the crisp frosty grass for a while in silence, then she murmured, "What news do you have for me sir?"

"I visited the Reverend Rogers two weeks ago."

Maddy relaxed a little, and for the first time in months a warm sense of safety spread through her. She smiled and looked up into the gentleman's strangely familiar eyes. "How is he, and how are the family?"

"They are very well my dear. I had a reason for paying him a visit. I wanted to find news of my daughter Maisy and my grandchildren. I am your grandfather."

Maddy halted as though she had been struck by a bolt of lightning. Shock tingled through her, and it gradually mutated into powerful and long harboured fury. This was the man who had fiercely disapproved of her father, disowned her mother, and abandoned her entire family when they needed help. The indignation grew until her cheeks were stained by fierce red blotches. "You are Grandfather Braithwaite?"

"Yes. Imagine my surprise when I discovered you were living on my doorstep..."

"Don't say any more," she whispered fiercely. "If you imagine that I have anything to say to you then you are mistaken. You should have contacted my parents years ago, not now when it's too late."

"It's never too late to repair the damage, Madeline," he murmured gently, and placed his hand on her shoulder.

She shook the hand off. "Don't touch me. Do you know what you've done? You *killed* my father, and my mother is dying because you totally abandoned her. You can never repair that harm. If you'd been more forgiving, they could have lived a far more secure life. I have nothing to say to you."

"Wait," his hand shot out and he grasped her fingers with stern authority. "I'm deeply sorry about your father but listen to what I have to say. I saw Maisy last week."

Maddy turned back to look at him. She had not seen her mother for nearly a month, and suddenly she was helpless with longing for her.

"She's very frail, but we talked for hours. Damn it, girl, she's my daughter! Don't you understand?"

He paused for a long moment but Maddy was too angry to think. She glared at him, then shock surged through her as she recognised shades of her mother in him. Small mannerisms and beloved expressions that hurt her a second time and fuelled her anger still further. "Oh yes, I understand. You feel guilty at last for your callousness."

He looked down into her blue eyes, and his face stiffened. "The doctors are merely waiting now. I've done everything I can to make her more comfortable. I promised her that I'd take care of you and Matthew. I've already put Matthew into a new school, and he will go to stay with the Rogers family during his holidays. He will be a great deal happier now."

"So, you believe you have sorted Matt out." Her voice shook with contempt and she continued in a whisper. "And you think you can organise me too, after all these years of neglect?"

"No, I don't think that." He drew himself slowly to his full height. "But if there is anything I can do for you, I will do it. You are my granddaughter, Madeline. I'd like to care for you if you'll let me." His expression softened. "Do you know, there's so much of your mother in you, and she in turn was very much like me." He touched her cheek gently.

Maddy's eyes flared wide in pure instinctive dread.

Did he want to possess and touch her in the same way Belaugh did? She froze rigidly and her face drained of all its colour. Whatever was she doing to make people behave like this?

She took one step backwards, then another and another, then at last she spun round and ran.

♪♫

CHAPTER 22

HARBOROUGH HALL PROVIDED an intensive study environment for the three young people. They were constantly stretched, learning and experiencing various aspects of their art. Already Madeline was feeling the first thrill of excitement and nervousness. She was preparing for her London debut, where she would be taking part in ambitious concert of Rachmaninov with the BBC Symphony Orchestra. If she performed well, this would launch her into the musical world.

To relax in her free time, and to provide a musical contrast, she had tremendous fun playing all sorts of popular songs and dances for Phyllis. The two of them would get together when Belaugh was away at work, invite a few of Phyllis's friends to the house, and Maddy would play for them so they could dance and sing along. The moment Belaugh returned, though, she concentrated entirely on the serious work.

Then in March, a catastrophe happened in the Belaugh business empire, casting a dark shadow over everyone. Whenever he was home, Belaugh was a brooding presence that overawed his three protegees. He would work long hours alone in the library and then emerge to watch their practices sombrely, an aura of desperation surrounding him.

The tension became unbearable. Even Phyllis, who cared for the children with the warmth and understanding of a natural mother, withdrew into herself and they would find her staring blankly through the window, utterly immersed in her thoughts.

Maddy tried just once to talk with Phyllis about it but found herself brushed away in a distracted fashion. After that, she was deeply reluctant to intrude on these private struggles. So she, Patrick and Janet made a pact to focus exclusively on their tuition and practice, to behave quietly and discreetly around the house and do nothing to cause contention.

Then one day, Phyllis sent for Maddy.

This was it, she thought. Were the three of them about to find out that their sponsorship was ending? Her heart was thumping as she hurried to join her in the drawing room.

The older woman looked up and smiled, patting a stool by her side. "Come and sit with me for a while Maddy. I have something important to ask of you."

Relief washed through Maddy as she saw a warm and friendly smile instead of the anxious frown of the last few weeks. She had become very fond of Phyllis and hated to see her so deeply distressed.

"Bernard and I shall be entertaining a large group of business associates here in a few weeks' time, and we would like to ask an enormous favour of you, Maddy. I expect you've realised that something has been wrong recently. We've experienced a significant business disappointment, but we are hoping to reverse that by putting on a very special event."

"I will help you in any way I possibly can," Maddy assured her quickly. "What would you like me to do?"

Phyllis smiled warmly. "Thank you, my dear. I was explaining to Bernard how you've been playing for my friends recently. We were wondering if you would play for our guests at the business meeting, and turn the evening into something unique and memorable?"

"But of course I would," Maddy's cheeks pinkened slightly. "I can play any amount of dance music, and I could sing..."

"No, no, no," Phyllis squeezed her hands to halt the enthusiastic flow. "Dearest Maddy, we had something far more ambitious in mind. Would you like to give a proper half hour recital? We could have a stage and lighting installed in the ballroom…"

Maddy's eyes sparkled suddenly. They were asking her to do what she loved best. "I could play some Chopin and Schubert if that's the sort of thing you want."

Phyllis nodded. "You could select the music you love best. Would you do that for us?"

"Yes, I'd love to, and it will give me some valuable experience ahead of my concert in London."

"Yes, that is very true. We'll discuss it with your tutor, and I'll leave the programme entirely to the two of you. I have to admit, I shall really look forward to hearing you."

♪♫

The marketing event they were planning was to be even

more sumptuous than the one of the previous year. It had been made necessary when, just two months ago, Sir James Monaghan had suffered a major stroke and the lucrative contracts he had made with them failed to materialise. Now, Phyllis and Bernard were urgently seeking new buyers for the range of gowns. If they failed, the losses to the business would put the entire Belaugh empire in jeopardy.

Finally the critical day came. Downstairs, the guests began to arrive. They were entertained and dined lavishly, whilst the three young people remained out of sight upstairs.

In the privacy of her room, Madeline was being dressed in a luxurious evening gown that Phyllis had chosen from the Belaugh collection, and her golden hair was carefully brushed and pinned back. Janet lay on her tummy on the bed, chin resting on her hands, watching the proceedings solemnly. She did not speak a word. Although she was a quiet and introspective girl, the two had become close, and Maddy was glad of her company. She knew Janet would listen to the entire recital from the top of the stairs.

Nanny talked constantly as she dressed Maddy, coaching her as she always did on etiquette and poise. Then, ten minutes before she was due to play, Maddy made her way downstairs to the peace of the library. She needed a few minutes of complete silence and tranquillity so that she could concentrate inwardly, focus every part of her awareness on the music she had chosen to perform.

She had not been there long when an unexpected noise broke her concentration. She turned quickly and dismay filled her.

Belaugh stood on the threshold, impressive in his sheer bulk and presence. The brooding tension of the last few weeks had gone and his face was curiously alive with excitement. He smiled. "Are you ready my dear?"

"Almost," she replied cautiously. "I just need a few minutes alone to prepare myself."

She could almost feel him touching her as he examined her from head to foot, studying every aspect of her appearance. She prayed he would quickly be done and would leave her in peace.

He nodded. "Phyllis has a good eye for colour and style, and you wear that particular gown very well."

"Thank you."

He came up close to her and stroked her neck with his plump fingers. She cringed inwardly and took a quick step back.

His eyes flashed like fire. "Stand still, girl! I just want to make sure you'll do. A great deal depends on your performance tonight. I'm hoping you will persuade them."

His eyes were changing now as he looked at her, warming in a way that made her flesh creep with revulsion. He nodded. "You'll have them all at your feet." Curiously, he touched the smooth line of her jaw then her cheek. "Such perfection..."

In desperation, Maddy murmured, "Please sir. I only have a few more minutes and I need to concentrate."

"Quite right." He glanced quickly at his watch and nodded. "I must get back. I just came to wish you good luck." Then he turned and hurried away.

Maddy stood where she was for a moment feeling utterly distracted. Turmoil was raging through her. What on earth did she do that made him touch her in that way? She certainly did not want it.

♪♫

Ten minutes later, Madeline Brooks walked slowly through

the darkened ballroom towards the piano. She carried herself with poise, but the outward calmness simply hid the fact she was still trembling from that disturbing encounter.

There were many prominent and famous figures from Belaugh's business world concealed in the darkness, sitting at their tables sipping wine.

The piano was standing in bright spotlight. Clapping rose eerily from the darkness, adding to the tension of the moment and spurring her on as it always did.

She reached the instrument and turned to make a small bow, then she seated herself and closed her eyes for a moment to rid her mind of extraneous thoughts and concentrate her efforts on the spirit of the music. She reached inwardly to that great well of music.

There was nothing there, just an empty void!

Panic hit her. What was she to do? She took a deep steadying breath and extended her hands to touch the ivory keys. She knew the sequence of notes by rote, but the passionate love of music had simply dried up, as though the flame had been extinguished.

The applause was dying away and there was an expectant silence. She had to perform, for Phyllis and for herself.

Forcing herself to concentrate, she launched into the music. The notes came, everyone in perfect order. But to her appalled ear there was no spirit, no truth, no magic in the rendering, and no satisfaction in the making.

When she finished, a wave of clapping arose around her and she rose automatically to smile and take her bow.

She was trembling in every limb now, but she held her chin up and retired gracefully through the enthusiastic throng. How could they applaud when her playing had been so utterly barren?

Once out of sight the emotion came. She ran up to her room, ignoring Janet who was waiting for her in the shadows. She slammed the door, shutting the world out, and in the privacy of her own space she stared down at her slender hands. She had taken it for granted all these years, the gifts she had inherited from her father, and it had gone! Tears sprang in her eyes. "Oh Daddy," she whispered. "What's happened to me? Help me. Please, wherever you are, help me."

She reached inwards once more and found only a terrible emptiness where there should have been warmth, emotion and passion, and she threw herself down on her bed and wept.

Her head was still buried in the crook of arm more than fifteen minutes later when Phyllis silently pushed the door open and paused on the threshold.

It was not until an arm circled her shoulders, and that gentle, firm voice murmured close to her that Maddy realised she was no longer alone.

"What is it my dear? You've never played like that before. It was so mechanical. Oh poor lamb, don't cry like that."

"I don't know what's wrong!" Maddy forced herself up and whispered despairingly. "But the music has just gone. What *ever* am I going to do? It hurts to be so utterly barren and empty."

Phyllis smiled encouragingly. "I think you need a complete rest. You've been working incredibly hard recently. You'll see. It will all be back in a week or two."

"You could hear it then?" she looked searchingly into Phyllis's eyes.

Reluctantly the lady nodded. "But it's not to be wondered at. We'll take a holiday together, a week at Bournemouth or Brighton, just you and me. A few ice creams on the beach and a swim in the sea, listen to the brass band, and you'll be as good as new in no time."

"Just the two of us?" Maddy demanded, imagining the effect of a peaceful time away from Belaugh and his unwelcome attentions, and a grateful smile returned to her eyes. "Oh yes. I think that would do it. You are so kind to me, and I don't deserve it."

"Yes, you do," Phyllis touched Maddy's hair tenderly. "All three of you are very special to me, almost as though you were my own."

Maddy looked at the kind smiling face and murmured, "Sometimes I wish we were. But then..." her voice dried up and she shuddered at the thought of Belaugh for a father. A surge of pure shame flooded through her, and she hugged her arms tightly around herself as though trying to build a protective barrier.

"What is it?" Phyllis asked quickly, trying to draw Maddy back to her.

"Nothing, honestly," Maddy tried to smile.

"Never mind. I'll speak to Bernard once tonight's over. He's busy entertaining the buyers just now, and this meeting is extremely important. I'm sorry I have to leave you, but I must go back and join him. Just remember, this is *not* the end of the world, my dear. You'll be back to normal soon, once you've rested. Promise me you won't worry anymore?"

"I promise," Maddy murmured huskily, but she knew it would be a promise she could never keep.

Phyllis patted the girl's shoulder then rose to her feet and returned reluctantly to the busy ballroom.

♫♫

Once more throwing herself into the bustle, Phyllis went in search of her husband, and to her experienced eye Bernard looked anxious. His round face was smiling and animated, and there was a persuasive sparkle in his eye. To most, it would appear to be enjoyment and triumph. To her it was a sure sign of mental effort.

She stepped over to join him and took his arm, pinning an expression of charm and pleasure on her face. Arthur Manning glanced at her and a smile flickered briefly on his sharp thin featured face. In a husky voice that was almost a bark, he said, "Astonishing girl you have there, Phyllis. She has class. Can see it in her face and carriage. I was explaining to Bernard, she would be an excellent advertisement for your gowns. The two go hand in hand."

"Our young Madeline?" Phyllis glanced quickly at her husband and her heart sank. She thought of the poor young woman crying upstairs, so close to breaking. She would never cope with the pressure. Yet Bernard was desperate enough to agree to anything in order to sell the dresses. She pursed her lips. "Madeline is under a great deal of pressure at present and needs rest. She's working hard preparing for her debut in London. She's playing Rachmaninov with the BBC Symphony Orchestra next month and the works are ferociously hard."

"All the better," Manning murmured and smiled. "I can picture the entire marketing campaign: articles in the Tatler, the Telegraph and the Times accompanied by a series of photographs of her at the piano dressed in a range of your gowns. That face and grace would appeal to the clientele I want to attract, and we can turn the images into an effective advertising campaign. The gowns will sell for twice the price you would have got from Monaghan, so you will see double the profit."

Belaugh nodded. "I'll consider the proposition, but *nothing* must jeopardise Madeline's career. Being photographed is highly stressful."

"She need only spend a day or two with the photographer. We'll try her at the Ritz, give her a little of the bright lights and glamour. Or perhaps I'll send him here to capture her in this environment, with her piano. Yes, she'd excel in this background."

Belaugh nodded again, slowly. "I will give it careful consideration." He waved his hand towards the dining room. "Meanwhile, would you care to see the gowns once more?"

Manning's intelligent sharp eyes smiled, and Phyllis thought he looked rather like a predator homing in on a juicy prey. "Yes. I have to be completely certain about this. We're talking a great deal of money here."

♪♫

CHAPTER 23

JOSIE SAT WITH the letter on her knee, staring distractedly out through the window. The trees were just beginning to show leaf buds, tiny pale green bulges that would soon blossom into vibrant life. Daffodils splashed the garden with yellow, but her eyes did not register the happy fact. The suitcase on her bed lay open and half packed, and until a short while ago, she had been running around collecting her very best clothes and imagining the treats in store for her in London. She had been promised a trip to the theatre and a day out shopping. But now, her fingers were as anxious as her mind, unwittingly pulling the edges of the paper, again and again.

Something was very wrong. It was not that Maddy said nothing in her letters. On the contrary, she recounted the happenings of the month, describing the horses, the music she was learning for her debut and her planned holiday with Phyllis. She even told Josie about the irritating habits and arguments she had with Patrick, the boy living there. He sounded just like her brothers, an utter pest!

So why did she get this ominous feeling that Maddy was in trouble?

It was because everything her friend said was superficial, as though she would shatter into pieces if she spoke of anything that delved more deeply. Once upon a time they had talked about all sorts of things that were personal and intimate. They had confided their feelings, fears and joys in one another just as though they were still together. Now, Maddy was holding Josie at arm's length, treating her as a mere acquaintance.

What if someone was being really beastly to her? Perhaps the environment did not suit her. Or perhaps they did not like her and were making her life unbearable. What if she had discovered she could not achieve what they expected of her? She would hate living with failure. It was terrible to think of her so desperately unhappy. And something about the letters gave her the sense that her friend was coming close to the edge.

Josie came to a reluctant decision, and for a moment she looked longingly at her packing. She had been looking forward to this holiday for months. But she shook her head. She would not enjoy it if she was worrying about Maddy.

She took the letter and went in search of her father. He was in his study writing Sunday's sermon and he looked up over his spectacles sternly. He had a strict rule about being interrupted. But something in her face must have betrayed her thoughts, for the stern expression faded, to be replaced by concern. He rose to take her hands and looked down at the letter. "Is it Maddy again my dear?"

"Yes, and I'm really worried. I've got to go and see her!"

"If you're that concerned then I think you should visit her, but when? You can't be away over Easter, and you're due back at school in fifteen days."

"I know. But if…" she took a deep breath. "If I go to Harborough Hall tomorrow instead of London, I could be back here before Good Friday."

The stern expression returned. "You can't let Aunt Rebecca down. She's been planning your visit for months."

"I know, but something frightens me… something really horrid!"

He frowned and rubbed his forehead. "It concerns me too, and I have to say I'd feel a little happier if you went to see her." He took a deep breath and nodded. "Very well. I'm sure Aunt Rebecca will understand if you write her a proper letter. But before you do, we ought to speak to Mrs Belaugh and see whether it's convenient for you to come. Wait a moment whilst I contact her."

Josie breathed a sigh of relief and followed her father into the depths of his study. Getting his approval was the first enormous hurdle achieved. She watched him lift the telephone receiver and dial the operator, and she discreetly crossed her fingers behind her back. He asked for Harborough Hall in Leicestershire, and within moments he was speaking to Maddy's guardian herself. Josie hoped that Phyllis was as kind as Maddy said and would not mind this intrusion.

The conversation was only brief, then the Reverend Rogers put the receiver back on its cradle and smiled at his daughter. "She'd be delighted to have you, Josie. She sounds a charming woman. Now for Aunt Rebecca. Then we'll have to plan our journey."

"*Our* journey?" she asked in surprise.

He nodded and peered at her, a small smile on his face. "You don't think I'd let you go all that way alone did you? There will be several train connections to make and a trip across London. In fact, I might visit Rebecca myself for a few days while you're there."

Josie smiled, then flung her arms around him and hugged him, glad to the bottom of her heart that she had such an understanding father.

The arrangements were quickly made, train timetables studied, and plans drawn up, and early the following morning father and daughter set out on their journey across the heart of England.

♪♫

That same morning Maddy rose early and found it hard to settle. Josie was the one person in the whole of her life who had remained a sincere and loving friend, and she was both longing to spend some time with her and yet afraid that Josie would see through her cheerful facade and try to touch the trouble that afflicted her.

She shook her head. She should not dwell on such dark thoughts. It was quite possible that in her best friend's company she would be able put these strange fears aside and overcome the echoing emptiness inside her. Josie was such a lovely person. Perhaps she could make her whole again and reconnect her with her musical soul.

It was mid-afternoon when Briggs drove to the station to collect the visitors. Maddy watched and waited at her bedroom window and eventually spotted the car in the distance, making its way up the straight tree lined drive. At last she her doubts began to ease away, and enthusiasm took their place. She made her way down the grand staircase and out onto the marble steps.

The car was just drawing to a halt as she emerged, and the first thing she saw was Josie's face in the back window, peering up in awe at the facade of Harborough Hall. As a vicar's daughter, she was accustomed to dealing with people from all backgrounds, but nothing could have prepared her for this historic grandeur.

Josie hesitated nervously and then climbed from the car, and Maddy's heart went out to her. She came down the steps and held her hands out. "Josie!"

"Maddy!" her friend smiled in utter relief and ran up the steps to embrace her. "You look so well! Oh, and I love the dress you're wearing."

"Thank you," Maddy laughed and tucked her arm through Josie's. "But do come straight in. Briggs will bring your bag up for you."

Josie looked once more at the marble facade that towered over them. "My goodness, what a place this is! Do you know I've been longing to come and see you. But you didn't warn me! Never once did you mention how enormous the Hall is, nor how grand! I'm just glad Daddy managed to find time to bring me!"

Maddy glanced hastily over her friend's shoulder and sure enough, the Reverend Rogers was climbing stiffly and slowly out of the car. A sudden pang of nervousness made her stiffen slightly. She had not expected to see Josie's father, and she could feel herself recoiling inwardly. Had Belaugh really tainted her view of men that much? She only prayed she would be able to behave naturally with him.

"Good afternoon Reverend Rogers," she said with what she hoped was an assured manner. Then she turned back quickly to Josie and tried to recapture that first enthusiasm.

She could see her friend's brown eyes were troubled, and she gracefully took Josie's hands.

"There is no need to be nervous, Josie. We are really very relaxed here." Maddy gave her a quick hug, and the feeling of stiffness evaporated. "Oh, it's so good to see you," she breathed. "You've no idea how much I've been longing for you to visit. We can do so much while you're here. Come straight on in." Then she managed to smile a little more naturally at the Reverend Rogers and gathered about her all the formal graces she had been learning. "Will you come and take some refreshment with us too, sir? What time does your train leave?"

"Not for another hour and a half my dear and yes, I'd love to take some tea with you."

The two girls were soon completely at ease in the marble and gold of the drawing room, and they gossiped easily and intimately, under the watchful eye of the Reverend Rogers. He added very little to their conversation, not wanting to interrupt the natural flow of the reunion. But he watched Maddy closely, observing every expression and reaction. It bothered him that she did not seem at ease with him. She had once been so spontaneous and generous.

Later that afternoon, as he left Harborough to continue the journey to his sister, his worries about Maddy had abated somewhat. But he still had a lingering impression that something was wrong.

Once they had waved the Reverend off, Maddy took Josie back into the house. "Phyllis has had a bed set up for you in my room, so we won't be separated. It will almost be like old Westcott days when we used to stay with each other. Oh goodness, that seems like a lifetime ago."

"It does. And it's been years since I've heard you play

Maddy. Will you show me this beautiful grand piano of yours? You've told me so much about it."

"Perhaps later," Maddy tensed for a moment. She could not do that. Josie would instantly hear the difference in her playing, and she did not want to talk about that just yet. It hurt too much. So, she drew Josie towards the stairs. "We have so much to catch up on. Let's go up to my room now. You must tell me all the latest news about the girls at home, and I'll show you where you're going to sleep."

♪♫

That night, after an evening of friendly gossip, the two girls began to undress for bed. Maddy looked across the room at her friend and tried to make her voice sound casual. "Will you be able to stay for long, Josie?"

"Only for three days, I'm afraid," her friend said sadly. "Daddy needs me back for Easter, so he's coming to collect me on Thursday. But we can cram a great deal into that time, can't we?"

"Oh yes." The relief Maddy felt was immense. Of all things, she had dreaded Belaugh coming anywhere near Josie. It would be like bringing the radiance of an angel into the shadow of corruption. But now she could laugh freely and could look forward to the next few days. "I have so much to show you."

"And we have so much gossip to catch up on, too." Josie was continuing. "Things that can't be put into a letter. What's it *really* like living here?"

Maddy smiled and climbed into bed. "There's always a great deal to do. We spend the majority of our time working, but that's not really a hardship. In our spare time we have the horses. I'll take you to see them tomorrow, perhaps we'll go for a ride. And we have a den…"

"I know, you told me all about it. But what's it like actually *living* in a house like this? With servants and everything. You're surrounded by people who aren't even family."

Maddy curled up, pulling the blankets close around her ears, and for a moment she could feel herself stiffening. The truth came too close to her personal problems. But she knew she had to find an answer for Josie, she could not snub her. With a tremendous effort she crushed her reluctance to talk and began to explain. "We don't see much of Mr Belaugh. He's busy in London all week and has had some problems with his business. But Phyllis is really wonderful, she's here all the time and is just like a mother. I have to admit it was daunting when I first arrived. Everything was utterly different. But we have a nanny who makes it easy for us to adapt. Even now, she tells us how we should behave and what we should do. If she didn't, we'd all be in a terrible mess."

Josie looked at Maddy across the small gap between their beds and a nostalgic expression appeared on her face. "You used to spend so much of your time playing your father's piano. I've never heard anyone play as you do. It's as though you can colour the music with subtle lights and shades, express emotions that could never be put into words. Oh please will you play for me tomorrow?"

A bolt of horror shot through Maddy. Her throat dried up suddenly and there was a peculiar silence. Then eventually she said with some difficulty. "I… I can't, Josie. I've… *lost* it. The doctor said I've been working too hard, and I must take a complete break from playing."

"Oh Maddy!" Josie's eyes opened wide in distress. "How terrible! It's… perhaps I shouldn't have come."

"Oh no!" Maddy's hand shot out and she gripped Josie's across the gap between them. "You're the best tonic I could ever have. All I need to do is take a rest from playing."

Josie smiled encouragingly and nodded, but her fear and concern had just increased enormously.

♪♫

CHAPTER 24

FOR THE BELAUGHS, the days following the show were filled with long and tense business negotiations. Their entire fortune now hung on making this work, and their anxiety cast a deep pall over the house. To lighten the mood and help Maddy to recover, Phyllis took her on the promised holiday to the seaside. It refreshed and cheered them both as nothing else could have.

A month later, the new contracts arrived at Harborough Hall. Belaugh opened the envelope and looked keenly thorough the many sheets of paper. Success was sweet, and sheer relief thrilled through him like an exotic pleasure.

He looked up at Phyllis as she lay her hand on his shoulder, gripping it anxiously. The tension in her voice was painful to hear. "I hope it's good news, Bernard?" she said.

He could not help a smile spreading across his face. "Manning has agreed to everything. The photographer will be here next weekend. Where is Madeline? I must tell her."

"Resting. The holiday did her the world of good. She has her concert with the BBC Symphony Orchestra in a few days. I'll talk to her about it after that. Leave it to me, my dear. You'll just frighten her and ruin the good that's been done by the holiday."

He nodded and rose restlessly to his feet. "And her playing?"

"Back to normal."

He nodded again and moved towards the door. "I need a walk."

He left her standing where she was and went out into the gardens. He walked quickly, working off the tension and anxiety that had oppressed him these last few months.

For the first time in his life, he was glad to be here and not in London. He needed the open spaces, the freedom, the exercise. But nothing he did seemed to ease the unbearable tension of success.

The children were coming out to play now, and he stepped back behind the line of trees to watch them. Then he saw Madeline. It was painful. The boy was dashing out too, such grace and vigour.

He moved uncomfortably, aware of the tightening in his groin. God! He needed Phyllis. That would ease the tension as nothing else could.

He went to find her. She was standing in the drawing room window, looking out on the garden. Her well-proportioned statuesque figure was silhouetted against the sunlight. She was a splendid, mature and highly desirable woman, yet the heat in him dwindled from what it had been. He came up behind her and drew her gently back against him, and his fingers fondled insistently at her waist.

He could see the children again, lithe and

unselfconscious, running and playing together, but he tore his eyes away as Phyllis turned to him.

♪♫

CHAPTER 25

ONE WEEK LATER, the concert with the BBC Symphony Orchestra was a tremendous success. Phyllis was waiting for Maddy offstage and gave her an enormous hug, having to shout to be heard above the applause. "Well done Maddy. I'm so proud of you."

"Just listen to that," Maddy's eyes were glowing with triumph at the roar of clapping and stomping of feet.

Adrian Boult came up and touched her shoulder commandingly. "Come on my dear. They want to see you again. And rightly so. Well done."

Maddy squeezed Phyllis's hand and then returned to take another bow, and as she stood at the front of the stage with the conductor at her shoulder, tears of joy filled her eyes. If only her father could see this. This ovation was his, for it was he who had trained and inspired her.

Later that night, as Briggs drove them home, Maddy looked down at the beautiful bouquet of flowers in her lap, and then at Phyllis.

She was beginning to hope again. She had not seen Belaugh for nearly a month. Perhaps he had lost interest in her at last.

She closed her eyes for a moment and prayed so. She had done her best to avoid him. Softly, she said, "I couldn't have achieved any of this without you, Phyllis, and without that lovely holiday."

Phyllis smiled and glanced warmly at the girl's mature young face. "I don't think I've ever enjoyed a holiday so much either. But you deserve the success. You've worked incredibly hard for it."

"And so have you and my tutors. But you said you had a surprise for me after the concert."

"Yes." There was a hint of caution in her voice this time. "I don't know how you will feel about this. We have a photographer coming to the house next week, and if you don't want to do this, I'll send him packing. They want to take pictures of you in our new range of evening gowns."

"Of me?" Maddy's eyes widened in surprise.

"Yes. The buyer seemed to think that you would add exactly the right note of sophistication and class to ensure the gowns appeal to his elite clientele."

He wants me to be a mannequin?" she laughed suddenly. "But that's absurd. I'd have no idea what to do."

"I'll be there with you Maddy," Phyllis said a little too quickly, and reached out for Maddy's hand. "They won't ask anything difficult of you. It'll be just you, me and the photographer, and your piano."

Maddy slowly straightened up in the seat and leaned forward. She had detected some subtle changes in Phyllis's voice. "This means a great deal to you, doesn't it? How important is it that I do it?"

"That's not your concern, my dear," Phyllis squeezed her hand. "So don't…"

"Oh but it is," she insisted. "What will happen if I don't model the gowns?"

There was a brief silence, then Phyllis continued reluctantly. "We will simply have to find another buyer, that's all."

Maddy nodded slowly. "I know a little about business contracts. If I fail to play when I'm contracted to, there are significant financial implications. The orchestra still needs paying. Rental for the venue will still be due, and the public will demand refunds on their tickets. If *you* have to search for a new buyer, would you lose a great deal of money?" She waited a long while, and when there was no reply, she prompted anxiously, "How much?"

"We'd have to sell the estate."

Maddy looked down at her hands. She owned Phyllis so much and had grown to love her too. She took a deep breath and gathered up her courage. "Well, who knows, I might actually enjoy it."

She felt Phyllis's fingers close gently around hers. They did not speak again on the way home.

♪♫

The review of Maddy's concert lay open on Charles Braithwaite's knee for a long while, and he gazed up at the ceiling vacantly. He could not help but think that Reverend Rogers was right. Something strange was going on in that house. The girl had been taken away for a week unexpectedly, and every time he had seen her, she had appeared more and more withdrawn.

It was not good.

His gaze returned to the newspaper, and abruptly he passed it to his wife. "Look at that. I told you we should have taken care of her. She's done more to honour the family name than your precious young Jeremy will ever do."

Her face tightened as she read through the review. "Jeremy's young. He'll grow out of these foolish pranks, mark my words."

"Rubbish. You rejected the only child with any moral fibre."

"She left of her own accord, as you well know. Far be it from me to beg her to come back."

"She's dying!" He stood wearily, sickened by her callousness. "She hasn't got long to live..."

"You've seen her?"

"Yes. Now listen to what I have to say. Maisy wants to see her two children again, with me. I'm going to take them to visit her this weekend. I shall speak to Madeline, and if she wants to live here with us then my house will be her new home. That is my decision. I won't have any harm coming to her, and outside influences working on her. She is *my* granddaughter."

Mathilda Braithwaite rose slowly to her feet. Her splendid eyes were sparking with anger, her hands were trembling, but curiously she was unable to speak. She opened her mouth to make the attempt, but nothing came. It was impossible to defy him.

Charles nodded briskly and left the room.

♪♫

CHAPTER 26

HARBOROUGH HALL WAS peaceful all that week. Belaugh was away in London consolidating his success, and his young protegees relaxed as a consequence. On Friday, however, they arrived home from school to find that the house had been invaded by a colourful crowd of people who were unpacking huge crates of equipment.

Although they had known this was going to happen, they stood on the threshold for a while, watching the display of artistic adult behaviour in fascination.

They knew Nigel Davenport of course, the designer who worked for the Belaughs, and he was supervising a thin pinch-faced dresser who was fluttering around as erratically as a butterfly. Maddy sidestepped to avoid a hurrying workman and moved a little closer to the door of the small closet where they were carefully unpacking and lovingly hanging one glorious dress after another.

Patrick looked scornfully at the animated expressions on

the girls' faces. "They're a horde of fools, and so are you. Caught up in the glamour of fashion. Sheep!"

"Why don't you just go away!" Janet said sharply. But her wide eyes were fixed on the colourful gowns. "This is nothing to do with you."

Maddy smiled at the indignation in the young girl's voice, but she could not take her eyes off the activity either. "Don't let him tease you Jan," she said softly. "He's just jealous that the fuss won't involve him. Oh, look at these beautiful gowns. Aren't they exquisite?"

Both girls had watched Phyllis dress to entertain at Harborough Hall or leave the house for an evening in London. She was always beautifully attired. It was awe inspiring to think these gowns were here for Maddy to wear. The thin man was examining each one as it was revealed, muttering to himself fussily and making a note of any creases and marks on the material.

The other people rushing around in the hall were noisy workmen, unpacking and setting up an array of lights and cameras, and shouting loud instructions to each other as they laboured.

Amidst all this bustle, a short but beautifully dressed man in his middle years was completely ignoring everyone. It was as though he existed on a completely different plane. Swathed in a halo of personal serenity, he was wandering through the rooms, sizing up and examining the features, and viewing them from various angles.

This had to be the photographer.

The youngsters stood together at the edge of the hall for nearly ten minutes before their presence was noticed, then Phyllis emerged from the chaos and hurried over to them. "Come on my dears. Let's go and get you changed, then perhaps things will be a little calmer when we return."

"Please may I stay and watch, ma'am?" Janet asked diffidently.

Phyllis smiled and touched the girl's long brown hair. "Yes, you may. One more observer amongst this crowd will hardly make any difference. But I'm not sure Patrick will take much pleasure in it," she laughed. Then she glanced quickly at Maddy. "I am sorry Maddy. I didn't expect anything as overwhelming as this, but I will sort it out for you."

Maddy glanced one last time at the intimidating chaos and took a deep breath. "I only hope I'll be able to do what they want me to do."

An hour later, Maddy was looking at the gowns hanging in the closet, and a small confrontation was going on behind her. She knew who would win. Phyllis was indomitable when she was determined.

The thin little man was in a passion of tears and so too was the makeup artist, but Phyllis held the door firmly in her hand and was barring their way. "*No*. You may *not* come in while Miss Brooks is changing. She will be ready for you in a few minutes."

She snapped the door shut, then turned round and leaned on it with a weary smile. "There. That should do it. I'm sorry about all this fuss my dear. They're used to professional models and simply don't understand the modesty of the ordinary woman. But they're just going to have to learn!"

With Phyllis's help Maddy changed quickly into the first gown, and five minutes later the two men were allowed back in. The dresser waited patiently while the makeup artist draped a cloth around her shoulders and dabbed powder and colour onto her face. Then he stood back while the dresser carefully twitched and arranged the gown on her.

Maddy stood with her eyes closed while they worked. Every time she opened them and saw her reflection in the mirror, she felt a little less like herself. They were turning her from a growing schoolgirl into a sophisticated, aloof young débutante.

Finally, the makeup artist murmured quietly. "Whatever you do dear, don't laugh. Only the smallest of smiles."

Her eyes flew open in surprise. She looked at her reflection in the mirror and slowly drew her shoulders back, raised her chin and turned. She had matured by about five years and would not have been out of place at any high-class social event. The gown fitted snugly, hugging the developing curves of her hips. Then her cheeks warmed beneath the makeup as she realised the low-cut neckline revealed far more than she had ever displayed in public before.

She glanced quickly at Phyllis for her reaction, but they were no longer alone. Patrick and Janet were standing in the open doorway with a cluster of workmen crowding behind them. They were all looking at her.

She stiffened, deeply embarrassed by the exposure of herself, and wishing suddenly that the floor could open up and swallow her.

Then her eyes widened.

Belaugh was amongst the admirers and his plump face was alive with ugly excitement. He was looking at her was as though stripping her of the gown and touching her.

Below the makeup, she could feel her face growing pale now. The world seemed to shiver at the edges, shimmer as though the air around her had become water. She could hardly breathe. Hot weakness flooded through her limbs. The world blacked out and she crumpled to the floor.

She surfaced with a feeling of queasy discomfort and searing shame. There were arguing voices all around her.

"No! I won't have it!" Phyllis was saying firmly above the multitude of arguments.

"But it can't be done without us."

"The lights are extremely hot. The makeup will..."

"You will wait in the library please," Phyllis insisted. "Every one of you. I will call you if and when you are needed."

"This isn't going to work, is it?" Maddy could hear Belaugh's voice now, raised in irritation. "What's wrong with the girl? Send for a doctor."

"One moment, please." A calm velvety voice hushed them all.

Then the voice continued. "There's no need for all this excitement. We have three days, and this is just a preliminary photoshoot. Phyllis, will you stay with us please? The rest of you take a break. I want to see what the camera can do. It's a personal thing, very private, between the camera and the girl. I'm not surprised she's fainted, with all of you staring at her as though she were dinner on a plate."

Maddy was still feeling queasy and faint, but someone had covered her with a jacket so that they could no longer leer at her.

A pair of birdlike hands were holding hers, and above the hubbub she heard Janet whisper, "Oh thank goodness Maddy. Are you alright? You went so white!"

She opened her eyes to find Janet leaning over her, blotting out the hordes of people.

She bit her lip dazedly. "I feel awful."

"You fainted!" Patrick's face now appeared in her range

of vision. "What a stupid thing to do."

"Shut up!" Janet dug him fiercely in the ribs with her elbow. "You know very well what it was. It was *him*."

Patrick's face stiffened and his expression changed. "I'm sorry Maddy. He's gone now, Phyllis sent him away."

The tension in her stomach eased at last and she began to feel a little better. The world was slowly returning to normal. "What a fool I've made of myself," she whispered.

"They're coming back." Janet squeezed her hands reassuringly then shrank out of the way and Phyllis came to take her place.

She touched Maddy's disordered hair tenderly and said with a smile. "They don't understand. Men are such idiots, aren't they?"

Maddy smiled. But that moment of shared humour hurt. It was Phyllis who did not understand what was going on in her house, in her marriage. Thank God she had not seen Belaugh's face! If she ever found out, it would cause untold grief, and she did not deserve to be hurt by the people she loved and trusted.

She was turning away now, gently shooing Patrick and Janet towards the door, pointing out that they needed to focus on their own rehearsals.

A short while later, Maddy was once more on her feet and waiting while the dress was being smoothed out and arranged on her. She looked round apprehensively, but the dresser had disappeared. Everyone had gone. The drawing room was empty except for Phyllis and the photographer, and he was busy adjusting his cameras.

Finally, he turned back to Maddy, and she got her first real view of him in all his splendour. He was a vision of purple and pink. His short figure was clothed in a vividly coloured silk suit and shirt. He wore a spotted cravat around his neck instead of a tie, and a French beret, pulled down slightly over his left ear. Yet he was smiling in an understanding way, and Maddy felt herself relax a little more.

"Take no notice of them, my dear," he gestured dismissively towards the closed doors. "I have to ignore them too, or I would never get a scrap of work done. Now…" he fussed with his camera, "how old are you?"

"I'm fourteen."

He nodded, and his eyes crinkled attractively in a reflective smile. "I can just about remember being fourteen. I think we should dismiss the entire team for the rest of the day and work quietly together. We don't need them. Would you mind doing the honours Phyllis?" he rubbed his chin and looked thoughtfully at Maddy. "I'll have to experiment with different settings, but I have a feeling you'd look better without that ridiculous layer of makeup too. I want a strong natural character and plenty of atmosphere."

Phyllis watched him cautiously for a moment, then nodded and left them to talk.

Maddy looked around at the lights and equipment and smiled anxiously. "You'll need someone to operate this lot, won't you?"

"Tomorrow perhaps. We have plenty of time. Fourteen years old, well, well! Do you know, when I was your age, I wanted to be famous? I dreamed of all the fashions I'd design." He laughed in a self-deprecating way. "I ended up designing theatrical costumes. What an indictment on my taste!"

Maddy watched him and could not help but laugh.

"I leave fashion to the Nigel Davenports of this world.

My ideas are far too extravagant for polite society. But my pictures are a different matter. I can match a personality to its costume and background, and that's what my clients want. I've seen all the dresses. I've seen the house. Can you show me exactly what you can do with this piano of yours?"

Maddy led the way to her music room and sat at the piano. She ran her fingers speculatively up and down the familiar ivory keys. "What would you like me to play, Mr Jenkins?"

"Whatever you wish my dear. It's got to come from within you. And I want you to call me Larry by the way, or I simply shan't be able to work." He left his camera and tripod near the piano, then lifted the lid for her in the best concert fashion. "There, that's better. Play something you love and just ignore me. I've still got a few things to arrange."

Maddy closed her eyes for a long moment and stretched her fingers out, and after a few moments the music came, filling her soul, filling the room with sound. She was aware that he was walking round slowly. He left her playing for a while, and then returned carrying several boxes. He did not make any noise. For a plump man, he was surprisingly nimble. None of his silent manoeuvring with the camera interrupted her concentration because she loved her music. She played seriously for a while, then glanced at him and smiled. If he loved the theatre, he would love song and dance, and she began to play a series of popular modern dance tunes and melodies.

Immediately she could sense, just by the way he bustled around, that he was enjoying it.

Then a tremendous flash blinded her for a moment and she stopped.

"Keep playing, Maddy," he said encouragingly. "There'll

be more flashes, just ignore them. I'm experimenting. Play on. Play me the music *you* love best."

"Very well, but when..." a little thrill ran through her, "when will the pictures be ready?"

"I'll have this batch developed tonight. You'll be able to see them in the morning."

She nodded and bent her mind once again to playing. Several hours passed, and she was photographed again and again from all sorts of angles. Then she gradually became aware that there had been no flashes for some while.

She stopped, and concern filled her. Larry Jenkins was looking utterly exhausted. He had seated himself at the back of the room and was listening with his eyes closed. And now that his face had relaxed, she could see he was a lot older than she had originally thought. "Are you alright Mr Jenkins?" she asked anxiously.

He shook himself and mopped his forehead, then rose to his feet and came to place his hand on her shoulder. "I think it's time to call it a day, young lady. I wish I had your stamina. When you reach my age, work begins to take its toll. Did you enjoy that? I enjoyed your music. I would have danced to it years ago."

"Yes. I love playing. But won't tomorrow be different? All those lights and people crowding round us?"

"Once the pictures are developed I shall have a better of idea of what really works. My clients want atmosphere, and there's a great deal of that in your playing. I just need to capture it on camera. Come on now. I'd recommend a good dinner and plenty of rest."

Maddy rose to her feet and went to obey. In the small changing room, she found the dresser waiting for her and the workmen were hovering around too, desperately hoping they would be needed.

♫♫

The following morning, they set to work again. This time, pictures were taken in a whole series of locations: the drawing room, the hall, and again in the music room. The gowns were changed again and again, and the dresser and makeup artist fussed in attendance. But as soon as their task was done, they were shooed away, so that in the end they were nothing more than passing irritations, and the real work was done peacefully between Maddy and the photographer.

Several times, Belaugh came to observe the proceedings, and Maddy tensed through, conscious of his gaze on her. By the time he had interrupted them three times, the photographer straightened his back, glanced at her face and then at Belaugh. He sighed and came to place his jacket gently around Maddy's rigid shoulders. "Go and get yourself a cup of tea, my dear. We've worked hard and you deserve a break. Be back again in fifteen minutes."

Belaugh was gone by the time she returned, and he never again came to watch the photography.

After lunch Maddy dressed in yet another gown and took a quiet moment to consider her reflection in the mirror. Even with far less makeup on her face she looked very sophisticated, and the grown highlighted her maturing figure, her slim waist and curved hips, and the growing roundness of her developing breasts. She smoothed the material against herself and dared to imagine what it might be like to be taken out to dine by a handsome young man. It was something she often dreamed about.

When she emerged from the closet a few minutes later

the usual throng of people were waiting to arrange her gown and makeup. As they bustled around, she looked up and caught sight of Charles Braithwaite in deep conversation with Phyllis. She froze.

He looked up too, alerted by the voluble burst of activity in the hall.

Surprise suffused his face. He broke off his conversation with Phyllis to come striding towards her.

She blushed painfully, overwhelmed by self-consciousness.

"What on earth are you doing, child?" he demanded in disbelief. "You're far too young for this."

He pointed at the revealing evening gown, and she had a desperate desire to cover herself up.

He closed his eyes for an instant, then said deliberately, "I'm going to visit your mother tomorrow. She's relapsed and has asked me to bring you and Matthew to see her."

Maddy felt all the heat flood out of her face and concern take its place. She looked around at the multitude of people waiting for her. They were as nothing compared to her mother. If she was ill, then she needed to see her and be with her. "I will come with you, Grandfather."

"She is very ill, Madeline," he murmured in a gentler tone. "I know she tells you very little in her letters. That's her way. But you must be prepared for a shock when you see her."

Phyllis was at Maddy's elbow now and took her hand. "What about the photography Maddy? There's still a great deal to do. I will take you to visit your mother the moment we have finished, I promise you."

Maddy shook her head and took a deep breath to calm her racing heart. "No Phyllis. Larry and I will work hard today and get the pictures finished. If Mummy's really ill, I need to be with her. And..." pain caught in her throat, "I haven't seen Matt for many, many months."

The old man smiled warmly and nodded. "Thank you my dear. It will be a great comfort to her to see you. I'll be here at seven in the morning. It will be a long journey."

♪♫

CHAPTER 27

AFTER DINNER THAT evening, Maddy retired to her practice. She only had two weeks before her finals, and two months until her next concert. There was a great deal of work to do. She started as usual with her scales and arpeggios, working her fingers, exercising the muscles. Then she opened the music and began to play.

The practice took every ounce of concentration as she created and explored the music. Then suddenly a soft pair of hands touched her shoulders.

She surfaced from the music and turned quickly.

Belaugh was looking down at her. His eyes were oddly feverish, and Maddy shivered in dread.

She tried to pull away from him, but his hands became powerful and bit into her shoulders. With a gasp of hurt, she subsided into her seat and shut her eyes to block out his presence. Then one of his hands moved around her neck, caressing her bare skin. Her cheeks burned with shock and embarrassment. "Stop it," she cried fiercely. "Let me go."

"You're growing up Maddy," he was murmuring thickly, utterly oblivious to her repugnance. "I hadn't realised until I saw you in that gown."

She was struggling to break free now. "I... I have a tremendous amount of work to do, sir. Please let me go."

"Sh. Sit still and be quiet. I'm not going to hurt you. I'd never do that... you're too perfect... too precious." He hauled her tight against him, pressing her hard against his groin.

"Don't... please don't." She tore at his inquisitive fingers. "Stop it now. I don't want this."

"Don't you?" He was forcing the buttons of her school blouse open, and those hot sweaty palms groped across her breasts. "Do you know what you've been doing to me all this year Maddy? You're crying out for this."

Maddy was beside herself with shock and revulsion as the most private, most vulnerable and tender parts of her body were exposed to his revolting touch.

"Let me go!" she screamed frantically, struggling with every ounce of her strength. Yet not even her powerful pianist's fingers could prize his grip loose. "Oh please... leave me alone."

But he was fiercely strong, too engrossed in growing excitement to understand her horror. "There. I knew you'd enjoy it. You're so perfect, so beautiful..."

Powerless to stop him and desperate not to witness what was happening to her, she screwed her eyes tightly shut.

He did not speak again. He was beyond words and the hard eager rubbing of his groin against her back became urgent. Then suddenly he gasped for breath and shuddered.

She half expected him to collapse in some horrendous fit.

Instead, his grip on her slackened.

Free at last, she distractedly drew her blouse together with hands that shook. She could not bear to look at her skin nor round at him. She had to get away from him, find somewhere to clean herself of his touch, of this feeling of contamination.

Before he could stop her, she rushed from the room and ran straight up to the bathroom. Whatever had she done to make him think she wanted to be touched like that? She didn't. He was her guardian, Phyllis's husband and old enough to be her father!

She turned all the bath taps on, stripped off her clothes and jumped into the steaming hot water. The heat scalded her skin, but she was glad of the pain and scrubbed furiously at herself until her skin was red and raw.

It did not help. The sticky feel of his palm print was seared into her flesh, branding her.

Finally, her efforts stopped, and she sat there in silence. She could still feel him on her.

Nothing could change the person she had become, and she was bad.

♪♫

Charles Braithwaite was met the following morning by a withdrawn and aloof young lady. She replied politely to his conversation, but he had the peculiar feeling that he was communicating with a statue, the remains of a person who had shrunk away from human contact. She sat in silence in his car, only speaking when addressed, and when he broached the subject of her coming to live in his house, she stared at him in open horror.

She would not allow him to take her arm, and when she

met her mother, she recoiled from the sick woman's touch.

As they were leaving, Maisy clutched at his hand and wept. "Look after her... please... find out what's happened... my poor little girl... she's so hurt... take care of her!"

♪♫

CHAPTER 28

PHYLLIS HAD FOUND the photographic sessions both physically and mentally exhausting. Protecting Maddy while managing the sensibilities and anguishes of the various artistic souls, something she would normally have achieved with little effort, had utterly drained her. She retired to bed each evening too tired even to eat, which for someone whose endurance and capability had always seemed limitless, came as a considerable shock.

Initially she put it down to stress and the disruption of normal household routine. But she felt no better once they had packed up and departed, and it was not long before she began to suspect that this might be the first signs of the wonderful event she had been longing for all her adult life.

When her physician confirmed that she was to be a mother she was so overjoyed that she did not notice Maddy had withdrawn into herself again. She wrote immediately to inform her husband, and then began planning for the little one's arrival.

Bernard hurried home earlier than usual that Friday, which did not surprise her. He would undoubtedly be delighted by the news, God knows they had been trying for so long. But the moment she saw him she knew, by the expression on his face, that he had good news to tell her too.

She came to take his hands, her spirits rising instinctively. The only thing that could gratify him so deeply was a business triumph. "You have news, Bernard, I can sense it."

"Arthur Manning!" he replied with a smile of triumph. "He's spent the last two days boasting about how clever he is! The photography is absolutely superb, and he's already begun planning a large Christmas advertising campaign. If the public responds in the way he has, then those gowns were going to be an outstanding success."

"That's wonderful news Bernard! You'll be able to pay off the loan, and Harborough Hall will be safe. We shall have a home for our family."

He nodded and took her hands tenderly in his. "Our family. What a wonderful phrase."

♪♫

Phyllis rose early the following day feeling calmer and more energetic than she had in a while. During the night she had decided that she would speak with Madeline and let her know how grateful they were for the help she had given them with the photoshoot. But she paused for a few moments in front of the mirror, distracted. There was no sign of her pregnancy yet, except that her skin was a little coarser and blotchier.

She looked up as a tap came on her door. "Come in."

Bernard entered and he smiled. "Up already? I'd expected you to be resting, my dear. You've got two to consider now, you know."

She looked wistfully at her warm and comfortable bed. "I'd love to be there still, but I want to speak to Madeline this morning before she begins practicing."

"Hmmm, well I think one of us should," he said tartly and frowned. "Her exam results have just arrived, and she has some explaining to do. You go back to bed, my dear. I'll see her."

"Why, what's happened?" she asked in quick concern, and hurried to his side.

"Read this."

She took the printed sheet from him, and her eyes scanned down the marks. Then she read the examiner's handwritten comments and her face faltered. "Oh no, not again! Poor child. It does hurt her, you know, Bernard."

"If that little monkey hasn't been working, then she'll have me to answer to."

"But she *does* work, she practices for hours. Leave this to me. You'll only make matters worse if you go in with a heavy hand." She drew her dressing gown on and tied the belt. "Wait for me here." Then she slipped out of the room.

Madeline's voice called out sleepily when she knocked on her door, so she entered and sat down on the edge of Maddy's bed. The face looking up at her seemed suddenly heartrendingly young, and she could see something very vulnerable and hurt in her expression. She touched the young girl's forehead tenderly. "What is it Maddy? You can tell me, can't you?"

Maddy shook her head and shrank away slightly. "There's nothing wrong. I'm just very tired. I'll be alright again soon."

Phyllis frowned. "Your exam results arrived this morning, and they're not what we expected."

"Oh no!" the girl's eyes widened in dread, and she whispered, "Have I failed?"

"No, in fact you've got a merit. But it's happened again, hasn't it? I thought the holiday had done you so much good. The examiner said the music was performed to technical perfection but was mechanical."

"At least I haven't let you down badly. But..." pain flamed in Madeline's eyes, and she whispered in a hollow voice, "it's like living with a howling void where the music should be."

Impulsively Phyllis took her two hands. "If you're tired, why don't we take another holiday? I could do with a rest too after the stresses of the last few months."

Madeline shook her head and withdrew into herself, once more hiding behind an impenetrable barrier. "Thank you, you're very kind to me, Phyllis," she said firmly. "But the expression will come back. All I need to do is keep practicing."

Confused, Phyllis touched Maddy's hand gently. This was such a difficult age, full of contradictions. She was part child, part adult and both parts of the person were warring within. The problem was probably no more than that. "You're growing up quickly, sweetheart, and growing up is a difficult business. Don't worry about things all by yourself. If you want to talk to someone, come and talk to me. Now, your teacher will be here in an hour." Phyllis stood up briskly. "I'll leave you to get ready for him."

♪♫

Maddy dressed slowly, then went to the music room and sat perfectly still in front of the piano. She stretched her hands out, but there was no feeling left in her. There seemed to be an impenetrable barrier somewhere inside that was holding her innermost thoughts and feelings beyond her reach. As though the real her did not want to emerge and touch the person she had become.

She looked at her hands, turning them over slowly. She remembered visiting her beloved mother. She had not even been able to respond to her. She loved her mother tremendously. She loved Phyllis too. Yet all she seemed able to do was hurt them. The only feeling left in her was a deep disgust at herself.

She remembered the applause that had been hers only a month ago. There would be no more of that if she could not break down the barrier inside her. But she did not know where to begin. Every time she played, the notes came out but the music was locked away. She could express nothing but emptiness.

In desperation she began to play, striving and aching to reach that inaccessible part of herself, the sensitivity and emotion that brought the notes to life. She failed and her hands slid helplessly from the keys.

Playing was the only thing that she really cared about, and now it was locked away and inaccessible deep within her. It was the single most precious gift that father had given her and she had destroyed it.

By so doing, she had lost her father again.

♪♫

The churchyard was warmed by gentle sunlight. There had

been rain in the night, and the drops glistened like diamonds in the long grass. Maddy breathed in deeply of the fresh air, then she heard arguing voices and her eyes flashed open. Her grandfather and Phyllis were in deep conversation and Belaugh was looking in her direction.

She raised her chin and approached Phyllis, trying her best to avoid Belaugh's gaze.

"...I assure you, Mr Braithwaite, nothing has happened," Phyllis was saying. "This is simply a traumatic time in a girl's life. She's growing up and under a great deal of pressure. I promise you, I am taking great care of her."

Maddy could feel her face tensing as she realised that they were discussing her.

"That child has changed." Her grandfather sounded angry but fell silent as Phyllis made a small warning gesture with her hand. He turned with a frown.

When he saw Madeline, his face softened and his voice grew gentle. "Would you walk with me a moment Madeline? I would like to ask you some questions."

She nodded, glad to escape the realm of Belaugh's influence. Her grandfather was strangely aloof, as though he was struggling with himself and did not know how to begin. They had walked some distance before he asked, "Are you happy Madeline?"

What could she say? She tried to smile. "Yes, Phyllis is very kind, almost a mother to me."

"And what of the life you're leading? How are you coping with the work and study, the exams and concerts?"

"I enjoy it, Grandfather. Music is my life. I promised I would succeed. I swore it, for my mother and father, and I *will* do it. For them."

His frown deepened. "Then what has upset you? Was it

that abominable advertising campaign? Did the photography disturb you?"

"No."

"Then what is it?" he turned to study her anxiously.

They had left the gravel path now and were standing among the peaceful dampness of the tombstones. The wet grass was waving at Maddy's ankles and she looked away from him, touched in spite of herself by the subtle resemblance to her mother.

She shrugged her shoulders. Perhaps he was someone she could talk to and trust. He was her grandfather, and she could feel the ties of family, like a bond between them. If only she could unlock her pain to somebody, that might help. She glanced back at his aging dignified face, and she knew he would never understand. He would probably not even believe her. He would imagine she had asked for it to happen. Perhaps she had.

He smiled gently and touched her cheek. "Ah Madeline. You remind me so much of your mother when she was your age."

Maddy stepped back involuntarily, horror flaring in her eyes.

"What's happened Madeline? Tell me, for God's sake, I may be able to help." He took her hands gently. "Listen to me. We have a spare room for you. I'll provide anything that the Belaugh's do. And I guarantee that there will be no pressure on you, nothing that you..."

Maddy stiffened, and a surge of despair washed through her. It was happening again. What was wrong with her? She did not want Grandfather Braithwaite to touch her in the same way that Belaugh had. She would not let anyone touch her ever again!

She wrenched herself free of his grip and ran wildly, tripping and leaping over the tombstones as she went.

She needed to make her own life, build her plans and break away to a place where no one wanted anything from her.

♪♫

CHAPTER 29

THE CONCERT AND reception were over at last, and though Maddy had played without feeling, the music had allowed for that, and she had performed well. She shut the door of her dressing room and the noise of conversation eased away.

Phyllis patted her hand. "You look exhausted dear. Change out of the evening dress and I'll take you home."

"Did you notice the horn player?" Maddy asked with a tired chuckle. "I'm surprised he didn't make a complete hash of his part. Every time he leaned over to empty the water from the horn, he took a secret nip from a little hip flask. I don't think it was just to lubricate his lips. He started drinking during rehearsals this morning."

"He must have been half cut," Phyllis draped a shawl placidly around her young charge's shoulders. "I didn't hear any wrong notes, though. Now come and sit down."

Maddy let herself be led back to the chair and eased gently into it. As her hair was unpinned, she began to relax.

The mental tension and stimulation so necessary for performance, began to melt away.

When a knock came on her door, Phyllis wrapped the shawl a little more snugly around her and murmured softly, "I'll send them away dear. I'm sure they'll understand."

Maddy opened her eyes and roused herself from the edges of slumber. "No, it's alright. It could be important."

Phyllis nodded reluctantly and called, "Come in."

The door opened and it was Sir Edward Elgar, the great old man of music himself, who came into her room. Maddy rose quickly to her feet, tiredness falling from her as though it had never been, and she greeted him with a smile of delight.

"Good evening, sir."

He smiled in response and held his hand out formally to her. "Miss Brooks. I'm glad to meet you at last. I've been looking for the opportunity to speak with you all evening."

She found her hand grasped briefly in a firm quick shake. "I'm honoured, sir. I had no idea you would be in the audience tonight."

"I heard you play earlier this year and could not resist coming to hear you again. The Mozart was a great contrast to Rachmaninov, very restrained, utterly perfect. My compliments."

"Thank you. I'm making a study of Mozart at the moment."

He nodded. "Do so, you need all the variety and experience you can get. I can see great things ahead of you. What plans have you made for your career?"

"Mr and Mrs Belaugh are arranging the details, with guidance from my tutors. I have a number of concerts arranged over the next few months. But for myself… oh, of all things I'd like to study at the Royal Academy of Music. It would be wonderful to be in such a creative environment."

He nodded. "You would certainly fit in well. You'd be with other young people like yourself. And there's nothing more stimulating." He glanced questioningly at Phyllis. "The Academy is excellent at inspiring young performers, and if Madeline were living in London, she'd be able to take tuition from the great Matthay himself. In spite of his age, he would relish a student with such talent."

Maddy's cheeks felt as though they were burning. Surely if she were able to go to the Academy immediately, with music all around her she would find her soul again. She turned quickly to Phyllis. "That would be wonderful, Phyllis. It could make all the difference to me."

Phyllis smiled wearily. "We were advised that the best thing for Madeline was to gain experience in performing, which is what we are focusing on."

"Excellent advice, dear lady. But with such talent, the stimulation of a creative environment would progress her skills even more. She would meet people of real excellence, and there would be innumerable opportunities to further her career."

Phyllis glanced at Maddy's alert, keen face and nodded slowly. "I agree."

Sir Edward turned to Maddy. "It's a lively environment and you would have a great deal of fun too, which would mitigate the hard work."

Phyllis was looking very tired now and rubbed her forehead. "I shall have to consult with my husband about this. The final decision will have to be his, but it does sound like an excellent suggestion."

It was as though Madeline had been drenched by cold water. Belaugh! It was going to come down to him again.

And she knew instinctively that he would not permit her to go. But she could not allow this opportunity pass, even if she had to find a way to do it by herself.

"What would I need to do to gain a place there, sir?" she asked.

"You would need to audition." Sir Edward smiled kindly. "Perhaps you would allow me to write to them on your behalf."

Her heart pounded with sudden hope. "Would you do that for me, sir?"

"With pleasure, my dear. With Mrs Belaugh's permission, of course?" he glanced enquiringly at Phyllis.

She was frowning now, but she nodded slowly. "Yes. Please do so."

"Thank you." Maddy straightened her shoulders slowly. "Thank you very much."

♫♫

Maddy was quiet and appeared to doze against the car cushions throughout the journey to Harborough Hall. Phyllis did not try to converse and when they reached home, she whisked the young girl up to bed, tucked her in and left her to her slumbers. Maddy was exhausted, and usually the long journey home was enough to soothe her spirits and induce sleep, but not tonight. She was far too excited at the prospect of escaping from here.

She lay for ages with her eyes closed but nothing happened, and eventually she sat up and switched the bedside light on. It illuminated her room in a warm cosy glow.

All around her were the things that Phyllis had provided to make her comfortable and happy. There were the books, the doll's house, writing and drawing materials, riding clothes.

Phyllis had been more than kind, treating her like a daughter. She covered her face suddenly, overwhelmed by a deep sense of guilt. The last thing she wanted to do was hurt Phyllis, but she knew she had to get away from here.

Already she doubted whether they could unlock the block on her emotions simply with a holiday and a rest. She hardly seemed able to feel natural and normal joy or sadness. She felt alien and cold.

Surely if she could study in such a centre of excellence with some of the world's greatest musicians, that channel of joy would open up again.

She climbed out of bed and went to open the box of music that had belonged to her father. She touched the pages tenderly with the palm of her hand and recalled the things he used to tell her about the Academy. Her thoughts turned longingly to the lounge in their flat, her father playing to her and the sense of security that had enveloped them. It had felt as though nothing would ever change.

But it had.

Now, if she seriously wanted to achieve the success her father should have had, then she *must* make the break and change her life again, or she was afraid the ability to play might never fully return. She sat at the table and drew a page of writing paper towards herself and began to write.

She realised suddenly that her bedroom door had opened, and her hopes dissolved around her. She spun round and froze, shocked by what she saw.

Belaugh stood on the threshold, a stocky figure in his pyjamas and dressing gown. His face, illuminated by the dim peripheral glow of her bedside lamp, looked black and thunderous. He entered and closed the door behind him, then looked at Maddy.

"What's all this about you wanting to study at the Academy *this* year my girl?"

Maddy rose to her feet, pulling her dressing gown protectively around herself. "Nothing, sir. I simply asked about entrance requirements."

"I have everything planned for you over the next three years, a series of concerts followed by study. Why didn't you talk to me about this? Why did you go behind my back and work your wiles upon another bloody musician?"

"I haven't worked any wiles. Sir Edward simply asked me a question and I answered him truthfully. Surely to have a recommendation from such a person will do my career a great deal of good."

"After all the things Phyllis and I have done for you? You don't need anyone else's recommendations, you ungrateful, disloyal little brat."

"That's not fair! I've been very loyal and done everything you've asked of me. It's you who have behaved badly."

"Rubbish." He stepped towards her purposefully. "I think you deserve a good thrashing for that."

"No!" she gasped and backed away from him, lithe and slender as a kitten.

His eyes flared suddenly with open ugly desire, and she knew with sick dismay that whatever she was doing, she had done it again. Desperately, she cried, "No, stop it. Not again."

"What did you do to make him want to help you?" he grabbed at her, but she eluded his grasp. "Did you use this pretty little body of yours? You know just how to use it don't you, and beguile a helpless man?"

Maddy shrank away from him until her back was against the wall and she cried vehemently, "I haven't beguiled anyone. You have it all wrong." He still came at her, and in desperation she hit out at him with her fists.

He laughed and caught her struggling body against him. He looked down into her face and nodded. "I know what will do you good."

Desperately Maddy scratched with her nails at the awful face looming over her. His plump pampered body touched hers and moved demandingly against her, forcing her painfully against the wall.

"Let me go!" she shrieked. Then she moaned in shock as he tore her nightdress from top to bottom. "Don't!"

"Sh," he murmured softly, quivering now with excitement. Maddy tried with all her fierce strength to break away, but he was stronger than her. He pinned her against the wall, and she cringed inwardly. Slowly he forced her hands up above her head and held them there, and with his other hand he explored the upturned roundness of her breasts, the flat smooth stomach and warmth of her thighs.

Belaugh was muttering hoarsely now. "Sh, you'll feel better in a moment, so much better. You don't know yet. Such tension. You're like a cat on heat. It'll all be better soon... I can help you... just let me... set you free..."

She could not bear to witness what was happening and tried to shut her mind to it. She was being slobbered over by this fat lump of a man, touched and possessed. No matter how she struggled, she had no power whatsoever to stop him. He pulled her to the ground, wrenching her arms above her head again in a hold that left bruises on her wrists and all but dislocated her shoulders. He was hunched over her, and she howled in pain as his fingers bit into her flesh and prized her thighs apart.

Then raw agony flared through her and she cried out raggedly. He forced his way into her body, with urgent vigorous thrusts that seemed to tear her apart and squash her against the floor. She could not breathe. She was going to die.

It did not last long and mercifully the brutality ended. The weight of his body slumped heavily on top of her and his grip slackened.

Then he rolled over and sighed deeply. "Christ Almighty, that was good."

Maddy tried to move, but she hurt too much. A flaming wall of pain shot through her. Her eyes flared open in terror. What had he done to the inside of her?

He took her by the hair, forcing her face up to his. "There. It's what you've been crying out for. You'll enjoy it next time. But don't you dare say anything about this to anyone, or there will be trouble. I'll come again tomorrow night."

She shook her head fiercely. "Oh no, you won't."

He was tying his dressing gown in a business-like fashion but glanced across the room at her and lust reared in his eyes again.

Gritting her teeth, she tried to cover her nakedness from his smouldering gaze, but her night dress was hopelessly torn and her dressing gown was wedged beneath her.

She forced herself up on one elbow and managed to climb to her feet. Pain burst through her at the movement, leaving her trembling with weakness and shock.

The door clicked shut and she was alone with herself. Her eyes shied away from her reflection in the mirror, but not before she saw the blood and bruises on her skin!

She whimpered in fright and pain and ran her fingers

through her hair as horror set every nerve in her battered body screaming. She had to get away from here.

She tried to walk and found that it did not hurt as much as she expected. Trembling with effort, she staunched the warm trickle of blood and semen that was seeping down her legs. But no matter what she did, she could not wipe away the feeling of utter degradation.

Half an hour later, Maddy Brooks crept down the stairs. She was carrying her old suitcase, and had taken only the things that were hers, and a few items of clothing that she could not survive without. Quietly she opened one of the large sash windows and climbed out into the garden. She pulled the woollen coat close around her beaten body and set out across the park with fierce determination.

♪♫

Phyllis Belaugh woke early the following morning and spent some minutes lying in bed, gazing up at the ceiling. She still could not accustom herself to sharing her early morning thoughts with the plump sullen cherubs that had been painted there.

Softly, eagerly, her fingers touched her abdomen and joy filled her. Everyone was trying to pamper her. No more early morning rushes or hectic days. She was going to treasure this precious little life, nurture and love it.

Some while later, she gently threw back the covers, intent on a gradual and sedate rise. But then she frowned. A square of paper had been poked under the door. She went over and picked it up, unfolded it and read.

Dear Mrs Belaugh,

I hate to distress you, but I cannot stay here any longer. I'm so very grateful for all that you've done for me, and I wish I didn't have to disappoint you like this.

Please forgive me.

Don't worry about me or try to find me, I shall be alright.

Love from Madeline.

"Oh my God!" Phyllis wrenched the door open and ran along the corridor to Madeline's room. The door was ajar, and she could see cupboards and drawers pulled out, items of clothing strewn around. She stood in the midst of the disarray, unable to move for several seconds.

Then she knelt down in front of the mirror and scooped up a handful of glistening thick golden strands. The child had cropped that glorious crown of hair.

"Maddy. Oh, poor little girl. Whatever have you done this for?" She pressed the hair softly to her cheek and tears filled her eyes. She had been so preoccupied with her own joy that she had failed to see the young girl's distress and help her. Whatever had gone so wrong?

It must have been something of great importance to Maddy, because it had seemed last night as though all the right doors were opening for her career.

Perhaps that was it! Perhaps it was the intense pressure she had been under!

"How could I have been so blind and not understood?" She would have to find Maddy, bring her back to safety and then persuade Bernard to be more lenient with the tuition programme.

She nodded slowly. The most important thing was to remember she was only a child, and children should be happy.

♪♫

CHAPTER 30

HUNGER WAS A familiar friend and Maddy was completely used to it once more. How could she ever have forgotten? How could she ever have allowed herself to become so pampered? She had eaten nothing but scraps for more than a week. Her feet had hardened to walking, and she had learned the hard way how to take care of herself. The streets of the capital provided many places to hide, and she was certain they would never find her here. A fierce independent spirit had grown in her. No one would ever organise and influence her life again.

It was a warm summer's evening, sunny, humid and calm. The normal smells of the city were sharpened and concentrated so that the air became difficult to breathe to one who was not accustomed to it. Even now the sights, sounds and smells overwhelmed her senses. The buildings rose tall and stately above her, so much history and success displayed in the architecture. The constant bustle and purpose, trams, buses, horses, cars, underground trains, and of course people.

She hoisted her battered suitcase purposefully, straightened her slender shoulders and continued on her way. She passed a grand establishment that was emitting a delicious aroma of cooking meat and the busy sounds of people politely talking and laughing. She was ravenously hungry, but she ignored it.

She peered up anxiously at the street signs as she passed. This was it. Then she saw the hotel in the distance, and nervousness stirred in her stomach. She had to get this job. Confidence was the only approach, and her public training and experience stood her in good stead. She mounted the wide steps of the establishment and entered, treading the red carpeted stair as though she belonged there.

A footman in smart livery was standing just inside the door, and he raised his eyebrows and stepped forward purposefully to intercept her.

She was painfully aware of the crumpled state of her clothes, but she raised her chin and met his gaze with quiet confidence. "Perhaps you would care to direct me? I'm looking for the Disraeli room."

He looked down his nose with utter disdain. "For the audition?"

"Yes," she nodded.

"Staff door is further along the street." He hurried her back out down the steps and pointed to a narrow flight of steps that descended to the basement at the corner of the building. "You'll have to hurry. And if I were you, I'd clean yourself up before they see you."

She hurried down the dark basement stairs. At the door, she took a moment to compose herself and sweep her hair back into some sort of order, then she pushed the door open and stepped into bright light.

Everything happened very quickly. She was escorted along a starkly illuminated corridor and given a place in a line of distinguished looking gentlemen. She went immediately to the cloakroom, filled the basin with steaming hot water and treated herself to a wash. Her surroundings were bleak: whitewash flaking from the walls, cracked wash basin and stained floor, but the act of cleaning herself was luxurious. She removed her coat and cotton dress and changed into the only beautiful evening gown she had brought with her.

Calming her nerves, she combed her naturally curly hair until it shone like a halo around her face, then looked long and hard at herself. A slow smile touched her eyes. She could easily pass for twenty, perhaps more. She examined her wrists anxiously. The bruises had faded at last and were nothing but shadows. They had been the reason she had failed the first audition. There had been many more auditions since then, and she was becoming desperate.

She took her place in the line of applicants, and her appearance now caused them all to turn and look.

Twenty minutes later it was Maddy's turn. She was escorted into a large empty tearoom. The wrought iron tables and chairs stood deserted, and stretched in rank upon rank into the darkened recesses of the vast room. Exotic plants, hanging elegantly from huge china pots, were the only witnesses to the occasion.

"When you're ready," a voice intoned from the darkness.

Maddy seated herself at the piano and launched calmly and gently into a long series of modern dances and songs. It was no difficulty. She had played so much of this over the last few years for Phyllis and her friends, for the ballet classes and for her own enjoyment, that she hardly needed to consider what she was doing. The room was utterly silent, and she found the lack of an audience rather disconcerting.

"Can you give us any Strauss, Miss Brooks?" a soft textured voice asked from the darkness. "We expect our clients to dance after their refreshment."

She smiled and nodded, and changed immediately into a Strauss waltz, following that with a medley of dances from previous eras. Several requests were made, and finally a different voice murmured, "Can you sing, my dear?"

Maddy obliged them as requested, and several minutes later a third voice snapped, "Thank you, that will be enough."

Maddy stopped abruptly and turned in the direction of the voices. Her throat felt dry as she waited. They were talking together. After several agonising minutes, the cold voice said, "Please wait outside."

The auditions continued for several hours, and by the end of that time there were only two applicants waiting for the verdict, herself and a handsome mature looking man.

Madeline glanced across the bleak corridor at him. He was watching her, and she averted her eyes quickly. Then finally he rose to his feet and came towards her and gestured to the chair at her side. "May I?"

Maddy shrank into herself and nodded. "If you must."

He sat down and leaned forward, elbows on his knees, and glanced sideways at her. "I've been racking my brains trying to remember where I've seen you before."

"I don't think we've ever met."

"We must have, your face is so familiar. Ah. I've got it. My God! You're the cover girl on the big new clothing advertisement, aren't you? And that's one of the gowns."

"A cover girl?" Maddy spun round to stare at him. "Those pictures aren't supposed to be published for months yet!"

"They're plastered all over town. And there's a story to go with it too. I remember now!"

There was a slightly contemptuous laugh in his eyes that made her itch to slap his face.

He sat back with ease in the chair. "I thought so. They won't employ you in a place like this you know, not with a face that's been blazoned across the magazines and papers. Though I have to admit you're very beautiful. No one would know you're only fifteen..." he touched her cheek with insulting condescension.

Maddy slapped his hand away and shot to her feet, trembling in every limb. "Don't you dare touch me. My private life is no concern of yours, and I'll thank you..."

"Don't be a fool. Once they realise who you are, you'll have no chance. You may as well go now."

"And you'd tell them who I am, I suppose?" The contempt in her voice was like acid.

His face froze at the tone of it, and he rose to his feet with dignity. "Yes, I would. I have a family to support. I'm not a spoilt brat who's run away from a very generous home. You should go back where you belong."

Maddy felt tears stinging her eyes. The anger and indignation in her had no voice, the horrors that had happened to her were too private to be spoken. She glanced down at the fading bruises on her wrists, then her anger flared out of control. She leaned over and snatched up her suitcase. Her voice shook with fury, the child she had once been had gone for ever. "You have the job then! But just remember, when you feed your family tonight, this spoilt brat hasn't eaten in more than a week."

He rose quickly to his feet and took a step towards her, but Maddy took a step back and spun around. All she could remember was Belaugh. She felt sick with anger at all of manhood. They were all the same. She gripped the handle of her case fiercely and walked as quickly as she could down the corridor.

"Hey, wait a minute!" the voice called, and she broke into a frightened run.

He took several steps after her, then shrugged and turned back to await the outcome of the audition.

Several minutes passed, and the man sat frowning moodily at his hands, then the door opened and a soft velvety voice called, "Miss Brooks."

The gentleman looked up. "I'm afraid she's gone."

The door opened further and there were three policemen in the room. One of them came into the corridor and demanded quickly, "How long ago did she leave?"

The man was silent for a moment, then for some reason he told a lie. "About half an hour ago, I think. Is there something wrong?"

♪♫

Maddy was shaking as she hurried away from yet another failed audition. Part of it was due to hunger and disappointment, part was rigid sick fear. Looking down on her was an enormous poster of herself dressed in evening attire. Whatever was she to do? She could shelter the night again in the old derelict building, but it was not safe. It was used by tramps, and the structure itself was unsound. She could risk queuing for soup again with all the other jobless and destitute, but they were looking for her. She could not continue like this much longer. She was so hollow and hungry that she felt waves of faint weakness washing over her. If she became ill, she would never raise herself out of this mire.

Gradually she began to pull herself together and think logically. She had nearly two miles to walk, and she could not do it dressed like this. She crept down into one of the public lavatories. There was no one using it at this time of night. Very quickly, she stripped the evening gown off and climbed back into her ordinary dress and zipped it up. Then she pulled her coat back on and returned to the street.

For a moment she did not notice the plump figure waiting at the corner, until she realised that a man was approaching her purposefully. She was filled with blistering contempt for men who propositioned her like this, and she had had to deal with enough of them now. She turned her back and began to walk away quickly. All men were foul.

"Miss Brooks."

It was as though a bolt of electricity shot through her. She took to her heels and ran.

Behind her, the voice called urgently, "No, wait Maddy. I'm not going to harm you. It's no good, I can't run after you, young lady. Come back. We've got to talk. It's urgent."

Maddy recognised the voice at last, and she stopped running. He was one man who had never treated her with anything except kindness. She felt utterly weak from the effort of running and she turned slowly, letting the suitcase slide from her hand. "Is that you Mr Jenkins?"

The colourfully clad figure of Larry Jenkins puffed up, and he stood looking at her, a little out of breath. "You walk too quickly for me. Did you know that the police are searching for you? It's alright," he smiled and held his hand up. "They're not following me."

"The police? But I've done nothing wrong."

"No, but you're underage my dear." He was silent for a while, then nodded. "When I took all those pictures, I knew you were in difficulties. It's not hard to see below the surface of the subject you're photographing. You have to get under the skin in order to capture the essence of the person. That wistful depth is there in the pictures for those who have eyes to see. I noticed the bruises while you were playing tonight."

Maddy drew back inside herself. But even as she did so, a little voice told her that he was no threat. He had coaxed her, understood just how she felt and cajoled her, but never had he looked with admiration or lust at her. Her voice was a little shaky as she asked, "What do you want of me then?"

"Nothing. But I'm worried about you. What are you going to do now?"

"Try again I suppose," she shrugged.

"Hmmm. I think you'll have problems now the pictures are out." He looked around at the busy street. "Look, I'm famished. I've been taking pictures all day and haven't had a bite to eat yet. Would you mind dining with me, and we can talk in greater comfort? I know a very nice little restaurant just round the corner, I'll treat you."

Maddy's hungry stomach churned at the very idea, and she replied a little weakly. "Thank you. I'd like that."

Ten minutes later, she was studying the menu in the intimate environment of a small restaurant. She made her choice, then glanced a little shyly at the elderly man opposite her. "Are you very tired, sir?"

"Shattered. I haven't been able to stop worrying about you all month." He glanced thoughtfully at her thin hungry face, and a smile touched his eyes. "I've been looking for you all over London ever since you ran away. I'm glad you've made the break. That environment was stifling you."

"But how did you know where to find me? Surely if you can do it, then they can too."

"Yes, and they're looking. Ah," he sat back as the waitress presented them both with a steaming bowl of soup. "Tuck in my dear. I hear that you haven't eaten in a week."

"That awful man yesterday!" she cried indignantly.

He laughed suddenly. "You made him feel very uncomfortable about himself. If it hadn't been for him, the police would have caught you yesterday."

Maddy choked suddenly over the soup, and when the coughing had subsided, she murmured quietly, "I won't let them take me back."

He shook his head. "The only trouble is that you're doing what they expect you to do."

She frowned in perplexity, and rubbed her forehead then shrugged. "What else can I do? I have no other talents."

He looked at her for a long moment then took a piece of bread and broke it and stared intently at the pieces. At last, he murmured under his breath, "I can see myself when I look at you. When I was your age, I was forced to work in a bank. Can you imagine? My father was a Yorkshireman, proud and successful. He wanted his son to follow in his footsteps. The only problem was that I had a different vision. So, I ran away. The difficulties for a girl are even greater than those for a boy, and I'd hate to see you encounter them."

Maddy found herself looking at his gentle face in fascination, and she noticed that his hands were slightly unsteady. Whatever had happened to him, had left him deeply scarred. She reached out hesitantly and touched his hand. "I'm sorry."

He smiled with difficulty and patted her hand. "It's a long time ago, and I can look back now and know that I've climbed out of it. Eat up. I've got some ideas and a proposition for you, but remember I'm on your side."

Maddy nodded her head and tucked into the food with a greater feeling of security than she had experienced in a long time. She ate an enormous meal and finished it off with a big plate of profiteroles, smothered in chocolate and cream.

"Better?" he asked, taking great delight in her pleasure.

"Mmmm. Much, thank you."

"Have you got anywhere to stay?"

"No," she shook her head.

"Then you can sleep on the sofa in my flat tonight."

Horror flashed across her face. "No, no. It's alright, I *have* found somewhere, I've been there for nearly two weeks now..."

"So, that's it!" he said sternly, "I'll have you know that I'm old enough to be your grandfather, young lady, and you don't interest me in the least. You have nothing whatever to be afraid of. I'll find you somewhere of your own tomorrow. Now, came with me."

Surprised into silence by his anger, Maddy followed him out into the street. He did not offer to take her case but marched along, still simmering with indignation. They took a short ride on the underground, and within twenty minutes, arrived outside a smart Edwardian house and he led her inside.

The interior of the hall was formal and echoing, but once he had opened the door to his apartment, a profusion of comfort and colour reached out to enfold her. Maddy stood absolutely still on the threshold, spellbound. He had said that he was closely involved in theatrical costume design, and she could see the drama of the stage in his taste here. It was comfortingly feminine.

"Larry? Is that you?" a clipped male voice came from behind one of the doors. "I was beginning to worry. Did you find her?" The door opened to reveal a tall slim man, relaxing in his pyjamas and dressing gown. He was puffing luxuriously on a long cigarette, and as he saw her he smiled ironically around the ebony holder, not even removing it from his mouth. "I see that you have. God, she's young!"

"Maddy, this is Rudy Crawshaw, he shares the flat with me."

"I'm pleased to meet you sir," Maddy held her hand out to him.

He gripped it briefly and smiled. "Larry has been worrying about you for days, young lady. I hope we'll be able to get a little sleep now that he's found you."

The photographer frowned at his friend, then ushered Maddy in. "Come and sit down, and I'll explain what I have in mind. Rudy, be an angel and make us a coffee, would you?"

The tall man nodded and left them to talk.

"Among my interests, I sponsor and run Rudy's touring theatrical company. We produce shows and musicals, then take them around the country. I need an accompanist, and I know you've done that sort of work before. Think Maddy, if you were to play here in London, to any audience, whether it was 'knees up Mother Brown' in a pub, or Mozart with an orchestra, you'd be recognised. If you're hidden behind the piano in a small theatre in the provinces, no one would see you. I need an accompanist to tour with the company."

Maddy looked at his friendly face, at the flamboyant generous comfort that surrounded her, and she wished she had some insight into this job. She did not know whether to trust him or not.

Finally, she nodded. "I'll take the job. And... I'm very grateful. I was beginning to think that I would starve." Her throat was closing up, and tears were filling her eyes unbidden.

"Sh, poor lass," he handed her his handkerchief gently. "You'll be alright. Now I'll just hunt out something for you to wear for the night, then we'll sit down to supper and get a good night's sleep."

Maddy wiped her eyes, comforted by her surroundings, the feeling of friendship and the pleasant perfume that pervaded the handkerchief.

♪♫

CHAPTER 31

THE FOLLOWING DAY, Madeline Brooks was transformed into Grace Mayers. With the exotically decorated apartments all around her, themselves resembling a film set, her new appearance fitted perfectly. She was dressed in a flimsy chiffon tunic and trousers, adapted from Larry Jenkins's extensive wardrobe. Her much shortened hair had been scooped back dramatically in a rolled up purple scarf, and she wore strings of coloured beads around her neck. The photographer looked over her shoulder at her reflection in the mirror and smiled. "There. I doubt even Phyllis would recognise you now."

Maddy laughed and rose to her feet, watching her reflection as she moved across the room. "I look like Greta Garbo with my hair like this."

"And you'll be able to command an audience just as she does. One small tip, my dear, coming from one who has learned the hard way. Clothe yourself in eccentricity. It's a strong shield. Adopt dramatic mannerisms, and you'll always have the last word. It's important. People expect artistic behaviour from artists, and you mustn't disappoint them."

An hour later, Maddy was surrounded by a bustling throng of artists the like of whom she had never seen before. She was the instant subject of very sharply critical speculation by several of the females, whilst another came to hug her and press a perfumed, powdered cheek to hers. "My dear. Welcome. I'm sure you're going to be much better than the silly woman who played my music before. Such a fool. She didn't know when to allow me time to breathe and expand the music. We must rehearse. I haven't sung for three days..."

"Presently, Desiree. You sing perfectly and you know it. It's your lines you need to rehearse." Rudy Crawshaw the producer swept Maddy through the throng, introducing her to each artist in turn, until her mind was reeling with a confusion of names, perfumes and colour. Then he called, "Silence please. Act two on stage immediately. We'll go from the curtain. Now, come this way, Miss Mayers."

Maddy was shepherded to the piano, where she was relieved to find Larry Jenkins waiting for her, already sorting the music and placing it in order on the piano lid.

Rudy looked severely at his friend. "I sincerely hope this works. We haven't got time to make any more changes to suit your whim."

"It'll work. Now come and sit down my dear. I'll be with you today and help you sort things out. After that, you'll be on your own."

Maddy nodded and made herself as comfortable as she could.

The rehearsal was long and arduous. The actors received constant instruction and support, but the accompanist was largely ignored. It was only when she resumed playing in the wrong place or failed to adapt to unexpected changes in tempo or key, that she brought the whole proceedings to a sudden halt and drew down on her head a scream of abuse. But Larry chuckled softly. "Ignore them, or better still, return the dramatic gesture. I'll show you some tricks tonight, and you'll have them eating out of your hand."

"There's so much to do and be aware of," her cheeks coloured with indignation. "How can he expect me to sight read the music and observe everything else? It's unreasonable."

"Exactly. You must be equally unreasonable with him. You can only expect to be perfect by the time we play to our first audience. What you've got to do is carve your place amongst them."

Maddy nodded dubiously and looked up at the players. Rudy was watching her critically. "When you are *quite* ready Miss Mayers. May we have the correct music this time?"

Taking her time Maddy closed one set of music, placed it in correct order, then with an artistic flourish, she sought out and placed the appropriate music on the piano and nodded with a sweet smile. "In your own time Mr Crawshaw."

But she spent that second night sleeping on the sofa at Larry's flat, too tired after such a stressful day, to go hunting for accommodation. She had serious and painful doubts about her ability to cope with the job, and spent several quiet hours studying the music and script, until finally things began to fit into a pattern. Then sleep overcame her and she crashed out, surrounded by disordered music, as though it were the feathering of an exotic nest.

She was unaware of it when the tall thin figure of Rudy Crawshaw eased the door open and moved silently into the drawing room. He looked down at her sleeping form for a moment then gently slid the music from her grip and tucked the blanket in around her.

A few moments later, Larry Jenkins appeared in the doorway. He watched his friend's elegant outline as he silently turned the light out and came to join him.

Rudy took a cool discreet draw on the cigarette in its long ebony holder and nodded. "She'll do. She's good."

"Then for heaven's sake, dear man, tell her. Just look at her now."

Rudy glanced again at the sleeping figure on the sofa. Lying there swathed in blankets, she looked almost a child. He smiled gently. "I can't. I'll have to treat her like the others, or it will raise suspicion. She's going to have to grow up very quickly."

♪♫

Phyllis Belaugh, meanwhile, waited anxiously at Harborough Hall. A city dweller all her life, she knew in detail all the disasters that could befall a young girl on the streets of the capital. She tried to keep herself busy so that the horrifying images of brutality and exploitation did not fill her mind. The child had said not to worry about her. How could she not? She was still nothing but a sweet trusting child.

She blamed herself completely. She had been so preoccupied with her own joy that she had failed to notice the child's despair.

Now it was too late, she was able to look back and see it quite clearly. It had been going on for a long while, the pale haunted face and the lack of expression in her playing. No child should be made to suffer like that.

♪♫

Mathilda Braithwaite stood at the door of her rambling old home and held her arms out to welcome her daughter. It was not Maisy, it was her favourite younger daughter, Jessica, whose elegant figure gracefully stepped up the path to the house. A boy of twelve followed her, but neither woman took any notice of him.

Jessica was smiling in satisfaction. Her mother, observing that smile, immediately took her into the drawing room.

The boy followed obediently. He made himself comfortable by the fire and occupied himself looking through the newspaper that was lying on the table. His eyes were restless, darting around the room, delving into curious corners, and after a little while he got up and snooped around, moving so quietly and inconspicuously that the adults took no notice. Every now and again he glanced at them, listening to and absorbing every word they said. Their conversation became more interesting as time went on.

"I've got it at last, Mother. Look. That dear friend of mine, Chief Inspector Partridge, sent me a copy of the latest report, knowing that the brat was family. They still haven't tracked her down."

"Well done, Jessie. We need to remain well informed." Mrs Braithwaite picked the paper up and peered at it, frowning hard with the effort to read. A slow smile spread across her thin face. "Just as wilful as her mother, and as ungrateful. She deserves everything she gets, that one."

Charles Braithwaite had appeared quietly in the

doorway while they were speaking, and his parade ground bark silenced everyone briefly. "Put that down, Jeremy!"

The boy hastily put a letter back on the mantelpiece. "I wasn't doing any harm Grandfather."

"You shouldn't be reading private correspondence, young man."

Jessica hurried to her son and put her arm around his shoulder protectively. "Don't shout at him, Father. The poor boy has been through a terrible experience at school, and shouting will only make matters worse."

"Have you now, Jeremy?" Charles Braithwaite's face tightened grimly, and he looked the young man up and down. "And you've been sent down again, have you?"

The boy stiffened and looked quickly at his mother.

Jessica squeezed his shoulders gently. "Go and sit down, dear. I'll tell Grandpa." Then she glanced resentfully at him. "Father, you must be gentle. You know how sensitive he is. We've decided to find a new school for him. I'm not having him accused of such terrible things."

Charles Braithwaite nodded and strolled thoughtfully across the room. "Perhaps you should pay attention to the accusations and consider them more carefully, Jessica. You've spoiled the boy to ruination."

"Rubbish." She stood her ground, glaring at him. "What would you know about children? You were never in England during our childhood."

"True." He smiled sadly and picked up the envelope that Jeremy had been opening. "If I had, then many things would have been different." He opened the letter and took it into the sunlight streaming in through the window. "This arrived for me this morning. Your sister Maisy has relapsed again. They've only given her a few days." His voice rasped oddly as he spoke, then he looked sharply at his wife. "Had I been here, this tragedy would never have happened. You can't crush courageous spirits, Mathilda! And from what I gather, Maisy and Angus had plenty of that. As it is, I intend to bring Matthew here this summer. He's a good lad, well brought up, which is more than I can say for that young whelp," he nodded at Jeremy.

Mathilda's pale blue eyes sharpened, and she gathered around her the pride and dignity that had always been her shield. "You, Charles, will do nothing of the sort. I will not have that common brat in my house."

"Ah, but you will." He turned his back on her and began searching the mantelpiece for something. Whatever he was looking for was not there. He stiffened slightly and frowned. "Jeremy! Come here."

"No, you will not, my darling!" Jessica murmured softly in his ear and placed her hand on his shoulder.

Charles Braithwaite looked sharply at his daughter. "You are an utter fool, Jessica." Then he strode across the room and looked down at his grandson with cold authority. He held his hand out. "Give it to me!"

The boy looked up at the strict, fiercely military face of his grandfather and shivered. His young face puckered suddenly, and he began to snivel. But his act made no impression on the elderly gentleman. Charles had spent his life handling men, and there was something undeniable about him. Finally, the boy delved into his pocket and handed over the gold pocket watch he had taken.

"Jeremy!" his mother rushed to kneel in front of him. "Whatever did you do that for? You know it'll be yours one day, my dear. Now, you must apologise to Grandpa."

"I won't. He shouted at me. And if this Matthew boy

comes to stay here, he might give the watch to him."

Charles turned away in disgust and returned to the fireplace. He leaned his hand on the chimney breast and looked at his wife. "And when Madeline is found, I will provide for her too."

Mathilda Braithwaite rose to her feet with dignity. "That girl is a criminal, Charles. She's wanted by the police. They've almost caught her three times. Look, I have a report here about it. I'm not having her in my house."

"She's no criminal," he interrupted sharply. "And if *you* won't have her in the house, then I can see only one solution. I would suggest that you take a prolonged vacation my dear. I'm sure Jessica and Jeremy would enjoy your company in London."

"Charles!" she cried indignantly. "This is my home."

His face was implacable. "Jessica. You and the boy will leave us for a moment."

He waited until they had gone, both of them overawed by the tone of the command.

He lowered his voice to an icy whisper. "Maisy told me of the ruination of young Brooks' career, and the lives they led. She never really imagined you could have engineered it. However, in the last few months I've come to know you very thoroughly. So, I made enquiries. You cold bloodedly framed and ruined that young man. That's why he was unable to secure a good job and support his family."

"I thought it would bring her back, when she saw him for what he was."

"He was no criminal and she loved him. I find it impossible to understand how you could do such a thing to your own daughter. I find your company intolerable. Matthew and Madeline will complete their childhoods with full family support. They are good children, not criminals, unlike that pathetic creature outside who will end up in prison before he finishes school. If you cannot contribute to Matthew and Madeline's future, then I would suggest you help Jessica to further ruin the child. I want you out of here by tomorrow."

♪♫

CHAPTER 32

MAISY ONLY LIVED three more days, and when she died, it was with her father and son by her side. She was buried four days later alongside her husband in the churchyard at Westcott, with their good friend the Reverend Rogers officiating.

Brigadier Braithwaite stood at the graveside in full military uniform, and he looked splendid in his fierce dignity. His face was grave and drawn. Matthew, now eleven years old, stood at his side trying to be brave. As the first clod of earth descended on the coffin, the boy moved closer to his grandfather and suddenly reached out for his hand.

Charles looked down at the tear-stained face and took the boy's hand gently in his own. They stood in silence, strengthening each other unknowingly.

When it was over they turned away, passing close to the other mourners. Several kindly hands reached out to touch the young lad. Then they climbed into the car and left

Westcott.

Most of the mourners were chatting quietly now, people of the town who had known and respected the Brooks family. But one lady, dressed in black, her face hidden behind a veil, refrained from any communication and was a stranger to them all.

♪♫

Phyllis Belaugh had been watching the Brigadier, and when he finally left, she turned to scrutinise the entire gathering thoroughly. She remained patiently by the grave for a long while after everyone had dispersed, until at last she had to admit that Madeline was not coming. That frightened her more than anything of the last few months. Something terrible must have happened to the sweet girl. Tears filled her eyes and she too turned to go.

She returned to Harborough Hall having spoken no words to Briggs throughout the long journey. He was worried by this unaccustomed preoccupation, for she was usually a relaxed and communicative passenger.

In the drawing room, Bernard Belaugh rose from his chair and strode towards her. "She wasn't there I suppose. I told you. You're worrying for nothing. That little madam is running rings around us." But his plump face grew pale as he studied the expression in her eyes. "What is it my dear? Christ, you look terrible."

Her face contracted suddenly with pain, and she pressed the palm of her hand to her stomach, low down where the precious little bump had recently begun to be obvious.

"I warned you not to go all that distance!" He clenched his fists suddenly in towering fury. "Heavens above woman, I told you!"

Her face crumpled. "Don't shout Bernard, I have such a pain. I don't think I can climb the stairs. You'd better call the doctor. It's only been like this for half an hour. Perhaps he can do something."

"Yes, yes." He pulled himself back from the edge of anger and reached quickly for the telephone.

A few minutes later he turned back to her. He had never seen her appear so fragile. Her face was white with shock, and her statuesque figure seemed to have shrunk as she lay back in the embrace of the chair. His expression softened. "Come on then. You're better off in bed, and I'll send Rebecca up to you."

He leaned over with some difficulty to pick her up. He was putting on weight and bending was difficult, but the sight of her suffering gave him the strength he needed. He cradled her to his protuberant belly and puffed heavily as he struggled up the long flight of stairs to her room.

He was gasping for breath by the time he lay her on the bed, and he had to sit down beside her for a rest.

"I had to go," she murmured and lay her hand coaxingly over his. "She wasn't there. If she had been with Braithwaite or with the Rogers family, she would have gone to the funeral."

"Forget her, Phyllis. You've been worrying yourself sick about that girl when you should have been taking care of yourself."

"She was my responsibility, Bernard."

A discreet tap came on the door and a homely middle-aged woman let herself in quietly. Belaugh looked up and some of the tension went out of him. "Ah, Rebecca, thank goodness. Mrs Belaugh needs you. I've sent for the doctor and he's on his way."

"Oh, my poor ma'am. Now don't go worrying yourself. It may be nothing more than a little warning." She quickly began loosening the high neckline of the black dress, and unpinned the veil and removed it, then she studied the pale face that looked back at her. "That's better. Now just rest yourself. I'll fetch you a warm drink of tea," and she frowned suddenly. "It hurts, doesn't it?"

Phyllis nodded but her lips tightened in determination, and she caught the maid's eye urgently.

Rebecca nodded her understanding and turned away to fiddle with the mirrors on the dressing table. Phyllis took a deep breath and reached out to touch Bernard's hand. "If we do lose the baby, don't be too disheartened. At least we know that we *can* have children. It's not the end of the world."

"That's true. But after so many years of waiting!"

Her face faltered for a moment, but she fought desperately to keep control of her feelings and squeezed his hand. "Will you wait downstairs for the doctor and explain to him exactly what's happened?"

He nodded and rose to his feet. "I'll go and wait for him now."

Once the door had closed on him, the agony of despair overwhelmed Phyllis. She covered her face with her hands and wept. "Oh God! After all this time!"

Rebecca dropped what she was doing and ran to her, gathering her close and sharing her anguish. "My poor dear. Hush now. It's so unfair!"

Phyllis reached out hastily for the older woman's hands, and they wept together and comforted each other, under the eyes of the little cherubs that adorned the ceiling, a constant reminder of the joy that fate was denying her.

♪♫

CHAPTER 33

THE DAYS STRETCHED to weeks in London, and Maddy became much more confident in what she was doing as the routines and patterns fell into place. She was very comfortable with her lodgings. The old lady who owned the house was partly deaf and relied on her lodgers to help her with the cooking and cleaning, so it was almost like being at home. All too soon, she was packing up her few belongings and preparing to go on tour.

The company travelled the country, carrying their props and costumes in a large transport van, and Maddy found herself confronted with pianos in all states and conditions: those that needed to be thumped in order to obtain any sound, and those whose tone was unbearably tinny. But the more she played, the more she enjoyed being with her flamboyant companions. They lived in a kaleidoscope world of colour and character from which she learned a vast amount. Within weeks, she had mentally developed into an adult, one able to stand up for herself and take her own place in this demonstrative environment.

Very soon she had created a personality for Grace Mayers, a buoyant fun-loving creature who behaved with loud familiarity, and established herself perfectly amongst them. They worked, ate and existed together, and not once did any of the men in the company show any interest in her. They were attracted like flies to Desiree Glendenning, their glamorous leading lady, and as the months passed Maddy was able to remain in the background as a sisterly figure.

They were rehearsing as usual one morning in a rather cramped church hall on the south coast. It was a dull gloomy day, the sort of weather that disappointed holiday makers but ensured that their opening afternoon matinée would be well attended. Periodically, the manager poked his head round the door and rubbed his hands together. By lunch time he interrupted them to announce proudly, "Sold out! Excellent work! Excellent."

Desiree had been singing touchingly on stage and she froze indignantly at the interruption.

Rudy sighed and raised his voice. "Right everyone, take a break for five minutes will you."

Maddy stretched her fingers and arched her back, glad to do a little exercise when a break came in the accompaniment. The dancers on stage had gathered into groups to gossip, and several were looking with interest at the empty hall behind her. Heavy footsteps crossed the wooden floor.

Maddy had her back to the rows of vacant seats and took little notice until a heavy hand fell on her shoulder. She looked round enquiringly, and her heart missed a beat.

"Miss, we have reason to believe that you are Madeline Brooks."

She rose to her feet, and her newfound maturity wrapped her round like a shield. She was not going to be caught.

She smiled, and then laughed with all the vulgar familiarity she had learned to act. "Me? I'm Grace Mayers, I was born that way and will probably die that way too. Who is this Miss Brooks anyway?"

"You must come with us for identification, miss," the constable tried to take her by the wrist.

"Oh, give over love," Maddy slapped his hand away playfully. "Don't make a fool of yourself."

"Constable!" Rudy Crawshaw's tall willowy figure stepped towards them, and he placed a friendly arm around the policeman's broad shoulders with a smile. "That's quite unnecessary. Miss Mayers has been accompanying our players for some time and is well known to us. There must be some confusion of identity."

"Nevertheless sir," the policeman straightened his shoulders, shaking off the unwelcome familiarity. "I have my duty to perform. If the charge is false, then the young lady will return to you immediately."

Rudy threw his hands in the air in an extravagant gesture of exasperation. "Look around you my dear constable. We're in the middle of dress rehearsal and the curtain goes up in three hours. She cannot leave us now. Out of the question!"

"Oh constable." Desiree Glendenning swept down dramatically from the stage, a vision of feathers and flowing gauze, and she smiled enchantingly at the policeman. "I know you would not take my accompanist away, would you? I couldn't possibly sing this afternoon if my rehearsal time is ruined."

"Sir!"

The police officer reluctantly dragged his eyes away from the ravishing creature before him, to see one of his men enter the hall.

Maddy's breath caught in the throat, and she looked around desperately for a way to escape. The man had her battered old suitcase in his hands, and it contained all her family treasures.

She was trapped. She would never get away even if she ran for it.

The officer turned and studied her face dryly, noting the sudden pallor. He nodded and smiled slightly. "Well, Miss Brooks?"

Maddy shrugged her shoulders. She could not bluff it out in the face of such evidence. So in her own voice, she said, "This is ridiculous, I've done nothing wrong! What do you intend to do with me?"

"Send you back to your guardians. We've contacted Mr Belaugh. He'll be here in another two or three hours."

"No! You can't do that!" Panic washed over her then and she could hardly breathe. It was as though she had been punched in the stomach. She sank weakly onto the piano stool, fingers across her mouth as a wave of nausea rose through her. Dear God! Belaugh! He was on his way!

Vaguely she heard Desiree gasp and cry, "No. You can't take her away! I don't care who she is, she knows my voice and ways better than any..."

"Officer," Rudy's voice interrupted. "If we have no accompanist, then we have no show. You cannot do this to us. The tickets are sold out for this afternoon and evening..."

Maddy hardly heard any of the furore that was going on around her. Belaugh was coming for her! Even the sound of his name aroused vivid mental flashbacks to the way he had brutalised and used her. She could not bear to be touched like that again, dominated and subdued by such violence and pain.

"Mr Crawshaw. You have been employing a child of fifteen without the consent of her guardian. I would suggest you stop protesting, or you may find that prosecution will follow."

"Good heavens!" Desiree spun round to stare at Maddy.

The silence that followed the policeman's statement was electric.

Slowly the dramatic fire faded from the actress's face, and genuine concern took its place. She knelt down and put her arm around Maddy's shoulder. "Fifteen! And look what you've done to her you beastly men!"

"Come on now, miss. We haven't done anything." The constable grasped Maddy firmly by the elbow. "Now will you come quietly?"

"You can't send me back," she looked fiercely up at his stolid, unimaginative face. "You have no idea what it's like."

The policeman's expression hardened. "Your guardian is a highly respected man. And from what I hear, he's moved the world for you."

Desiree squeezed Maddy's hand and turned to the policeman. "I'm coming with her."

The police station was several miles away, and Maddy was bundled into the back of the police car with Desiree protectively hugging her. The highly made-up actress had always confused her, and this unexpected kindness was even more surprising. The woman patted her clenched hands. "I shall always think of you as Grace. Don't let them hurt you sweetie. Whatever happens, hide the real you away so he can't hurt you anymore."

Maddy nodded and peeped sideways at the powdered face. "You understand?"

Desiree smiled, and the smile was worlds different to her public persona, there was genuine warmth there. "Larry's an angel. He's been good to us all. We've all had problems. But he can't help you now, so just remember what I said." The car was drawing to a halt now, and the actress hugged her once again. "Goodbye, sweetie, and good luck."

"Goodbye, and... I'm sorry I've let you down." Maddy gripped the woman's hands tightly. "I don't know what you'll do now."

"We'll be alright, you silly thing," Desiree laughed. "Rudy will play for us this afternoon. Just take care," a quick kiss was planted on her cheek. "Be brave."

The car door opened and Maddy was roughly pulled out and taken into the police station.

In the office, she found a big man in uniform looking through the contents of her case. He had scattered her father's music all across his desk and was piling on top of it the clothes she had bought with her wages. Indignantly, she exclaimed, "What do you think you're doing with my things?"

He looked up at her, and then at a picture on his desk. "I'm surprised he recognised you, young lady. You look an awful lot older, and utterly vulgar." Then he sifted once again through her treasured sheets of music. "I can't for the life of me see why you ran away, Miss Brooks. You've come down a long way."

Maddy clipped her lips together and stared at the desk, her hands knotted fiercely into fists at her side. There was no way he would believe that the life she was leading was far better than the one she had escaped from.

Suddenly she could see the black bruises on her wrists again, she could feel horror creep over her as though it was a physical presence touching her skin. She cringed from within and fear overwhelmed her. He was coming for her, and the law was going to force her back to him.

"All the opportunities you were given!" the man was continuing. "My kids would give an arm and a leg to get such help."

Maddy's eyes widened slowly, and she raised them reluctantly to the solemn stolid face.

"I've seen pictures of the house and estate. It baffles me. But then the more you do for some kids, the more they resent it. You had everything you could possibly want, young lady."

Maddy tried to shut her mind to the insistent goading comments, but he leaned towards her suddenly and forced her chin up. "Was it for the glamour? Did you want to be an actress? A dance girl instead of a pianist?"

"Don't be ridiculous," she shook him off in revulsion.

"I've read all about the Belaughs in the papers. They've spent their lives helping the likes of you, how could you have distressed them like that? It's made her ill you know."

A firm knock came on the door, and another uniformed constable poked his head into the room. "Car's come sir. Shall I show him in?"

Maddy spun round to face the threat, trembling in every limb now, her numbed mind leaping to life in agitation. "Please don't send me back. He'll only do it again. Please, I beg of you..."

"Alright miss, just calm down. Ask him to wait a few minutes would you Collier. Now, what will he do again Miss

Brooks?" the constable's face was suddenly intent on what she was saying.

Maddy could feel the colour draining from her face, and her mouth went utterly dry. "He... he beat me. I... I..." she came to a shocked halt, unable articulate the name of the horror.

There was a painful silence in the room, then the constable approached with a slow measured stride. "Every child needs a good beating now and then. It's nothing new."

She screwed up all her courage. She had to say it, though she felt as stiff and rigid as ice. She forced her hands to her sides and straightened her shoulders in determination. Her voice was husky as she whispered, "Alright, I'll tell you. He raped me. He ripped all my clothes off and touched me... he hurt me so much. He shouldn't have done that."

Outrage reddened the man's face and he slapped her. "Silence, you little baggage. Bernard Belaugh is a highly respected public figure. No wonder he thrashed you. But you won't take such filthy thoughts back to Harborough Hall with you. Bates fetch me that cane. I'll teach her a lesson she won't forget."

"No, you can't do that!" Maddy backed away. "I'm not telling lies. Please... It's the truth!"

"Enough!" the two men closed in on her. "These good people have been kind to you, provided all that you could ever hope for. They should have thrashed the filth out of you years ago." Maddy struggled fiercely, but she was helpless against their strength. They turned her round, forced her over and thrashed her until she wept.

♪♫

Madeline Brooks was returned to Harborough Hall late that

evening by Briggs the chauffeur. He attempted to talk to her during the journey, but she had nothing to say. She hurt too much from the thrashing and cringed away from him when he tried to be friendly. In the end, he too was simmering with anger.

His calm reliable face reddened with indignation as he stared through the windscreen at the dark road unfolding ahead of him. "I sincerely hope you apologise to Mrs Belaugh for worrying her. You've cost her dear, you know." He cornered sharply, the headlights picking out the hedgerow in a blur of green as they swept past. "She's been ill. And you've been too busy having fun to know that your mother died last month." He slowed marginally as the lights of a village approached, but there were no other vehicles on the road, and they swept on through. "You didn't even go to the funeral, did you? What sort of daughter are you?"

A stab of anguish pierced Maddy. She had not known!

For a long agonising moment, she could neither move nor breathe. Then slowly air eased into her lungs.

Her beloved mother had died, alone and without her daughter at her side. And because Maddy had not known about it, she had not even been there to say farewell as they laid her in the earth.

In the blackness of the back of the car grief came to her.

At Harborough Hall she was handed over to Nanny who swept her up to her room and clothed her in a pretty dress ready for the evening meal. It seemed surreal, she was being treated as though she were still a child and nothing untoward had happened. There were a few words of lament as her short hair was brushed, then Phyllis came to her room and Nanny left them to talk.

Maddy turned to face Phyllis, and her eyes widened in

shock and concern. The older woman had lost weight, her strong statuesque, vital figure had shrunk and she looked gaunt.

"Oh," Maddy cried, and wrung her hands. "Have I done this to you, Phyllis? I'm so, *so* sorry. I didn't mean to."

Phyllis took a deep breathed and came quickly across the room, drawing her close in a tender embrace. "Dearest Maddy. It wasn't you. But I've been so worried about you."

Blind panic flamed through Madeline. She could not bear to be touched and possessed any longer, and the contact was stifling. She struggled free of the oppressive grip, and stared around wildly, shivering with horror. "I'm s... sorry. I can't, I just can't bear..."

"What is it Maddy?" Phyllis reached out urgently but restrained the gesture as Maddy flinched away from her again. Phyllis's face tightened. "What made you run away from us? Look what it's done to you! Surely you were happy here."

Maddy longed to speak, but there was nothing she could say or do. She could not tell the truth. She had learned that the hard way. And she could not bear to think what it would do to Phyllis. It would wound her to the core. It was terrible to see the pain she had already caused, and she knew it would not end here. As long as she remained in this house the pain and hurt would continue to grow.

"Tell me, Maddy. Did we push you too hard? If that's what caused your distress, you can have a break for as long as you need."

Maddy shook her head. "It's not that. I love my music, but even that has dried up and gone."

"Then what is it?" Phyllis asked gently, yet there was a quiet desperation in the way she watched Maddy's face. She waited for a long while for a reply, but none came, and she looked away and continued. "I have some very difficult news for you. I know you loved your mother a great deal..."

"Don't!" Maddy interrupted in a hoarse whisper. "I know what happened. She's dead."

"Maddy!" Phyllis stared at her in disbelief, then the kind lady's face twisted. "You knew, and you didn't go to the funeral. I lost..." and she turned on her heel and marched from the room.

Maddy remained where she was as though she had been pinned there.

♪♫

That night after dinner, she retired to the privacy of her room. She had no key for the lock, so she pulled a heavy chest across the floor to block the door, and she climbed into bed.

She lay there for hours and knew that she would not sleep. The disgust in her was like a devouring black hole. She knew what she ought to feel, but it had been shocked out of her and the void was appalling.

Her eyes shot open when she heard a scrabbling at her door. She saw the handle turn. The door opened a fraction and then stopped, blocked by the chest. She leapt nervously out of bed and put a chair between herself and the door. "Who is it?"

"Open this door, Madeline." Bernard Belaugh's voice commanded.

"No!" She clenched her fists tightly at her sides. "Stay away from me."

"Open this door," he commanded quietly but firmly.

"If you take another step into this room, I shall scream," she warned.

"You'd better not. You've done enough damage already young lady."

She watched the chest slowly slide across the well-polished wooden floor as the door was forced open inexorably, and then he was standing there, studying her.

She was shivering violently now, and gasped, "One step and I *will* scream."

He nodded slowly. "Phyllis has been very ill, worrying about you. You know how much she wanted a baby of her own?" he crossed his arms angrily. "She was to have had a child, my child. That's why she looks so ill. She travelled to *your* mother's funeral, and the journey caused her to miscarry. You've already caused my family agony and despair."

He paused a moment longer in the doorway, a plump, pampered, hated figure. But the expression on his face slowly lost its anger, and desire began to take its place. "You won't scream, you wouldn't cause her anymore hurt."

He walked forward slowly, and Maddy backed away. She was helpless to stop him, and she knew that if she was not careful, he could devastate her again.

She was as tall as him now, but slender and feminine, and she could see an ugly lust firing in him until he was trembling with desire. He touched her cheek. The very touch sent cringing shivers through her, and she closed her eyes to shut out the sight. "Please, if you have any honour or pity, leave me alone."

"My, you have grown up," he murmured, oblivious to her comments, and reached out to touch her breasts. "And you've come back to me. I've missed you, missed the feel of you... the sight of you..."

Maddy did not scream, she could not cause Phyllis this

final distress, but her mind was screaming madly! Was she worth so little that he treated her like this? It seemed to her that this utter degradation was a punishment for the things she had done in her life, for abandoning her dying mother, for failing her father, for hurting Phyllis, for being the sort of creature to tempt this horrible man.

Numbly her mind switched off, regressed within itself so that she did not have to witness what was happening. She did not struggle this time, but it still hurt terribly. He did not seem to notice her distress, or care. Instead, he worshipped her body with his own as though he hungered for the feel of her, and that was even more degrading and sickening.

Once he had finished, she rolled over in her bed and wept achingly into the pillow, curling up protectively into a small ball.

Was this to be the sum of her life?

She only prayed that wherever her parents were, they could not see what had become of their daughter. She had had such high hopes for the future. But even the music that she loved above anything else, was paralysed and quenched within her, as though she was not worthy of such insight and beauty.

The weekend came, and somehow she survived it. Each night and sometimes during the day, he came to her, used her as though she was his by right, and in the dark hours of Sunday night, Maddy reached a deep nadir of despair. Then, as Monday morning finally broke, she had passed through the crisis and a new psyche began to climb back to reality and face the world.

♪♫

CHAPTER 34

MADELINE ROSE THE following morning, scrubbed her face to remove all traces of the events of the last few days, and went quietly down to breakfast and on to school. She had changed, and it hit her suddenly just how complete that change was, when she joined the other girls. She had nothing in common with their games and gossip, now. Belaugh had dragged her out of childhood, made of her a strange misfit. She left them to play, and spent her day thinking out her future.

There had to be a way.

Briggs drove them home to Harborough Hall that afternoon, and Madeline retired to her room. She could hear Janet and Patrick playing in the garden, their voices raised joyously in relaxation. Her eyes wandered around the room for a moment. It was time to stop feeling sorry for herself and to do something. She drew a sheet of paper from the pack, picked up her pen and bent her fair head to write.

It was hard. She took her time, and after several attempts, constructed a careful letter to the Royal Academy of Music, quoting her references and her conversation with Sir Edward Elgar. Then she went in search of Phyllis. She found her in the drawing room, and she too was writing a letter.

Phyllis looked up and her eyes became cold. Maddy took a deep breath and murmured, "Excuse me ma'am. I wonder if I may speak with you."

Phyllis studied face as though she was raking through her personality. Then she put her pen down. "Yes, you may, Maddy. Come in. It's time that we spoke to each other honestly. You have a great deal to explain."

The young girl entered the room and straightened her shoulders with determination. "I would prefer to be called by my full name now, ma'am."

Phyllis nodded slowly. "Very well, Madeline."

Madeline swallowed and gathered every scrap of courage she possessed, then began. "I should have spoken to you last Friday night. It was silly of me to be so silent, but I just couldn't utter a word."

"And why not?"

"I… it was too painful. Briggs had just given me the news about my mother."

The older woman's face tightened, and her voice was sharp with disbelief as she demanded, "Are you trying to tell me you didn't know about her death, until Friday?"

"Briggs told me in the car." Madeline's voice choked slightly with emotion. "It hurt… a great deal."

Phyllis rose restlessly to her feet and went to gaze out of the window at the frosty December landscape, her hands clenching tightly together at her sides. Then with a small gesture of helplessness she turned back and examined Madeline's face again.

Madeline opened her mouth to speak, but nothing happened. Tears filled her eyes as she thought of her mother. This was not how she had planned to speak to Phyllis, it was all going wrong. She had wanted to be calm and logical. But the horror and disgust in her was like a yawning black hole. It froze her courage, scattered her wits. At last, she managed to whisper, "I'm so sorry, I wouldn't have hurt you for the world."

Phyllis sighed softly and nodded her head. Then she came to take Madeline's hands gently in her own. "Whatever drove you to run away? I've thought and thought about that. It's been hell, worrying about you."

Madeline looked down at the hands holding hers, and abruptly she broke the contact, turning away from the kindly, enquiring face. The truth was too awful to share, and she would do anything to spare Phyllis that knowledge. She spread her slender powerful fingers out and turned them over slowly. "I've lost... I've lost the ability to express real feeling in my music. It's as though the sensitivity and emotion inside me have been blocked, dammed up. It hurts unbearably. It's so bleak, sterile."

Phyllis nodded and said softly, "And we were putting more and more pressure on you. That must have made it worse."

Madeline nodded. "Whenever I tried to practice, the emptiness tore me to pieces. Whilst I was away, I was playing for a theatre company. They didn't want beautifully interpreted music, just a reliable tempo and melody. It was great fun. I didn't have time to feel the awful loss and pain."

"Poor child," Phyllis sighed softly. "Come and sit down,

and we'll see if we can work out what to do." She drew a chair forward for Maddy. "I'm glad you've come to see me. This has been wrong all year, hasn't it? And it's getting worse."

"Yes."

"This is my fault. I should have done something for you earlier. I'll tell you what I'm going to do. I'll set up a meeting between us and your tutors at the weekend. Meanwhile don't touch the piano. Just relax and settle back into home life."

Madeline nodded, and gathered about her all her calm determination. "I know what would help me. If I could study under someone like Sir Ronald Ashwood right now, the music *will* return. It just needs the right key to unlock the door. Would you read the letter that I've just written? With your agreement, I'll send it."

Phyllis took the letter and read it carefully, then she looked back at Madeline, and her eyebrows rose a fraction. "Goodness me, you have grown up."

Madeline frowned and her desperation peeped through. "I think it's the only chance I have left, Phyllis. If I don't, then I'll be left like this all my life, and I couldn't bear that."

Phyllis gripped her arm reassuringly. "Send the letter my dear. It's important that we do what's right." Then she frowned slightly. "I'll approach Bernard tonight. He always needs a few days to come to terms with a new idea."

Maddy's face whitened at the thought. He would be furious and he would undoubtedly take it out on her. "Could you not ask him just before the meeting?"

Phyllis laughed gently and touched her stricken face. "Don't be afraid. He's not an ogre you know. He's a very kind and thoughtful man in his own way. Now tell me all about your experiences and what this theatre company was like."

♪♫

Bernard Belaugh returned from work several hours later. His first action was to change from his business suit into something slightly more comfortable and casual, and as he was dressing and studying his increasingly corpulent figure in the mirror, his dressing room door opened, and Phyllis entered. He glanced up at her briefly. "Evening m'dear."

She smiled fondly. He was looking older these days. There was a certain dignity in his presence that had always impressed her, and it was becoming more clearly defined with the years. "Did everything go well?"

"Excellently. We did well to issue the advertising early. We've caught the early autumn rush and the brand should be well established by the time the ladies begin their Christmas shopping."

Her face lit with relief. "Till receipts are good then?"

He rubbed his hands together with relish. "I've asked Davenport to bring forward two of his newest designs and adapt them specifically for the Christmas season. We'll have the product in the shops by December."

Phyllis nodded. "Good. Now I want to talk to you about Madeline."

He begun hunting in the wardrobe for a tie. "Oh?"

Phyllis seated herself comfortably in the chair. "She's changed Bernard. She's learned how to think for herself and argue intelligently for what she believes is right. She needs far more than we can provide for her here at Harborough Hall. I've had a long talk with her, and I think she's right. She needs the guidance of a truly creative genius, someone who can help unlock the problem she has."

She glanced up at him, but he was busy adjusting his tie, so she continued. "The poor girl has developed an emotional blockage, and it's tormenting her. I can understand that," she sighed. "I've arranged for her tutors to meet us here on Saturday, and we'll discuss what is to be done. We've written an enquiring letter to the Royal Academy, but there is no guarantee that they'll take her."

"No," he said quietly and turned to face her.

"But why not Bernard? She has the maturity of an eighteen- or twenty-year-old. She's learned the independence, and she needs the help. If we fail her, we could destroy her."

"She's only fifteen, m'dear, far too young to leave the security of home. She's not to go. We will bring her tutors here."

She rose to her feet and sustained his gaze. "We have to think of her needs and talents, not of her age."

"Listen and listen well, Phyllis. The child will remain here where we can watch over her until she reaches the age of eighteen. That is my final decision."

Baffled, Phyllis simply stared at him. Then she took a deep breath. He thrived in the business world by seeing the right path and adapting to it, so if she worked on him gently, he might perhaps change his mind. His round mild featured face smiled as he watched her. "I won't change my mind you know. Come. We will inform that young lady of my decision right now. Then perhaps she'll cease to torment you with her schemes."

♪♫

Dinner that evening was silent and uncomfortable. Phyllis watched Madeline's fair head lowered over her plate. She felt deeply for the girl, growing up was a difficult matter at the best of times. After the meal the girl slipped away quietly to the music room and Phyllis followed.

Even from beyond the doors, she could hear her struggling and striving to bring the subtle flow of genuine expression to the beautiful music she was playing. The notes were all there, the touch perfect, and yet something deeply fundamental was missing.

It hurt Phyllis when the music stopped with a crash. She pushed the door open, and found the young girl holding her head between her clenched fists.

The door creaked slightly on its hinges and Madeline spun round. A fleeting shadow crossed her face, but it was gone in a moment.

"You shouldn't try so hard, my dear." Phyllis touched her shoulders gently. "You can't force it to come back."

Madeline's fingers reached out longingly to the keys. "My whole life has been music, and it still is, I can't imagine anything else..."

"Look, why don't you play some of the things you've been doing this last month or so? I'd love to hear them."

"Oh yes, I think you would," Madeline smiled, her face brightening. "Come and sit down then, and I'll play to you." The music that came was full of fun, and it brought the girl to life, remembering happy times.

When Bernard appeared in the doorway, Phyllis put her finger to her lips and beckoned him in. It would do him good to see the child enjoying her music. Perhaps then he would think more kindly of her.

A little while later, she glanced at his face and shock ran through her. She looked away again quickly, but a chill touched her stomach. No. It could not be! But that expression was unmistakable.

She hardly heard any more of the playing, neither could she think very clearly.

Presently Madeline played a grand ending. "There, what do you think? It was such fun." And she turned enthusiastically to Phyllis.

Her face froze as she saw Bernard. Then she shot to her feet and looked quickly at Phyllis and then away again. The older woman rose with a tremendous effort, feeling as though the weight of the world was suddenly resting heavily on her shoulders. She knew she would have to be very wise and careful, or all their lives would shatter around them.

Hollowly Phyllis replied, "It sounded very good my dear."

"But," her husband approached the girl and placed his hand heavily on her shoulder, "that period of your life is over, young lady. You must dedicate yourself to worthwhile music, not such rubbish."

Phyllis could see that Madeline was desperate to avoid him. The young girl was trembling visibly, but somehow she managed to articulate a reply. "I won't play that again, sir. Will you please excuse me now? I must change for my riding lesson."

"Yes dear," Phyllis said. "Go ahead." Then she watched her husband's face in unwillingly fascination. She could not drag her eyes away. He was observing the girl's quick, lithe movements with possessive relish.

What she saw on his face at that moment finally destroyed her belief and faith in him.

She could not talk to him. Not yet. Not until she had had time to think. She hurried to her own room. She looked around at the luxury and comfort, but it had somehow changed. She had to sit down and make her stunned mind think.

♪♫

CHAPTER 35

MADELINE LOVED RIDING. She escaped the claustrophobic atmosphere of the house with a sense of relief. She saddled her beloved Sunny Suzy, patted the mare's long nose and looked up into her velvety, almond shaped eye. "I've missed you, old girl."

The horse whinnied in joyful recognition, nuzzling her snout against Madeline's cheek, knowing that her appearance meant a long exuberant ride.

Madeline smiled happily. The horses were vigorous simple creatures. At times they could be temperamental but presented none of the complex problems that humans did. There was a clear relationship between horse and rider that was dependent upon the character of both. She was becoming a good rider, skilled at the delicate balance between controlling the powerful beasts and allowing them their freedom, and today she shrugged off all the traumas of her life.

It was a bright but chilly afternoon. She led the horse out into the courtyard and mounted eagerly, then swung round and galloped across the park, stretching herself and the big animal in an extravagant gallop. As the wind tore at her hair, the clean exhilaration of movement swept through her.

Then after more than fifteen minutes, she reached the field where the fences and jumps had been set up. Her instructor was there already, adjusting the height of the fences for her, and she waved a greeting to him.

He acknowledged it, and finished raising the bar on the last jump, then moved to the centre of the field. "Right now, miss. Show me what you can do. I've raised number five for you today, so watch the run up."

She signalled her understanding, and began the round, concentrating every effort, every sense she possessed on correct posture and technique, on the length of stride and speed.

Her instructor watched her every movement. He expected a high level of concentration from her and shouted abrupt reminders and instructions the moment she made a mistake, and the time sped past.

She returned from her riding lesson more than an hour and a half later, glowing with health and confidence. Phyllis was waiting in her bedroom, staring blankly out of the window. Madeline paused in the doorway and shivered. Phyllis looked haggard.

The older woman turned quickly and examined her face, and she longed to be able to conceal herself in her old school uniform. The jodhpurs and jacket accentuated the curves of her fully developed figure. Phyllis's eyes moved from her head to her feet and back again, and her face tightened. "You've packed the doll's house away, I see. Do you no longer like it?"

Madeline's eyes flickered to the closed box under the table. She had done that on Friday, unable to bear the idea that any of the things from her childhood should witness what was going on. "No," she managed to reply. "It's something for a child."

"You're certainly not that any longer, are you?" The voice was hard and sharp.

"I wish you could persuade him to allow me to go," Madeline whispered. "I don't want any of this."

"Neither do I, but I don't think that will eradicate what's been going on, do you?"

There was a long awkward silence, then Phyllis shivered and rubbed her arms as though she sought to warm herself. "He's the reason why you can't play isn't he? What happened Madeline? Tell me exactly what's been going on."

Madeline's face froze. Her entire body was reacting beyond her control to the shock of confrontation. It was as though she had been stripped naked, and she could not bear the reality of herself. She shook her head. "I can't," and turned away from contact.

Phyllis rubbed her forehead in perplexity, then she seemed to make up her mind. She fetched a dressing gown and put it around Madeline's shoulders, her voice softening with gentleness. "I'm sorry. I'm not thinking very clearly. You need to change out of your riding clothes don't you."

Madeline drew the dressing gown tightly around her shoulders and nodded.

Phyllis touched her golden hair softly. "I keep thinking of you as a child still. What did he do, did he hurt you?"

Madeline's face stiffened, and she simply could not speak.

"For heaven's sake," Phyllis's voice shook with sudden

fury. "Whatever did you do to make him like that? He's such a kind man."

"I didn't!" Madeline screamed fiercely. "I didn't want him to. I tried my best not to... I... God, I *tried* to stop him!"

Phyllis was calming slightly now. She turned away and stared at the packed toys. Then she turned back and looked closely into Madeline's face, searching every expression.

Those minutes were agony to Madeline. It felt as though Phyllis was laying her soul bare and judging every one of her actions and motivations. Then abruptly the older woman turned away and snapped, "Get yourself dressed. If you won't tell me, then I shall have to ask him."

"No. You mustn't do that," Madeline cried in horror.

♪♫

Phyllis turned on her heel and stalked stiffly through the splendid house. Even now, she could not believe the things her senses were perceiving. Surely this was a nightmare, and she would wake suddenly to find life normal once more.

Bernard was not in the drawing room or library, and she ran up the stairs to his room, but again he was not there. Then her instinct led her to the huge mirror enclosed room where Patrick was rehearsing for his final audition for ballet school.

Her hand rested on the door handle for a moment, and a stab of cowardice pierced her. She did not want to confront him. It would be better for everyone if she just ignored it. The other children were alright. It was not worth jeopardising her marriage and the whole of the Belaugh sponsorship, for one frightened girl.

She shrank back from the door and turned away.

Then she stopped, ashamed of herself. Madeline was not

a nervous or paranoid person.

She turned back and entered the room.

He was with Patrick, and what she saw in that instant sickened her. He had the same expression on his face and was touching the boy, a young teenager now, in a way that was obscene.

"Patrick," her voice cut across the room like the blow of an axe.

There was a moment of agony, then the boy shrank back into the corner. "Go to your room and change, Patrick. You can resume rehearsing tomorrow."

She hardly noticed him run away. Her eyes burnt with disgust as she watched her husband round furiously on her. His plump pampered face was red with frustration and blind fury, and he moved towards her, his shoulders hunched forward, and fists clenched to strike.

Her heart pounded in sudden fear. But she faced up to him and loaded every bit of scorn she was capable of into her voice. "You pitiful inhuman little man. I believed you were a kind and thoughtful guardian. How could I ever have been so duped? I thought you cared for the children. Instead, you've been using them."

"Phyllis..."

"Don't you come near me. Don't you ever touch me again. Not after what you've been doing."

"Phyllis..."

She shook his hand off as though it were poisoned. "They were children! You didn't even have the decent honesty to take a mistress. I could have understood that...!"

"Silence woman!" he bellowed and hit her across the face with a blow that knocked her back several steps.

"No, I will not be silenced," she raised her hand to her

throbbing, aching face, her eyes flaming with disdain. "I promise you this, whatever you do to me will be visible for the world to see. And I *will* ensure they see it."

Slowly he lowered his raised hand, and the mad fury died from his face.

As she looked at him, she saw the reality of what he had become, and horror sickened her. "Did you rape her? Is that what you did?"

His plump, pampered face was haggard suddenly, and he turned away from her and drew himself up tall. "Do you take her word against mine, Phyllis? I'm your husband."

"You sicken me. What you have done is foul. Even that poor young boy. A boy!" She looked around the room as though searching for an answer that made sense. "Did you touch Michelle too? Oh God, I can't bear anymore!"

"No!" he was trembling a little now and wiped his hand across his dry lips nervously. "They were lovely, but Christ Almighty, Madeline's a little witch. She was asking for it..."

"She hated it!" she screamed in distraction. Then she took several deep breaths to steady herself and drew herself up with finality. "You will not see the children again, Bernard. If you so much as speak to or touch any of them, then I shall ruin you. I have the power to do it. What you've done to these young people would damn you for ever. You will continue to sponsor them publicly, but you will *not* come to Harborough Hall again. Is that understood? You will pack your bags and go."

♪♫

An intense and ominous silence had fallen upon the house, as though all thought and volition were suspended by the events that had taken place.

Madeline followed Phyllis, desperate to stop the confrontation that was going to occur and yet knowing that she could not. She watched Phyllis hesitate, and prayed that the older woman would just turn away, but she did not. Then all hell broke loose. She shrank back into the shadows of an empty doorway as Patrick ran from the room amidst the uproar of shouting voices. The fury of the outburst made Madeline tremble, but she could not leave. Phyllis could so easily be hurt, and she wanted to be there in case he assaulted or harmed her.

Then finally there was silence, and the older woman emerged from the room, walking with her head erect, fury in every aspect of her stiff frame. Two minutes later Belaugh emerged, and his face was black with anger. He looked capable of murder.

He passed within inches of Madeline and made directly for her room. Dread made her shake badly now, and her thoughts turned to Patrick and Janet. They were in such danger. She dashed through the silent house and slipped into Janet's room. The young girl was lying on her stomach on her bed reading a book, completely oblivious to what was going on. She looked up and smiled. "Is it nearly dinner time? I'm starving."

"Janet come with me. For heaven's sake hurry. We've got to get out of here before he..." then she heard footsteps in the corridor. She spun round desperately and jammed a chair under the handle of the door, then shrank back against the wall. The handle turned and there was an exclamation of surprise as the door stuck fast.

"Who is it?" she whispered.

"Is that you Madeline?"

She felt limp with relief as she recognised Nanny's voice.

"Yes. I'm here."

"I'm glad you're together. Mr Belaugh...! Mrs Belaugh is in such a state. Now listen carefully." The older woman's voice was unsteady with shock. "Keep this door locked and stay in this room until I come back. I've got to find Patrick. Is he with you?"

"No, he's not here, Miss Nichols."

"Whatever you do, don't venture out. Mr Belaugh is in a terrible fury. If Patrick comes to you, can you ring the bell twice to let me know he's safe. We're all in the kitchen."

"Yes, I will."

"Thank you dear. I'll come and get you as soon as it's safe."

"Whatever's happened Maddy?" Janet gripped Madeline by the arm in fright.

Madeline looked down into the young girl's pale face. "Phyllis has found out about Belaugh, and... she went to confront him!"

Janet shivered and her eyes grew round with pure terror. "Oh Maddy. He'll come here and beat us, won't he?"

Madeline could feel the panic rising through her, and she ran her fingers into her hair in distraction. Then she deliberately forced herself to think calmly. "We've got to find Patrick, that's what we must do. He'll be in terrible danger if he's alone."

"I think I know where he might be," Janet whispered nervously. "He always goes to the den when he wants to get away."

"Yes, of course!" Madeline rose quickly to her feet. "We'd better go there, then."

"Nanny told us to stay here and wait! We ought to do what she told us."

"But he would break through that barricade with no trouble if he wanted to get to us, Jan." She took the young girl by the hand. "Come on. It'll be safer out there than in here. No one knows about our tree."

Janet looked nervously towards the barricaded door. "It'll be cold out there! And what if he spots up?" she objected, then nodded abruptly. "Alright."

Together they dismantled the barrier and tiptoed along the corridor. All around them, there were unusual sounds as though the very fabric of the house had been disrupted.

Once they were past Belaugh's suite, they dashed down the grand stairs, snatched up their winter coats and hats, and emerged into the garden.

The lawn extended like an undulating green carpet before them, dotted with ancient trees that accentuated and enhanced the landscape. They ran across the velvety expanse, looked all around cautiously, and then ducked through the small cleft into the secret warmth of their hideout. They had made it.

"Thank God," she sighed. "Patrick, are you here? Oh heavens, are you alright?"

A whimper had issued from the darkness. It was a strange sound coming from such a confident, self-assured young man. Madeline shivered. Had Belaugh already caught him and taken it out on him? Then Patrick's voice issued tensely from the gloom. "I'm alright, but I'm not coming back."

The two girls sat down near him in the concealing darkness, and Maddy hugged her arms around her knees. "Something terrible is going on in the house. Belaugh is in a fearful rage."

"I know. Phyllis came to my room just now," he said,

"and saw what he was doing..."

Madeline looked up into the blackness over their heads, deeply grateful that the three of them were together. This spider and insect filled hollow was their only safe refuge. She swallowed suddenly as realisation hit her, and she glanced in Patrick's direction. She had thought she was the only one being treated like that. Softly she tried to articulate her thoughts and calm their fears. "It's quiet in here, isn't it? Safe and peaceful. I think we should stay here for a while until things have settled down."

"They've had the most terrible row," Patrick whispered in anguish. "She was screaming at him."

"Was she?" Madeline tried to see his face again, but the darkness was too intense.

Janet threaded her arm dependently through Madeline's and huddled closer for warmth. "What are we going to do, Maddy? We can't stay here for ever. We'll freeze! And if... if they've had such an argument over us, Phyllis won't want us here anymore."

Madeline put her arm gently around Janet. "We've got to stick together. I only hope he doesn't hurt her."

"He was in a terrible fury." She felt Patrick nod vigorously. "He looked as though he wanted to kill her."

"Don't even think of such a thing," Madeline whispered, and hugged Janet a little tighter as the girl shuddered.

They sat there together for a long while, and gradually the light began to disappear from the crack through which they had entered the den. The evening began to get seriously cold and then Patrick whispered, "I'm so hungry!"

"Are you? It must be long past teatime." Madeline suddenly nudged him teasingly. "You'll make a good soldier, you know. They always think of their stomachs first. Look, I think we ought to go back now. We can slip in quietly through the kitchen door and go to Miss Nichols. She said all the staff were in the basement. You've got your scholarship in a few weeks, and we can't risk you losing that chance Patrick. At least once you're there, you'll be safe."

Patrick rubbed his hands across his face and shivered, then sighed. "Alright. I suppose it's better than spending the night here and freezing to death."

They crept to the back of the house together, and almost the moment they descended into the basement, Parstow intercepted them. "Miss Madeline, thank goodness you're safe. Miss Nichols has been frantic with worry! Come through to the kitchen quickly, all of you, before Mr Belaugh comes down. He's in a fearful rage."

The children stayed with the servants in the kitchen for the rest of the evening. None of the staff ventured above stairs. What was going on up there was not their business and they were afraid that if they showed a presence, they could lose their jobs. Several times, they heard the muffled sounds of raised voices. But there was no news.

Once night had descended, the three of them crept upstairs and, with Nanny's help, made Janet's room habitable for three people. Two extra beds were made up on the floor, and they settled down to sleep with their door strongly barricaded, not knowing what the two adults might be doing and saying to each other.

Madeline lay in her makeshift bed listening to the sounds of the house, aware of a vast change and unease. Gradually the other two fell asleep and their heavy regular breathing gave the illusion of normality.

Then there came a gentle tap on the door and she froze to utter stillness, fear like an icy fist in her stomach.

"Are any of you still awake?" It was Phyllis.

"Yes," Madeline whispered and rose to unbarricade the door.

The older woman slipped into the bedroom, and Maddy gasped. By the faint glow of the night light, her face was disfigured and swollen, a large black bruise like an ink stain ran across her forehead and cheek.

"On no! What has he done to you?"

Phyllis met her eyes for a moment then her gaze shied away, and she peered at the two peacefully sleeping young people. "I'm glad they're asleep. I need to talk to you." She touched Madeline's forehead, swept a wisp of her short golden hair back and whispered softly, "You really are a remarkable young woman, do you know that?"

"No, I'm not! I must have done something very wrong for all this to happen." Madeline could feel her whole body tensing and she pressed both hands to her cheeks. She had no idea how it was that she had enticed Belaugh to behave in the fashion he had.

"I didn't mean it like that. I know how you've taken care of the other two today. They needed someone they could trust, who would guide and reassure them. You've given them the strength to get through it. Look!" Phyllis bit her lip. "What he did to you was completely wrong! It wasn't anything you did. It wasn't your fault, it was his."

Madeline shook her head. "I can't... I don't..."

Phyllis silenced her by grasping her hands. "If only I'd been brave enough to understand what was happening. But... I've been a very poor guardian to you."

Madeline whispered hollowly. "It wasn't your fault, you didn't know."

"But why didn't I see it? I've been living with him for six

years!" Phyllis shuddered. "That makes me his accomplice."

"*No!*" Madeline cried out vehemently.

Patrick stirred and mumbled something restlessly. Both women froze to silence and watched him cautiously. His eyes opened for a moment then closed again. He was still asleep.

Madeline took a deep breath and lowered her voice. "If I hadn't come here then none of this would have happened."

"We don't know that." Phyllis rubbed her swollen aching forehead in exhaustion, but there was a strength of conviction in her voice. "A proper man would never have done what he did. But you mustn't be afraid anymore, he's not going to touch you again, any of you. I've seen to that. Now we have to make some plans. You have all your lives ahead of you."

"If you want me to go away..."

"No Maddy! I would like you to stay here with me." Phyllis's voice shook with emotion. Then more rationally she continued, "You three children mean all the world to me, don't you know that? If you don't want to stay, I'll get you into the Royal Academy straight away. But whatever you choose, if he so much as speaks to any of you again, then I shall *destroy* him."

Then Phyllis's calm, determined expression crumpled suddenly, and the appalling shock of the last few hours became evident on her face. "How could I not have known what sort of man he was?" she whispered in horror. "I just didn't see it. And to think I was going to have his baby! I could have brought another little victim into his world."

Madeline's reserve finally collapsed, and it was she who hugged Phyllis. "Don't. Oh please. I'll stay with you for as long as you want me, if you're sure you really want me."

"Of course I want you." Phyllis took a deep breath and

returned the embrace. "Why didn't you tell me what was going on?"

"I couldn't," Madeline's voice was husky with the memories. "I'd already hurt you enough. They told me about the baby. And that was my fault too."

Phyllis touched her golden hair. "That was a merciful kindness. How do you think I'd feel about a child of his now? The very idea would just about kill me."

Madeline suddenly turned pale as a horrible thought crossed her mind. "And what if I am pregnant...?"

Phyllis went very white. Her strong-featured face tensed, and she hugged the girl protectively. "How on earth did you manage to survive?"

Madeline shivered and screwed her eyes up tightly. "I don't think I have survived," she whispered. "I'm not me anymore. I can't feel anything, I can't give anything, I can't play. I'm utterly useless."

Phyllis touched her golden gleaming hair tenderly. "We'll mend the hurt, Maddy. I promise you. If you'll just let me try."

♪♫

CHAPTER 36

MATTHEW BROOKS WAS allowed leave from school after his mother died, and he stayed with his grandfather for several weeks. It helped him, to share his grief with someone who had loved his mother too. But there was so much he did not understand, and he was frightened to trust and love the old man. It seemed that in so doing he would be betraying his father.

They spent a great deal of time talking, playing games of chess, and finally, Charles Braithwaite took the lad into the personal privacy of his library. It was a room he had forbidden even to his absent wife. He watched his grandson's face as the boy looked at the pictures that adorned the wall, and the small curios that were lovingly exhibited in glass cases. "Hmmm. That one was taken in South Africa more than thirty years ago. It was called Cape Colony then, of course! Can you see which one was me?"

Matthew studied the photograph seriously, then pointed

to a tall dashing young officer with a fierce moustache sitting astride his horse. "This one sir?"

"Yes," the old man stood a little straighter remembering the campaigns he had fought long ago. The boy was doing him good. He enjoyed the youthful company much more than he had expected to. But then his face grew sad. "Your mother was a little girl of four when I was posted to South Africa, Matthew. She was a beautiful little cherub, full of spirit and fun. She was eight years old when I returned."

The boy looked at him with longing. But it was all so awkward. He moved on to the next picture and studied it carefully. "This one is you sir. Northern Africa. Gosh look at all those strange costumes."

"It was very biblical and extremely hot. Those robes were sensible for the conditions," Grandfather Braithwaite nodded. "We even wore them ourselves on occasions."

"Did you bring some home with you?" Matthew looked eagerly through the cases.

"Yes," the old man laughed. "But they're packed away somewhere in the chests."

"I'd love to see them." The boy turned his attention back to the picture and frowned. "You were there quite a long time too."

Charles gripped the boy's shoulder solemnly. "I was away for years at a time. It was my profession, Matthew."

"I can see that sir. You must have seen most of the world." He moved on again and studied a more recent picture. "Ah, you look more like yourself here. India, it says."

"I was there until two years ago. Miss the place even now. I miss the hunting and riding, and of course the splendid entertaining."

Matthew's eyes were round with wonder as he looked at

his grandfather's wrinkled thin featured face and tried to imagine what such a life must have been like.

Then he moved on to another picture and his young face tensed suddenly. "Oh, that's a picture of Mummy, isn't it?"

"Yes. She was twelve then, and I had come home on leave between postings."

"So, you never saw your family very much sir?"

"No. I was home for six months, and then away again until she was sixteen. She should have come with me to India. She would have loved it, and made a wonderful hostess. She wanted to come but your grandmother wouldn't allow it. Said she'd never *meet the right gentlemen* out there!"

"It must have been very hard," Matthew said with some difficulty.

Grandfather smiled. "It's the only life I knew. I had no idea what I was missing until it was too late."

The boy looked back at the pictures and then nervously down at his hands. Finally, he plucked up his courage. "I've got something special to show you Grandfather. Would you like to see them? I've kept them very carefully."

"Yes, I'd like that Matthew," the old man nodded with growing fondness. "What is it?"

The boy gathered all his courage and looked up into the proud, finely featured face. "My father's medals from the Great War. He was a soldier. People think that because he was a pianist he was weak, but he wasn't."

"People are ignorant fools," the old man said quietly. "I'd be honoured to see them. I never knew your father, but he must have been a very special person to interest my daughter."

Matthew swallowed. It was as though the old man had

passed through a hurdle and had come out with honour. He was longing to be able to love and respect this splendid old man with a clear conscience.

Twenty minutes later, Matthew was lying on his bed. He had relaxed at long last and the two of them seemed very close. His face was alive with animation, and a small collection of precious medals was spread across the patchwork counterpane.

The old man's long strong fingers were lifting one of the medals with great respect. "And this one doesn't need explaining Matthew. I've seen a few in my time, they're not often awarded." He looked at the boy's face curiously. "I wish I'd known him. Are you like him?"

"A bit," Matthew shrugged, and then frowned. "Maddy's much more like him. Oh I do wish she'd come back, I really miss her."

"I received a note from Mrs Belaugh yesterday. She has returned. Perhaps we'll all be together in the end Matthew. But I'm afraid it will take a long while for her to forgive me for deserting your parents."

Matthew looked for a long time at the thin aristocratic face, and then simply said, "But you didn't desert them. You weren't there!"

♪♫

CHAPTER 37

HARBOROUGH HALL WAS a different place henceforth. Belaugh left in the morning and never returned. The first thing Phyllis did was to take all three children out for the day to London Zoo and it heralded the beginning of a new era.

They were aware of periods of tension when Phyllis travelled to London and fought to ensure Belaugh honoured his obligations to them, but she invariably won the battle and their lives settled down into a calm and peaceful routine.

Christmas came quickly, and they determined to have the best family celebrations ever, to mark this new beginning. Each of Phyllis's young charges invited their closest friends and family, and then busied themselves after school making and hanging the decorations.

Phyllis entered the drawing room one Saturday morning and froze to immobility on the threshold, holding her breath. Patrick had climbed onto a precariously balanced tower of stools and chairs and was being steadied by the two girls. He was leaning forward now, stretching out over the void to position the fairy on top of the Christmas tree.

"Hurry Pat, my arms are aching," Janet moaned, then shrieked, "Oh heavens, it's going to topple. Do be careful!"

He leaned further and further, until the fairy was nestled securely in place. Then with a whoop of triumph he leapt down, landing lightly on his toes. "You see? There was no need to make such a fuss, Jan," he laughed, looking at the young girl's pale frightened face.

Phyllis breathed a little more easily now and entered the room. "My goodness you have been hard at work. Well done. It's perfect." She walked slowly around the room, inspecting the holly, the tinsel, the pinecone decorations, and the colourful paper chains that adorned the ceiling.

Madeline smiled in delight. "It's been fun," she said. "But we have to get it finished soon. We only have three days before everyone starts arriving."

Phyllis met the young girl's eyes and her heart warmed to see the return of such enthusiasm. "Are the rooms ready for all your young friends, my dear?"

"Yes ma'am."

"And yours for your brother and mother, Patrick, and your aunt and friends, Janet?"

"Yes ma'am."

"Good. Now Madeline. You have a visitor waiting in the library to see you. It's your grandfather, and he has brought your brother with him."

"Grandfather Braithwaite?" Madeline's face suddenly became strained, and she frowned. "What on earth does he want of me?"

Phyllis sighed and touched the young woman's hand

reassuringly. "Don't be nervous. He's here at my invitation. He wrote me a very polite letter and so I went to see him yesterday. He's an honourable and courteous gentleman." She watched Madeline's face for a moment and then smiled gently. "I'm certain of it. There's nothing in his demeanour to suggest otherwise."

Madeline nodded slowly. "And you say my brother is with him? I haven't seen Matt in a long while," she said with a little catch in her voice.

"Then why don't we go and see them together?"

Madeline straightened her shoulders suddenly and took a deep breath. "You will stay with me, won't you, Phyllis?"

"Of course, if you want me to."

♪♫

Madeline glanced one last time at Phyllis's face, then took a deep steadying breath and opened the library door.

Her grandfather was standing in the window, silhouetted against the wintry sunlight, and his thin, taut broad-shouldered figure reassured her to some extent. Mummy had always spoken about her father with great affection and esteem, whereas she had rarely mentioned her mother. Then a young voice called, "Maddy!" and she was almost crushed by a vigorous, enthusiastic hug.

"Matt," she gasped, returning the embrace with heartfelt warmth. Then she held him at a less bruising distance and studied him from head to foot. "Goodness me, you've grown."

"So have you, Maddy. I've missed you so much."

"Oh, it's good to see you," she breathed, relieved beyond anything to see him looking so cheerful and confident. Then she glanced nervously in her grandfather's direction, and back at Matt again. "You look so well! This new school must agree with you. But you never tell me anything in your letters except the results of your rugby matches!"

Grandfather Braithwaite turned slowly from the window and watched the fond reunion with a small smile on his face. Then he came forward, leaning on his stick, and drew himself up tall. "Madeline."

"Come and meet Grandfather." Matthew took her hand enthusiastically and drew her across the room to meet him.

"I've already met Grandfather Braithwaite, Matt," Madeline murmured, and she drew herself up with dignity to meet the old man's direct gaze. "Good morning, Grandfather."

He smiled, and the expression that looked back at her contained a lively humorous twinkle that disarmed her. She felt herself responding. It was almost impossible not to.

He held his hand out to her formally. "Can we call a truce young lady? Open warfare between members of a family is a rather destructive thing."

She offered her hand in return and found it gripped in a firm business-like way, then released. She glanced at Matt's happy face and saw the eager expectation and hope there. Largely for his sake she murmured, "Yes, I expect we could."

"Good. I don't believe in beating around the bush, so I'll tell you straight away. Matthew is coming to live with me during his school holidays, and I'd like you to do so as well. The family should stick together."

"I don't believe it!" she cried indignantly, unable to restrain herself. "How can you say that after the way you deserted my parents."

"Maddy, don't say that. It's not fair." Matt took her hand urgently, his eyes suddenly anxious. "Please listen. It wasn't

Grandfather's fault. He was in the army. He's a Brigadier, you know. He was away in South Africa for years, and then India, and then the Great War came. He's only just retired and come back to England. He hardly saw any of our family. Mummy was brought up in England by Grandmother."

Madeline looked at her brother's earnest face. He obviously thought the world of Grandfather Braithwaite. But there was far more to it than that. She turned to her grandfather warily. "I remember how Grandmother reacted to me all those months ago. She would never allow Matt to live with her. She'd make life hell for him."

"She would, did I allowed her to do so," he nodded, and his eyes grew very hard. "She's not there. I've sent her to live with your aunt Jessica. You and Matthew deserve a comfortable home, we're family. If I'd known about your family's troubles, I could have done something about it before now. I could have helped your parents, but I don't expect you to believe that yet."

"I don't know what I believe." Madeline took a deep breath and looked from her grandfather to her brother. "I'm honoured that you would like me to live with you, but I would rather stay here with Phyllis and the children."

There was a long silence that hung in the air like a dead thing. Then finally her grandfather sighed. "I'd expected that. But I hope you'll allow us to get a little better acquainted. Would you care to join us for dinner on Sunday?"

"Please come Maddy. I've missed you so much."

"Have you Matt?" she smiled, and her heart gave a great skip of emotion. "Oh, then I'd love to come. I've missed you too." Tears filled her eyes, and she hugged him tightly. "We can still see each other often, even if we are living a little apart."

"Good." Phyllis came forward and placed her hand on Madeline's shoulder. "You three have a great deal to catch up on, I'm sure. Do you mind if I leave you for a while? I'll have Parstow bring you some tea and cakes."

Madeline smiled and touched the hand on her shoulder. "Thank you, Phyllis, that would be lovely." She looked from her grandfather to her brother, and for the first time in nearly two years, felt the deep bonds of family.

A little of her self-respect returned as she saw herself reflected in their eyes.

Then a thought came to her. Christmas was almost upon them, and all the families would be gathering here to celebrate. What could be better than that Matt and Grandfather should join them? If they wanted to.

She took a deep breath, a little frightened of the suggestion she was about to make. But she had to take a risk. "Would you... would you care to come and spend Christmas day with us?" She met her grandfather's eyes anxiously. "I know you've probably already made your arrangements, but we're having a party and all our families are coming to stay. I'd love my family to be part of it."

He smiled warmly. "We would be delighted to my dear. I'm sincerely honoured that you should ask."

♪♫

Jessica Durrant lived in a smart and expensive house conveniently located in Cavendish Square, and she was a busy lady. It suited her perfectly to have her mother move into her home. The two women enjoyed intimate and heated gossip that interested them deeply, for their tastes were very alike and they functioned well together. The younger woman was able to devote more of her precious time to entertaining and patronage of fund-raising events whilst her mother, a far more home loving woman, cared for the house in a way her daughter never had.

The old lady took delight in flower arranging, and in creating small items of personal comfort that turned the fashionable residence into a home that visitors delighted in. She was a more welcoming hostess than her daughter and had soon developed a wide circle of friends and took part in numerous activities that simply would not have been available to her in the confined and claustrophobic society of the country.

To the old lady fell the task of observing Jeremy, for his busy mother never had the time or the inclination to do so. He remained at home with her for several months while a new school was sought for him. During that time the old lady strictly corrected his behaviour and tried to instil into him a sense of values. But it soon became apparent to her that it would be a long-term job. He had been allowed to run wild for far too long, and his doting mother simply attended to his every complaint.

Several times Jeremy attempted to complain to his mother about the restrictions imposed upon him by his grandmother, but for the first time in his life his plaints went unnoticed, and he was subject to discipline.

Jessica left the house at ten each morning having eaten breakfast with her mother and sorted out the day's engagements in her diary. One morning, she found her mother unreceptive to her chatter, and looked up quickly from her note making.

"Is something wrong Mother? You haven't listened to a word I've been saying."

"Your father has sent me a letter, Jessie."

"Well, I'm glad he's in touch with you at last. I suppose he wants you to go back and look after him." She frowned and her lips tightened. "If I were you, I'd tell him you're far happier here. If he wants you, he'll have to come and apologise in person."

"Far from it!" The older woman's cheeks tinged slightly pink with indignation. "He's employed a housekeeper and has young Matthew living with him. They're planning to spend Christmas with Madeline at Harborough Hall."

Across the room Jeremy's eyes shot quickly to his grandmother's face. But he lowered them back to his book to avoid attracting attention.

"He's taken in Maisy's brats?" Jessica's voice held a note of incredulity.

"Yes, and the boy is charming him, just as his father charmed Maisy."

"Taking responsibility for children at his age is certainly not the act of a sane man. What he should be doing is coming here and mending the rift in his marriage."

"Jessie," Mathilda cut her daughter off impatiently. "I wouldn't live anywhere near him after the way he's treated me."

"But you've spent your life caring for him!"

"Hmmm. He was out of the country for most of our married life. No, I shan't go back to him." She looked down at her hands. "I think we'll let this relationship take its course. He'll soon weary of them and realise what a burden he's taken on."

"The whole situation baffles me, Mother. What does he think he will gain by it? They've had no education and will certainly let him down terribly."

"Funnily enough, I don't think they will. Madeline was

well spoken and well-groomed when I met her." Mathilda glanced round quickly and caught a glimpse of her grandson watching her intently, but he lowered his eyes instantly to his book, like a snake sliding away from trouble. "Being responsible for them may be a fate he deserves."

"But it's not fair on the rest of the family. He'll give those kids anything if they ask for, and there are a few things Jeremy particularly wants."

"Oh, hush Jessica!" she murmured in exasperation. "Little ears are listening. We'll discuss this later."

Jeremy's cheeks were staining red slowly but surely. He was staring fixedly at the page before him, his thin hands clenching like claws on the book.

Mathilda Braithwaite watched him, and the small nucleus of an idea came to her. Jessica was a fool. She *had* spoilt the boy beyond belief, ruined him, turned him into a selfish demanding monster.

Perhaps she could turn that selfishness to her own advantage. But she would have to be infinitely careful and patient.

♪♫

EPILOGUE

ONE BRIGHT BRACING day during the following autumn, Brigadier Braithwaite cantered up the long drive to Harborough Hall. He sat his horse as one would expect of a cavalry officer. He knew he would suffer for it in the days to come, but he liked to take Madeline and Patrick riding. He found it rewarding, the way the youngsters were building a relationship with a man of his age.

Madeline had become dear to him. She had all the spirit and tenderness of her mother. At times it was as though Maisy had been brought back to him, and yet Madeline had strengths and ambitions that his daughter would never have aspired to.

She must have inherited those traits from her father, and it outraged him that such a man had been brought down so despicably. But at last, she was beginning to believe that he had played no part in her parents' misfortunes.

It sometimes felt as though he had been given the chance

to be a father again, and he was not going to let that slip through his fingers.

Phyllis waved and smiled. "Beautiful day Charles," she called.

"Excellent for riding. Would you care to join us?"

She laughed and shook her head. "You'd find me a terrible drag. I don't ride well. But thank you for the invitation. I hope to see you later for tea?"

"That would be a pleasure, thank you. Are they in the stables?"

"Mmmm. I expect so."

He rode round to the stable block and found the two of them still preparing their mounts.

Madeline and Patrick both rode well. Although they were receiving formal riding instruction from the head groom, they always found riding with Brigadier Braithwaite a challenge. His skills far exceeded their own even though he was approaching seventy, and they used the comparison as a yardstick for measuring their own equestrian progress.

He had ridden to the hunt in countries around the globe, after prey they had only seen in picture books, and they felt a little of that exotic experience rubbing off on them when they were with him.

Within minutes they set out together across the open park. Madeline leaned down over Sunny Suzie's neck to dash under the overhanging branches of a gracious tree. By mutual consent, they headed for the woods that shielded the grounds from the north easterly winds. There were numerous pathways woven amongst the trees. In the summer months, the fully leafed canopy created a cool and shady environment, with inviting glades and picnic spots. In the winter, on a day like today, it was very different. There were fallen tree trunks that the horses could jump, a colourful montage of leaves turning all shades of yellow, red and brown, and curious fungi sprouting from the damp rotting vegetation.

They slowed to a sedate walk, picking their way along a woodland path that was fragrant with the musky dampness of the season.

Madeline glanced at her grandfather's figure proudly. She had become immensely fond of him. He was an upright, honourable man, respected in the world and, in spite of his years, still bristling with energy and enthusiasm.

The two youngsters reined in and glanced around the glade. It was empty but breathtakingly lovely, wet with dew and the dying ferns of early winter. Shafts of bright sunlight were darting down through the balding boughs overhead, glistening on the wetness as though picking out nature's own diamonds, a hidden and precious treasure.

Madeline murmured suddenly, "There won't be anything like this in London, Pat. You're going to miss it."

He laughed, the spark of taunting flashing in his eyes. "I shall be back to keep you on your toes, Madeline. I wouldn't want you to dwindle into a mere girl."

"Why thank you. I am proud to be female, and I assure you, there's nothing *mere* about me."

"Now, now, you two," Grandfather murmured with a laugh in his voice. "There are plenty of open spaces in London, Pat, and stables where you can hire very reasonable hacks. I'll take you to one when you've settled in at the school..."

There was an ear-splitting crack close by and Sunny Suzy, a spirited nervous creature, reared up vigorously with a snort of fear. Madeline cried out and clung to the animal's neck, her heart pounding with shock. Then the beast snorted and leaped forward at a strange angle to bolt.

Madeline had no time to wonder what had happened. She scrambled to sit upright, and was carried along, pounding and tearing through the tangle of trees, branches whipping and scratching at her face. Desperately she struggled to regain control over the terrified creature, hauling on the reins with all her strength. She could feel and smell her mount's fear and had to exert every scrap of skill and determination to impose her own will. At long last, the beast calmed to a more ordered gallop, and finally came to a halt, shivering and snorting, little jolts of anxiety passing through the saddle and the beasts flanks to her.

"Good girl," she gasped, leaning forward and patting the foam flecked neck. Then she glanced around. They had crashed through the undergrowth and left a broken trail to show the way they had come.

No one had come with her! What on earth had happened?

That had been a gunshot, she realised suddenly, and fear for her grandfather and for Patrick brought a tightness to her throat.

She turned her mount about, retracing their steps along the trampled path, coaxing the beast to return to that which had terrified her. She could feel the heaving shuddering breathing of the animal beneath her and felt more than a little shaky herself.

She emerged from the trees into the sunlit glade and her heart came up into her mouth.

Her grandfather was sitting calmly astride his horse, but a ragged looking poacher in a damp moleskin jacket stood just feet from him, his rifle aimed purposefully at the elderly gentleman's chest.

"Put the gun down, man," her grandfather was saying in an authoritative voice. "You've been caught red handed. You're only making matters worse for yourself."

"No. *You're* making things worse, sir!" The poacher settled the rifle stock more determinedly into the hollow of his shoulder. "You need to go and find Miss Maddy."

Madeline's heart thumped suddenly. She knew the poacher's voice. It was Jarvis their old game keeper.

"…that horse," he was continuing, "could have thrown her or dragged her through the undergrowth."

Madeline urged her frightened mount forward cautiously. "Jarvis, please put the gun down. What are you doing?"

Jarvis glanced fleetingly at her and then straight back at her grandfather. But the stubborn frown had relaxed slightly, and he asked of her, "You alright Miss Maddy? Carried you off smartish didn't she? Flighty thing, that one."

She nodded.

Her grandfather swivelled quickly in the saddle and relief swept across his face when he saw her. Then he too turned back to Jarvis and studied the man curiously.

His whole demeanour had changed, and he murmured softly, "Jarvis, is it? You can put the gun down now. She's safe, and I shan't prosecute you for any of this."

The truculence returned to Jarvis's face. "On your honour?"

"On my honour," the old man replied gently, with a small bow.

Slowly the barrel of the rifle moved away. Jarvis sighed and smiled ruefully. "It's alright Brigadier. I know you, sir. I wouldn't have pulled the trigger anyway."

Brigadier Braithwaite nodded. "You know my granddaughter?"

"Yes sir. I was game keeper and woods manager here, till Mr Belaugh decided not to keep the gundogs and birds. He don't like shooting you see. Nothing left for me to do."

"I see. So, you lost your job." The old man's eyes sharpened. After glancing again at Madeline, he turned back to the ex-gamekeeper, and said thoughtfully, "You look as though you know how to handle a gun. Did you bag the bird?"

"Yes sir."

"What work are you doing now, and where are you living?"

"Taken over Rose Cottage sir. But there's no work around. I just make and mend." A dog came crashing through the dying ferns, tail wagging exuberantly, a plump pheasant firmly grasped between its jaws. Jarvis automatically made a fuss of the dog who dropped the bird for him and strutted triumphantly.

"Can you handle a pack, Jarvis?"

"Yes sir." The man looked quickly at the Brigadier's face. "I used to keep the gundogs for old Lord Harborough, and took care of the breeding birds, sir."

"What about horses?"

"A tool of the trade sir. They're the only way of getting around an estate this size. Ask Miss Maddy or Mr Patrick. They were always coming to the stables to see the horses. I used to take them riding."

The Brigadier glanced once more at Madeline and raised his eyebrows. "Is this true my dear?"

"Yes Grandpa. Jarvis used to set the jumps for us and took us riding when Green was busy."

He nodded and rubbed his chin. "Come and see me on Sunday after church, Jarvis. I want to see Burrows first, but I may have job to offer you. I need a good man to take care of the dogs and horses while I'm in London."

The man's face coloured slightly, but he just said, "Yes sir."

The Brigadier smiled. "Well, pick up your dinner then. I'll see you on Sunday."

He turned back to the two young people and dismounted to examine Madeline's horse. Sunny Suzy was still twitching nervously and skittered uneasily as he approached. Madeline brought her gently back under control, calming the animal's nerves with a few words and a reassuring hand on the neck.

The beast responded by relaxing visibly as Grandfather examined the mouth and nostrils, then the chest, and finally the long powerful legs. At last, he straightened and smiled at his granddaughter. "She's fine, nothing more than winded. Well done my dear. You're quite a horsewoman."

She smiled, delighted by such a compliment. Later, once they had returned to the stables and finished brushing down the horses, she sent Patrick back to the house and turned to face her grandfather.

"Grandpa, are you seriously going to give Jarvis a job? He was holding a gun on you."

"He wouldn't have shot me. Most poachers slink off into the undergrowth like rats, but he stayed because he was worried about you, my dear."

"Can you trust him?"

"I've handled men all my life, he's a good man. I could see it in his eyes. I need someone like that who will give me loyal service."

She frowned anxiously. "Well be careful, won't you?

Make absolutely sure of him first."

He smiled fondly. "I will my dear, never fear. I don't like to see good men wasted."

Suddenly something seemed to touch him, deepen the lines of his face and he became hesitant. "I've never told you this before, but that's what happened to your father, Madeline. I've never forgiven myself for being so distant. Had I been here, things would have been different."

Tears filled her eyes. "You must not blame yourself. If only you had known my father. He was such a good man." She touched his hand tenderly. "I think you would have got on well."

"I think so too." He squeezed her hand, and the painful memories were still visible in his eyes. "Maisy told me many things during the last weeks of her life. I began to see him through her eyes, to see you all as a family."

She nodded and with an overwhelming impulse, she threw her arms around him and gave him a fierce hug. "I'm so glad I've got you now, Grandpa."

He looked down at her golden hair and patted her back gently, encouragingly, just as her parents had used to.

"And so am I. You and Matthew have given me something to look forward to in my old age. Now come." His voice was warm suddenly, and he held his arm out for her. "We had better be going to the house, or Phyllis will be anxious about you."

Madeline tucked her arm through his, and they walked together back to the Hall.

THE END

Dear reader,

Thank you for reading my book. I hope you've enjoyed it. If you have, I'd really appreciate it if you would take a moment to leave me a review at your favourite ebook retailer.

And please do come back for the next book in the series. I have such a tale to tell!

Thanks!

Gayle Wyatt
Author

ABOUT THE AUTHOR

Like many authors, I'm a compulsive writer. I started telling and scribbling bedtime stories at a really early age. By the time I was twelve years old, I had begun constructing plots for my first novel. I've been writing ever since.

It's only now, though, many years and several careers later, that I'm turning seriously to fiction writing. My plan is to bring several historical series to print over the next few years.

Life has had a habit of getting in the way of my literary aspirations, and I don't think that has been a bad thing. I have done so much and learned so much. My first career was as a Physiological Measurement Technician working in the Health Service in the UK, and then moving to Bahrain for three years where I worked at the Salmanaya Medical Centre.

The second phase of my life was as a mother bringing up two beautiful sons, but when I decided it was time to return to work, I had the most amazing stroke of pure luck. While temping for a few weeks at a publishing company, I was able to put my writing and editing skills to good use, and I was offered a job as an assistant editor.

It was a dream come true and was the first step in a satisfying career! I eventually become magazine editor, a highly stressful job working to immutable deadlines, directing the editorial content, overseeing the quality of the magazine, managing a portfolio of writers and of course writing a vast number of articles and news items.

After 20 years in that challenging role, moving from magazine to magazine, I decided to go independent, to spread my wings and perhaps de-stress a bit. I became a freelance writer and branched out to manage the marketing for my musician son. This inevitably led to marketing and web development for other budding and established musicians.

And is there time left in the day for writing? Oh yes. And I'm loving it.

MORE BY THIS AUTHOR

THE WESTCOTT GIRLS:
The Music Maker's Daughter
The Hours Before Dawn
Love Comes at a Cost
Song of a Nightingale
Speak Softly of Tomorrow

Next in series:

THE HOURS BEFORE DAWN

Beneath the outgoing facade, Madeline Brooks hides an agonising secret.

Gifted as a pianist, she is struggling to unlock the musical block stifling her career. Her only remaining option is to take a terrible personal risk.

Violinist Joshua Hanson reaches out to her through music. The explosion of creativity is instantaneous.

Can he help her overcome the traumas of her past or will this end in disaster? Get it wrong, the conflagration will consume them both. But old family jealousies are rekindling around her.

The hatred that destroyed her father's career is now reaching out to destroy her and Josh.

For publication dates of later books,
And to get your reminders go to:

www.gayle-wyatt.com

CONTACT ME

Check out my website:
www.gayle-wyatt.com

Follow me on facebook:
www.facebook.com/authorgaylewyatt

Email me at:
gayle@gayle-wyatt.com

Printed in Great Britain
by Amazon

80871443R00174